Mary,
Thank you.
Gregg

She Learned to Die

Gregg E. Brickman

Best Wishes
Gregg E. Brickman
3-24-16
2-6-23

This is a work of fiction. Resemblance to any person, place, or event is entirely coincidental.

Other Kindle and CreateSpace Works by the Author:

Stand alone:

the lord

Tony Conte Mysteries:

Illegally Dead

Sophia Burgess and Ray Stone Mysteries:

Imperfect Contract

Imperfect Daddy

Please visit: www.GreggEBrickman.com

ISBN-10: 149972361X
ISBN-13: 978-1499723618

DEDICATION

For my dedicated, caring, and compassionate
nursing faculty colleagues and students

Working with you brought joy to my life.

ACKNOWLEDGMENTS

This story is a work of my imagination, though I've made every effort to present accurate, true-to-life details. If I got it wrong, the blame is mine. If I got it right, those mentioned below share the credit.

As always, I must thank my husband, Steve, for supporting my writing, putting up with my fantasy life, reading my first draft, and listening to my endless chatter about my plots. I thank Benjamin for encouraging me and pointing out that I should write because it brings me pleasure. Sales are a bonus. I thank Mark and Laurie for their support as well.

My critique group is superb. Thank you to Randy Rawls, Victoria Landis, Stephanie Levine, Ann Meier, and Richard Hodes. They read and reread, and provide helpful, thoughtful, and usually kind commentary. Each one of us has a special editing focus that we willingly share with each other.

Jennifer Samuels was an early reader, making line edits and tracking the plot. Geraldine Sutton read last. She has a marvelous eye for catching mistakes and keeps me honest on the characterization of my nurses.

I don't believe any book can be the work of only one person. This one is no exception.

CHAPTER 1

Brambles snagged her slacks as Jillian Grey picked her way through the shrubbery edging the parking lot at Ft. Lauderdale's Conover College. While bending to tug free, she scraped her right arm against some branches. Then, having lost sight of the target—what looked like a burgundy backpack—she strained to see past the ixora hedge. A wisp of blond hair among the leaves. She stopped and sucked in a deep breath. Despite the oppressive mid-morning heat and the perspiration beads across her forehead, a chill swept up her spine to the top of her head, leaving gooseflesh in its wake.

Another few steps.

A slender young woman lay on her left side with her right knee bent and her arm twisted behind her back. A loose burgundy tee shirt gathered under her breasts, revealing the bottom edge of a black lace bra. The elastic band from a matching thong stretched above the waistband of designer jeans.

The girl—Bethany Newland—was Jillian's nursing student.

Her heart raced, and her breathing quickened.   She

1

struggled against a surging anxiety, holding her breath for a few seconds, then exhaling into cupped hands. The long, slow exhalation calmed her a bit. She wiped cold sweat from her forehead with her palms, then clenched her fists to quiet them. Transfixed, Jillian envisioned her daughter, Deirdre, who died in an automobile accident, in Bethany's place and wept among the silent trees.

Pushing aside the memory, she approached Bethany's body, crouched low, and palpated for the carotid pulse. Nothing. As a nurse, Jillian had no doubt Bethany was dead.

Jillian backed up several paces, being careful to keep to the same path, and pulled her cell phone from her pocket and dialed 9-1-1.

It was five minutes after ten. Only two or three minutes had passed since she entered the woods, but it seemed a lifetime.

A few seconds later, a woman's voice said, "You've reached 9-1-1. What is your emergency?"

Jillian identified herself and described the situation.

"Fire-Rescue and a patrol car are en route. Someone will arrive in three to five minutes."

"Thank you. What should I do now?"

"Go sit in your car and stay available. The officers will have questions for you."

The dispatcher's efficient tone sounded comforting, and Jillian's anxiety abated. "I'm okay." She realized the voice hadn't asked how she felt. "Sorry."

The woman repeated the instructions to sit in the car, reminded Jillian to not disturb the area, then disconnected.

Transfixed, Jillian stared at Bethany from a distance, remembering their meeting the previous evening. The girl was vibrant. Now it was obvious she'd been dead for several hours. Dark shadows, signs of lividity, loomed where skin met ground. No visible gunshot or knife wounds sullied her body. No blood marred the near-perfect form. The sharp angle of Bethany's head suggested neck trauma as the cause of death. The vivid scrapes and bruises on both arms hinted that Bethany resisted the attack.

"What am I doing?" she muttered, realizing her fixation on the facts avoided the reality of the situation. Too much CSI on television made a crime scene expert of everyone, she thought. Bethany, whom she knew and liked, lay dead—perhaps murdered.

Jillian shifted two or three feet further away and continued to study the area. A scrap of red fabric lay near Bethany's foot. A leather pouch-type pocketbook, half-covered with debris, leaned against a tree trunk ten feet to the right. Nearby, a Coke bottle lay on its side, the contents spilled onto the strap of the handbag and the ground.

She was certain the smooth leather bag belonged to Bethany. Jillian had moved the handbag with the etched pewter clasp to the end of her desk to make room for the papers Bethany needed to view.

Where was her canvas backpack? An overloaded burgundy satchel hung from Bethany's shoulder on a single strap as she had walked away. Jillian recalled cautioning the girl about back injury, earning a gibe for acting like a mother.

Then Bethany had turned to Jillian and said, "Thank you so much for seeing me, Professor. I'll try to take your advice. I can do better if I apply myself." Her manner seemed sincere, her smile genuine. A casual shake of her head sent long blond hair cascading over the backpack.

Now Bethany was dead.

Jillian scrutinized the ground but saw nothing more. She

retraced her steps to the parking lot, being careful to not get caught on the branches, then she climbed in the car to wait for the police.

Again, her mind drifted to the last time she saw Bethany alive. The girl had requested an appointment to talk about how to improve low grades. During the meeting, Jillian learned Bethany, the daughter of physicians, didn't want to be a nurse.

Jillian had said, "Bethany, you don't seem happy with nursing. You're like a fish out of water. When other students are studying their notes, you're in your own little world, staring into space. Sometimes in the hospital, you act like you wish you were anywhere else in the world. Last week, I found you sitting in the corner looking bored."

"It wasn't my idea to be a nurse. I went to a magnet school for the arts, and I wanted to major in fine arts in college. My father wouldn't hear of it. He wanted me to be a doctor, but, thank God, my grades aren't good enough to get into a state university, much less the University of Miami. My whole flipping family is in medicine. My brother is an orthopedic surgeon, and my sister is in her first year of med school."

"You didn't want to be a physician?" Jillian said.

"No way," Bethany said, biting off each word. "My parents thought if they let me dance in high school, I'd get it out of my system. But I'm talented. Gifted maybe. I really am." Bethany's thin body, long legs, and graceful movements supported the statement.

"How did you get here?"

"Mom insisted I try nursing. Gave me no choice. She wants to pacify my father. Keep me in a related field at least."

4

"What do you think about it now?"

"I'd rather be an employed nurse than an unemployed dancer, and I can do the work. I know I can. But I need to get a handle on the exams."

Jillian snapped out of her recollections and looked around.

Vultures circled above the trees. Two landed close to the parking bumpers and strutted across the narrow strip of grass. Then two entered the shrubs, moving toward Bethany's body.

Fighting waves of nausea, Jillian keyed the ignition, then mashed the car's horn.

The birds left the ground, joining their companions and elevating their flight paths high into the clear blue sky.

Jillian worried about the birds and didn't notice the patrol car until it stopped about five yards behind her vehicle. She grabbed her belongings and slid out of the car. A woman in her early twenties met her halfway between their vehicles.

"Ms. Grey?" the officer said.

Jillian nodded.

"Tell me what you found."

Jillian pointed in the direction of Bethany's body. "There's the body of a girl, Bethany Newland, in the trees."

The officer looked from side-to-side, then rose on tiptoes to repeat the process. "Can't see anything. How did you happen to find the body?"

"I pulled into the parking space and decided to finish my coffee before going into my office. I don't have class today—only office hours—so I came in late and wasn't in a rush. But that's also why I parked way back here, all the faculty spots were taken. I sat thinking, staring into the trees, and noticed some burgundy fabric. Many of the students have backpacks that color—it's one of the school colors. I decided to retrieve it, if it was a backpack, or toss it out, if it was trash." She angled a finger toward the path into the bushes. "Through there. Then I found her. She's wearing a burgundy school tee shirt."

"I see it now."

Jillian said, "Bethany felt cold. I think she's been dead for hours. I didn't touch anything except her neck."

The officer raised a brow.

Jillian read the nametag on the woman's chest. "Um, Officer Morgan, I'm a nurse."

Morgan nodded. "You knew the victim?"

"She's a first-year student of mine. In fact, we had an appointment late yesterday." Jillian summarized the meeting while the officer made notes. "We walked into the courtyard together when we finished."

"Any idea what went on here?"

"No." Jillian started to say ma'am, but it stuck in her throat. Officer Morgan appeared to be about the same age as Jillian's elder daughter, Allison, who was twenty-three.

"Bethany said goodnight in the courtyard, and we parted company."

A second officer—tall, well-muscled in a snug blue uniform—joined the two women. After listening to Morgan's brief summary, he said, "You wait here with Ms. Grey. I'll check things out."

"I went in there," Jillian said, indicating the path.

"Ma'am, I know how to approach a body."

Taken aback by his condescending tone, Jillian returned to her car and pulled out her iPhone. She ignored Morgan's cautionary stare and called the school. As Jillian waited for the dean to answer, the older cop treaded through the heather

SHE LEARNED TO DIE

in a manner sure to destroy any trace evidence in his path. At a loss about what else to do, and feeling exposed and insecure, she captured several pictures of the officer's actions.

Jillian lowered the device to her lap. She glanced at the second floor windows where several people stood in full view. Several panes away, someone peeped between the slats of the vertical blinds.

CHAPTER 2

Detective Simon Brewer completed a U-turn on Federal Highway south of Oakland Park Boulevard, then snapped a quick right into the Conover College campus. He graduated from their School of Criminology several years prior and now taught crime scene investigation techniques every Wednesday evening.

Five two-story, white concrete buildings sat like the points of a star around the four-story Student Services structure. Tree-lined walkways and manicured patches of lush grass connected the red-roofed buildings.

Brewer pointed left. "There," he said, glancing in the direction of his partner, Nate Zale, who rode shotgun. "The whole back of the property is covered with trees and shrubs. The victim is under the trees behind the northeast parking lot."

Brewer pulled the white Taurus in behind a row of cars. Without killing the flashing blue light on the dash, he popped the door and stepped onto the pavement. "Man, it's hotter than hell out here." He tossed his sport coat onto the back seat. He knew that without it he looked like a perspiring, paunchy civilian in a golf shirt and wrinkled Dockers, but he had no choice.

Zale buttoned his jacket over his trim physique, adjusted the four-in-hand knot on his silk Armani tie, and stepped between two cars. He approached the waiting patrol officer. "What do we have?"

Though fifty years old, the same age as Brewer, Nate Zale appeared five years younger—brown hair, firm skin, boyish dimples, blue eyes—while Brewer's countenance, with his graying hair and deep expression lines, suggested a hard-earned fifty-five.

From his position a few steps behind Zale, Brewer listened to Officer Morgan's recap of the situation. Brewer pulled a bound notebook from his breast pocket. In the white rectangle on the otherwise plain black cardboard flap, he wrote Friday, September 24, Conover Campus, book 1 of, leaving a space for the total number of volumes he'd use during the case. Later he would also add the victim's name to the cover. He flipped open the first page, jotted the officer's surname and badge number, and after glancing at the patrol car, tacked on the car number. He took a step forward. "What's your first name, Officer Morgan?"

"Yoli, sir."

"Partner?" Detective Brewer asked.

"Frank Goetz. Badge 1847."

"He's the guy who transferred in from Deerfield, isn't he? Had some sort of problem."

"I'm not aware of that, sir."

Brewer waved his hand around the area. "Get some tape up. Keep the onlookers away." He studied the gathering crowd and recognized several professors.

"I'm on it, sir." Officer Morgan started toward her cruiser.

"Wait a minute, Morgan. Where's the woman who found the body?"

"Jillian Grey. The lady with auburn hair and blue sweater over there with the teachers." Morgan jerked her chin a bit to the right.

Brewer observed Jillian for a moment, then scribbled a brief description—height five-four, weight one-thirty-five, age upper-forties.

"Morgan, get names, addresses, telephone numbers from the faculty and staff." He motioned toward the small group of onlookers. "And where they'll be later today." He checked his watch. "Find out where they'll be tomorrow and Sunday, too. When you're finished, send them back into the school. Ask Ms. Grey to stay on the premises until we talk to her. Oh, and tell her not to talk to anyone about what she saw." Brewer continued to write his crime scene observations—ambient temperature ninety-two degrees, clear and sunny sky, no wind, circling vultures.

"You about ready?" Zale asked, offering a pair of latex gloves.

Brewer ran his hand through his thinning hair, sucked in a big breath that he exhaled with a swoosh, and stepped onto the grass. "Yeah. Got the digital camera?"

"Right here." Zale patted his pocket.

Frank Goetz stomped through the bushes, creating crashing, snapping sounds. "Damn." He dragged the back of his hand across his brow.

Zale stopped in the middle of gloving and glared at Goetz. "What in the hell do you think you're doing?"

"What do you mean?"

"That's a crime scene," Zale said, his voice edgy. "You barreled through it like a bull elephant in musk after a herd of cows."

"I needed to check things out. Make sure the vic's dead."

"Your job is to put up the tape and keep the damn buzzards away from the body," Zale said, stepping closer to the big officer.

"What'd you touch, Goetz?" Brewer stepped between the officer and the detective. He wondered where his partner's references to wildlife came from. He saw the birds, but the only mad elephant seemed to be Goetz, who didn't appear to have learned from past reprimands.

"I touched the vic's neck, then I walked around the body."

"Find anything?" Brewer asked.

"No. There's a purse next to that pine tree." He pointed. "I didn't touch it."

"Go help your partner secure the scene and get names and addresses from the crowd." Brewer shook his head in disgust. "Let's do it," he said, nodding to Zale.

Zale took several long shots of the scene and attached voice comments specifying exact location and angle. Then Brewer and Zale worked their way to the small clearing where Bethany Newland lay dead. Even though the crime scene technicians would digitally photograph the scene, Zale and Brewer preferred to have their own shots available. Every few steps, Zale took more pictures, capturing everything from the thin canopy to the brush-strewn ground.

Brewer inspected the shrubs and the area, searching for a glint of metal, the white of a cigarette filter, or a more obvious killer's calling card, like a driver's license. It'd happened before, but not today.

"Here's a couple of footprints," Zale said. He bent

forward and snapped several vertical shots.

Without touching, Brewer measured the impressions—he hoped the bull elephant hadn't made them—then estimated their distance from both the pavement and the body. He shoved a stick in the ground to mark the site, planning to ask the crime scene technicians to make casts of the prints.

"Take a look." Brewer pointed. Parallel furrows ran from the bushes to the victim's feet. "Dragged." He shifted his finger to indicate a spot in the dirt. "The marks start there. I'll bet the son of a bitch carried her over the bushes and dragged her the last few feet."

After taking several additional shots, Zale moved in closer. "Can't weigh more than one-ten. She's light enough it could be a woman perp. A man would have carried her in here, I think. Less trouble."

"Maybe. We've got another crime scene around here someplace. Wonder where." He looked around for more broken foliage.

Brewer waited for Zale to take several pictures of the body from various angles, then squatted for a closer inspection. "Looks like her neck's broken," Brewer said, moving his finger to indicate the sharp, twisting angle between Newland's jaw and shoulder.

"Medical Examiner will tell us." Zale's camera clicked. This time the strobe flashed. "Did you call yet?"

"They're on the way. When I heard about the friggin' vultures, I told dispatch to hurry them along. We don't need to battle birds for the body."

Still crouching, Brewer pressed his gloved hand against Newland's jaw to turn her head. A bloody scrape ran from the hairline at her forehead to her left ear. "Get a picture of this abrasion. The perp probably struck her. Get the marks on her arms, too."

"Maybe she fell against one of those concrete bumpers out there. See how ragged the edge is?" Zale took a close-up.

"Yup." Brewer stepped away from the body. "Okay, let's check the rest of the area. I'll bag the purse." He squinted at a spot of color, then stooped to retrieve the scrap of red cloth lying near Newland's foot, putting it in an evidence bag, and labeling it. Then he measured the distance from the body to the handbag.

Brewer continued. "I'll tell campus security to clear the cars. They'll be able to get the word to the students and faculty quicker than we can. We need to look at the parking lot." He motioned to his left. "Those footprints are recent. They're almost dry. The grooves the victim's shoes made are moist with dew." Brewer stepped on an area of moist grass. When he removed his foot, the dew was gone. "She laid here most of the night. Been dead awhile. I don't know where she met her attacker, but it wasn't here."

"It wasn't sexual assault. Her clothes are intact." Zale took another couple of photos. "Call security. The parking lot might be interesting."

While Brewer returned to the car, Zale widened his search, walking the clearing in concentric circles until he disappeared into the trees.

Brewer helped himself to a roll of crime scene tape from the trunk and marked the path from the pavement to the victim's body. Then he walked across the jam-packed lot to where two men from campus security sat in a golf cart. "Gentlemen," Brewer said. He glanced in the direction of the Health Sciences building, where a steady stream of students queued behind a blue and white uniformed female guard. "You've got evacuation under control."

The cart's gaunt driver offered a firm handshake. "I'm Alfred Smoller, chief of campus security. We'll keep a man at each driveway to direct cars to alternate parking until you're finished. I suspect sessions will be cancelled for the rest of the day, so it shouldn't be much of a problem for you."

"I appreciate it. We'll also need to talk with anyone on your staff who was in the area last evening, during the night, or early this morning."

"That would be Carmichael until midnight, then Joe," he nodded at the man to his right, "from then until now." Smoller removed a folded paper from his shirt pocket. "I grabbed a lot layout for you. Thought it might come in handy."

"Thanks. It will." Brewer made arrangements to interview Joe Campbell, then trudged to where Morgan and Goetz stood. He used his handkerchief to wipe his brow. "Do you have the names of all the onlookers?"

"Yes." Morgan held out the top page from her clipboard.

"Keep it for now. I want you to escort each person to their car." He pointed to the students. "Get their stats. Tag numbers, too. After the drivers vacate each section, tape it off. Be sure no one else enters—even on foot—until we're finished here." He handed the map of the parking area to Morgan. "Use this to mark each vehicle's location."

Faculty relocated their cars in less than a half-hour, walking back from a distant staff lot in groups of two and threes. Jillian Grey wasn't among them. He wondered where she'd gone, then noticed her among a group of young people near the main entrance.

The medical examiner arrived. Crime scene technicians pursued their tasks. Brewer and Zale stood in the middle of the lot watching the student interviews.

Brewer pointed to a section of cars. "Did you notice how the groups of kids exit together and go to their cars in the same general area? I'll bet they park with their friends every day."

"So?"

"If we find anything, it'll be where the nursing students park, don't you think?" Brewer headed toward the northwest corner of the lot. "Newland comes out of the building after meeting with Grey, gets a soda, then heads to her car. It's late. She takes a direct path across the grass, then diagonally over the pavement."

Zale jumped in. "You're making some assumptions, but okay. The perp waits by her car or follows her into the lot. The place to start fine-combing is at the victim's car."

Brewer nodded, watching a thirty-something woman from the long line approach Officer Morgan.

With the exception of oil stains, an older model Mercury Sable, and the congregation of cars toward the rear, the lot appeared empty and clean. Brewer and Zale inspected each vacant space, making their way toward the solitary car at the front of the lot.

A crime scene tech called Brewer and Zale to the empty space next to the Mercury. "There's a trace of what appears to be blood on this parking bumper."

Brewer hunkered next to the elongated concrete block. "Nate, get a shot. Get one of the proximity to the entrance, too."

The camera whirred as Nate opened the lens.

"Blond hair." Nate pointed to a strand stuck on the edge

of the concrete. He crouched for a closer shot, then stepped away as the tech sealed the hair in an envelope. "Piece of scalp attached. My money's on this being the primary."

With the assistance of the crime scene technician, the detectives repeated the same procedures they followed earlier in the day, starting at the periphery of the scene and working their way in.

"All right," Brewer said when they were finished. "Let's talk to the teachers."

"Man, I hate this. Time to cut myself loose, I think," Zale said.

"You say that whenever we have a young victim."

"I'm serious. I'm working my plan. Pretty soon I won't have to deal with this bullshit anymore." Zale took a couple of quick steps to catch up with Brewer. "How do you want to handle it?"

"You find out the kid's address and next of kin. I'll start with the faculty. When we're done, we can interview Grey together."

"That works for me." Zale fell into step with Brewer.

"I want to know why Grey saw the vic late last night, then happened to find the body today. Mighty strange if you ask me."

"Keep your shirt on."

"Yeah."

CHAPTER 3

Jillian stood under the portico covering the main entrance and exterior staircase. She watched the students shuffle past, their expressions dismal. Several asked questions about the upcoming Monday's exam, some gave or accepted hugs, and a few gathered close to her without touching or talking.

Bethany's close friends, Carrie Kennedy and Tanya Li, clung to Oliver Cooley, the disheveled young man Bethany had dated for the past several months. Tear-streaked faces signaled their despair. Shanna Albano and Vincent Barrera, the others in the clique, followed close behind, arms interlocked, dry-eyed but somber.

Jillian embraced the last of the departing students, murmuring comforting words.

The scrape she got from the bushes stung. The small cut no longer bled, but it had. Deciding to take a moment to tend to it, she took the stairs to the second floor. Her heels clicked on the metal edges of the white concrete steps. At the top of the first flight, she paused on the balcony to view the scene below. People stood in a queue, two and three abreast, waiting their turn to be questioned and escorted to their cars.

The parking lot served two adjacent buildings, creating an ongoing parking problem. At the encouragement of campus administration, several classmates, Kennedy, Li, and Cooley among them, shared rides. Officer Morgan guided them to Cooley's Ford.

Bethany had been part of the car pool, but yesterday was an exception. She'd commented about driving to school alone because of her after-school appointment. Jillian wondered who, other than close friends, knew Bethany planned to stay late. Jillian wiped away tears, then continued upward.

The building was two stories and L-shaped. Windows filled both the east and west walls of the second floor, abutting one another. She walked to the skills lab at the far end of the long, tiled hallway, pausing for a moment at a sink to clean the blood from her arm. A bit of antibiotic ointment and a bandage from the first aid supplies finished the job.

Through the lab window, Jillian saw the activity in the parking lot. Yellow crime scene tape delimited the corner where first semester beginners usually parked. They tended to arrive early and fill the slots closest to the building. She often heard upperclassmen remarking about the long walk from Pluto, the outermost spaces.

Jillian took the central elevator to the first floor, deciding to stop in the staff lounge where she anticipated her peers waited for their opportunity to interrogate her. She found them gathered around two tables, their faces expectant.

"You poor dear. You must be in a state of shock," Geraldine Southern, the huggable-looking obstetrics instructor said, patting the chair next to her. She squeezed Jillian's hand, then held tight. "Tell us about it."

Jillian clenched her jaw to steady her nerves and squinted to stay her tears. She'd guessed the faculty wouldn't be shy. "The police officers told me not to talk about the details. I'll tell you what I can."

"That's fair," said Ursula Tankoff. Ursula was new to the staff. After years of working for the state caring for abused children, she hid her sorrow and cynicism among the pages of academia.

"I pulled into the lot around ten. All the faculty spots were taken, so I went to the back row. My coffee was hot— Ursula, you know I live about five minutes away—so I decided to finish it in the car rather than lugging it with my laptop and lunch." Jillian told the teachers about seeing the burgundy fabric and walking into the trees.

"You should have come inside. Now you'll have to answer a million questions from the police." Tankoff picked up her sandwich. "Then what happened?"

Jillian filled in a few details, then said, "I called 9-1-1. You know the rest."

"Did you see blood or anything?" Tankoff asked.

"I think that's the stuff the police don't want me talking about."

"You're a suspect," Tankoff said.

"Why would the police think I had anything to do with Bethany's death?" Jillian crinkled her face in dismay.

"Just like on CSI, you'll be a suspect because you were one of the last people, other than the killer, to see the victim alive."

"I hadn't thought . . . didn't imagine . . ." Jillian scrunched her eyes closed and shook her head. She found the notion distasteful.

"You better think. Write down everything you can

before you forget the details. Like charting, include it all."

"It'll be fresh in my mind until the day I die."

"Don't be so sure," Tankoff said, drawing out the last word, her voice musical.

Waves of nausea, which Jillian attributed to anxiety, lurched to her throat. She excused herself at the first possible moment, hurrying out of the office suite and around the corner to the bathroom faculty shared with students, staff, visitors, and the occasional wandering vagrant. She splashed water on her face and ran damp fingers through her collar-length hair, willing the upheaval in her stomach to stop. She returned to the suite, avoiding the lounge and co-workers' offices on the way to her own.

Jillian entered everything about the morning into a Word document on her laptop, then turned on the PC, retrieved the record of the counseling session with Bethany, and clicked on properties. She'd created the file at six-fifty the previous evening, making the counseling note as Bethany chatted about hospital assignments. They'd walked out together.

The memory of Tankoff's comments swirled forward, and Jillian wondered if Officer Goetz destroyed valuable evidence with his crash-through crime scene technique. Feeling unsettled and untrusting, she retrieved the photos of the big cop from her iPhone, saved them to a flash drive and added copies of the word documents. Then she sent everything to her personal email address. Overcautious behavior perhaps, but experience had taught her the only secure file was a backed-up file.

Hearing a tap, she looked up from the computer screen and saw a sweaty-faced, baggy-eyed man in the doorway. "May I help you?"

"Detective Simon Brewer." He entered the cramped

office, flashing the badge he held in his left hand while extending his right in a gesture of greeting. "My partner, Detective Zale, will join us in a few minutes."

She accepted the proffered handshake and gestured to one of two upholstered chairs wedged between her desk and the wall.

Brewer squeezed into the chair closest to the bookcase, taking a moment to browse the shelves before turning to Jillian. He settled himself, removed his notebook from his pocket, flipped a few pages, and cradled it in his hand, pen poised. "Mrs. Grey. Is it Mrs. Grey?"

"Ms. works for me, thank you."

Brewer flashed a warm smile. "I've seen you at a few faculty functions. I'm an adjunct over in the School of Criminology."

Jillian nodded, keeping a passive expression. "I thought I recognized you."

"I'd like to start by getting some routine information."

"Fine."

"Have you worked here long?" Brewer asked.

"About ten years total, but I've been full-time for two. Before that I was an adjunct. Did hospital clinical rotations."

"Married?"

"Divorced." Jillian watched his pen move over the pad and wondered why he cared about marital status. Ursula Tankoff's comment about being a suspect concerned her. She decided to be forthcoming and responsive without volunteering extra information.

"Where do you live?" Brewer reclined against the chair's back. Damp crescents poked from under his fleshy biceps, and a dark band of perspiration circled the waist of his light colored slacks.

He smelled of Old Spice and sweat. Jillian rolled her chair back until it tapped the credenza, increasing her distance and attempting to get upwind in the draft created by the air-conditioner. "South of Oakland on the Intracoastal Waterway." She recited both address and telephone number.

"Alone?"

"No. My roommate is Chantal Rice. Teaches chemistry." She pointed toward the southeast. "Next door in the School of Physical Sciences."

"Hefty rent, even sharing."

Jillian nodded.

"I'm familiar with the building. Several stories, inside garage, second level pool. I tagged along with a buddy when he looked at an apartment there a few months ago." Brewer paused for a moment. "Like I said, high rent. Even with a roommate."

"My work here is rewarding, but private colleges don't pay well. I work a few odd shifts in an emergency department to supplement. I don't understand why you need all this personal information about me."

"I like to get background information upfront. Helps me get a feel for people and saves me retracing my steps later." Brewer scribbled on his pad. "Take your time and tell me everything. Start with when you arrived on campus."

Detective Zale filled the doorway, an arrogant look on his face. "I got here right on time, I see."

She glanced at the detective. "I don't believe we've met."

"My partner, Detective Zale," Brewer said.

"Have a seat." She leaned back, crossed her legs, and took a deep breath, exhaling slowly through her nose, willing self-control.

Zale sat. "Continue."

"I arrived later than usual. There were no vacant spaces closer to the building, so I parked in the last row near the trees. Since I had several items to carry inside, I decided to sit in my car and finish my coffee. It was about ten. I had no appointments or classes today, only office hours." She repeated the details—burgundy fabric, the body, vultures.

Zale said, "You were the last person to see the victim alive. Is that correct?"

"Bethany is . . . was . . ." Jillian paused and exhaled with a sharp hiss, ". . . in my beginning nursing course. I wasn't the last one to see her alive, though. Whoever killed her saw her alive after I did."

Brewer held his pen at the ready. "When did you last see the girl?"

"A few minutes before seven. We finished our conference. She waited while I gathered my things. We left the building together. Then she told me goodnight. She wanted a soda for the drive home. Bethany walked across the rotunda to the vending machines, and I went to my car. I can see her in my mind. She settled the backpack on her shoulder—most of the girls use the rolling ones, but not Bethany—then she waved to me with her pocketbook."

"You left the young woman alone?" Brewer said.

"Yes. I didn't think about it. There was a group of men at one of the tables—it looked like a study group—and it was still light." Jillian drummed her fingers on the arm of the chair, realized what she was doing, then moved her hands to her lap.

"Is it usual for you to stay late for conferences?" Brewer said.

"We finish lecture at five. I have appointments for maybe an hour, sometimes longer. Bethany asked to see me about her grades. After class yesterday was the most convenient for both of us. I had others scheduled first, so she got in line. A couple were verbose." Jillian shrugged. "Bethany waited."

Zale said, "So the two of you left together at seven?"

Jillian sighed. "As I said, a few minutes earlier."

"Where did you go when you left?"

She paused for a moment. "I went home, changed clothes, ate a bowl of Cheerios for supper, and went for a walk on the beach."

Zale raised a brow. "Is there anyone who might remember seeing you?"

"I took the service elevator and left through the garage like every other night, so I didn't talk to the guard." Jillian looked at the ceiling, thinking. "There was no one around that springs to mind. On the beach, I chatted with some tourists—but there was nothing distinctive about them. We didn't exchange names."

"You don't remember much about your walk, but you sound sure about when you left work."

"Detective Zale, like always, I made a conference record at the end of our meeting." Jillian retrieved the electronic document and displayed the file properties. She pointed. "Six-fifty-five.

"Can we have a copy, please?" Brewer said.

"I suppose." She clicked the printer icon.

The printer activated with a whirl and a series of plastic-on-plastic chinks.

"Email it to me, too, if you don't mind."

After typing in the email address Brewer provided, she attached the document while he scribbled away. Jillian distrusted the note-taking. It made her curious and anxious at the same time. A small pit of nausea returned. She swallowed.

Zale said, "It's seems a coincidence you left Newland after normal hours yesterday, then happened to park in the exact, right place to find her body."

Jillian handed Brewer the warm copy of Bethany's counseling record, but focused on Zale.

"And you happened to notice burgundy fabric even though you were late for work?" Zale said.

"First, this is a college. Normal hours are whenever the buildings are open and classes are in session. There are activities in this building from eight in the morning until ten in the evening, five days a week. Second, I wasn't late for work. I arrived later than usual. I sat in my car to finish my coffee." Anger swirled within. Zale seemed to twist everything she said. She took a calming breath, thinking it's his job to ask these questions. "Faculty members have discretion about work hours. It's mandatory that we are here for our classes and posted office hours. That's about it. Since I see students on Thursday evenings, I don't make appointments for Friday morning. I use it as private office time. It's not even on my schedule." She pointed to the calendar taped to the office door.

Zale glanced at the document and nodded. "Did you have classes today?"

"This is redundant," Jillian said, her voice edgy. "No. I pulled in around ten."

"No reason to be upset, ma'am." Zale paused. "Dispatch clocked in the call at ten-fifteen."

"Seems right to me. I sat in my car a while before noticing what I assumed was a book bag and going to investigate."

"You're all dressed for work, but you wandered into the bushes, risking your good clothing. You said you had no particular reason to believe you'd find anything but a backpack." Zale nodded, punctuating his comment. "By the way, we didn't even find the backpack you said the victim was carrying."

Her willingness to be forthcoming dissipated. She waited for him to continue.

"Answer my question, please." He sounded annoyed.

"What is your question, sir? I don't believe you asked one." Jillian kept her tone polite, controlled.

"Why did you decide to enter the trees?"

"Detective, crime on campus is a big problem. A backpack could contain several hundred dollars' worth of textbooks. If someone stole the backpack, helping recover the property would be a good thing. Don't you agree?"

Zale said, "Why not call security?"

"Didn't think to do that. It was only a short distance away. Wasn't a big deal in my mind." She repeated the sequence of events. "By the time I realized it wasn't a backpack, I was already in the bushes."

"You're a regular campus do-gooder, aren't you?" Zale said.

Detective Brewer looked at Zale and raised a cautioning hand, then shifted his gaze to Jillian. "So, when you realized it was a school shirt, you continued into the trees. Do I have that correct?"

"A second later, a couple steps further, I saw blond hair. I hurried into the trees at that point. I recognized Bethany right away. I checked to see if she was alive."

"What did you do next? Call 9-1-1?"

"I looked around a few seconds first, trying to

understand. I found it shocking, confusing. I moved several feet away."

"Not an uncommon response," Brewer said, his voice gentle.

"Then I called 9-1-1. I stood there a couple of minutes after the operator disconnected, then went to my car." Jillian struggled to keep the exasperation out of her voice without success.

Zale leaned forward in his chair.

She tried to roll her chair back a couple inches, crashing it into the credenza.

He pointed to Jillian's bandage. "What's wrong with your arm?"

"Ah . . . In the bushes. I got caught, and I hurt myself getting loose." She touched the dressing, noticing a sting.

Zale's smile didn't reach his hard eyes. "What were you searching for in the trees?"

She took a moment and thought about ignoring Zale's question. "My father is a retired police sergeant." She shrugged. "I suppose, in my shock, I was looking for any piece of information that would tell me what happened to Bethany. When I realized how silly that was, I retraced my path to the car."

Zale edged closer to Jillian's desk, encroaching further into her space. "You're telling us you came upon the body of your student, called 9-1-1, then had the presence of mind to retrace your steps? Pretty impressive, Mrs. Grey." He raised both eyebrows, smirking.

"Sir, I'm the daughter of a career cop, and I'm an emergency nurse. If nothing else, I try my best to function in emergencies." Then feeling another wave of nausea, she added, "I might not have a calm stomach, but I usually keep a cool head."

Brewer said, "We appreciate the fact you controlled yourself." He paused. "Who's your old man?"

"Ron Grey. He retired from Ft. Lauderdale PD thirteen years ago. He was a sergeant downtown for the last few years. Before that, he was on patrol."

"I remember him," Brewer said. "He retired after his twenty in New York, came down here, did another twenty. We used to tell him he should've opened a restaurant or a garage like the rest of the retired New Yorkers. He said police work was in his blood."

"Ron's daughter. Huh." Zale bit his lower lip, looking thoughtful, his tone conciliatory. "He still into martial arts? I remember him doing his thing with the Explorer group. Man, he must have been fifty at the time."

"He was. But, no, he had to give it up when he had his first heart attack."

"Did he get you involved with the sport?"

"He sure did. My mother. Me. My daughters. Even my ex-husband. Dad insisted. Said we all had to learn to protect ourselves."

"You call your old man yet?"

"No, but I will as soon as you gentlemen leave me."

"We're about done here," Brewer said. "Nate, you finished with the rest of the nursing faculty?"

"Yup. They didn't have a lot to add, most of them never heard of the girl. They haven't had the victim or her friends in their classes yet. Mrs. Grey, here," Zale said, thumbing in Jillian's direction, "is the only one besides the Dean to have any consistent connection with her." Zale pushed back his chair and stood. "Mrs. Grey—"

"Ms.," she said.

Zale said, "We may want to talk with you again."

"I'm not leaving town."

Brewer extended his hand, "Tell your dad Sy Brewer sends his regards."

Jillian hesitated for a moment, then took Brewer's hand, thinking it best to stay on good terms with the amiable detective. She watched the officers walk down the hall and out into the lobby. When the glass door clicked shut behind them, she picked up the telephone and dialed. "Dad, I need to tell you what happened."

CHAPTER 4

Jillian sat across the table from Chantal Rice, her longtime friend and roommate. At five-five, Chantal stood an inch taller and weighed a few pounds less. Mixed heritage had graced her with even, fine-boned features and skin the color of the café latté she adored.

Aruba Beach Cafe, the casual hangout the women frequented, boasted an ample bar, plenty of tables, lazy paddle fans, the smell of roasted pineapple, open-air access to the outside world, and a view of the ocean. Both divorced, the women had decided to share rent for an apartment close to Fort Lauderdale's beach and live a more laid-back life style than either had enjoyed during their failed marriages. The bar exemplified their desires.

Jillian finished an update on the events of the day, ending with her uneasy feelings about the interview with Brewer and Zale. "They have no reason to consider me a suspect, but Zale, the arrogant one, seemed to treat me with suspicion." She sipped her Merlot, gazing at the expanse of white sand and the glassy blue ocean beyond. "Even Brewer, the nicer one, seemed accusatory at times. The whole thing unnerved me." She shook her head. "I can't believe this is happening."

"Believe it, girlfriend." Chantal paused. "They're the same two detectives who came asking questions in the Physical Sciences building late in the afternoon. A couple of uniformed cops came first, collected names and addresses, asked if anyone saw anything, who was where, that sort of thing. Then the suits came and interviewed specific people."

"Did you talk to them?"

"I did. Zale asked where I was this morning. He asked if I was home when you left and if it was usual for you to leave for work midmorning."

"What did you tell him?"

"The truth. You're a workaholic, and your habit is to arrive early. He wanted to know why you went in late today. I said he should ask you."

"He already did. Doesn't look like he was satisfied with my answer."

Chantal fluffed her straightened hair with her fingertips. A long moment later, she said, "Why did you go in late? It is unusual."

"I didn't sleep well again." Jillian nibbled a bit of grilled sirloin, washing it down with wine. "Seems like I never sleep well. The whole scene with Deirdre's accident plays in my head like an endless video loop. I want to stop the memory and sleep, but I'm afraid I'll forget her, or she'll look down from heaven and find me disloyal. When my alarm went off at six, I turned it off, stayed in bed. I felt so exhausted. I couldn't move."

Chantal touched Jillian's hand. "Maybe you should go back to the grief counselor. Couldn't hurt." She shrugged.

"I can't spend the rest of my life visiting a shrink." Jillian took a deep breath and exhaled with a huff. "What bothers me most is Pasquale hasn't lost a moment's sleep over his daughter's—our daughter's—death. Never did. Never will. He acted sorry, sure, did the usual guilt thing, but he just drank more and gambled away our savings." Jillian shook her head, thinking it pointless to rehash old hurts. "Maybe I'll call for an appointment. I guess I have issues."

"Of course, you do, sweetie. A drunk driver smashed into your baby girl while she drove the 'Vette you didn't want her to drive. It wasn't your fault. Pasquale handed over the keys. You weren't home. You would have insisted on the Volvo." Chantal repeated the familiar words like well-rehearsed lines from a long-running play.

"So, what you're saying is he should be up nights feeling guilty, and I should be having the dreams of the innocent." Jillian laughed without mirth.

"Something like that."

"I should have been home to stop her from taking that car. Young girl in a hot car—big target. Pasquale should have had better sense. The police said the other driver dogged her for a couple of miles. She called 9-1-1 on her cell phone."

Chantal nodded at the retelling of the story. "All the shoulds in the world won't change things. You know that. Assigning blame won't bring Deirdre back either." She turned in the direction of Aruba's entrance. "Speaking of the devil. Here he comes."

"Who?"

"Pasquale Lorenzo Pascasio," Chantal said, her faux Italian accent making the name musical and rhythmic.

"Ah shit, damn, son of a bitch," Jillian said, jerking her head side-to-side for emphasis with each curse. She glared in the direction of the tall, slender man.

Jillian started dating him while a high school freshman.

He was a senior. She'd found him irresistible with his clear blue eyes and thick brown hair. Time had turned him prematurely gray, providing an air of sophistication. Women pursued him in droves. He seemed to enjoy the attention, flirting at will, though she once believed he didn't cheat. For her part, she never had another boyfriend and, despite the urging of friends, hadn't dated since the divorce.

"Ladies," Pasquale said. He kissed each woman on the cheek, then pulled out a chair and sat. "Mind if I join you?"

"Be my guest," Jillian said, restraining a bit of apprehension. "What brings you to our humble hangout?"

Three months earlier, he moved into a high-rise condo overlooking the New River in downtown Fort Lauderdale. After suffering severe financial reversals in the stock market—and at the race track, too—he'd returned to day trading with apparent success. Gambling, apparently, still suited him.

"On the Internet this afternoon, I saw a clip about the girl murdered at Conover. The article mentioned you found the body. I wanted to make sure you were okay. When I stopped by your apartment and you weren't there, I decided to look here."

"Thoughtful." Jillian looked in his direction but avoided eye contact.

"You okay?" Pasquale said.

"Yes. But, how did it get on the Internet already? It's only been a few hours," Jillian said.

"There was a brief mention on the six-o'clock news— channel four—just enough to say the authorities weren't sharing any information yet," Chantal said.

"I saw it on a student nurses' blog," he said.

"You read that stuff?" Jillian asked, sounding

incredulous.

"You should check it out. Your name comes up a lot. Maybe Allison mentioned it. Anyway, I looked it up while surfing the Net one afternoon, waiting for a stock to move." Pasquale wrote the Internet address on a napkin and slid it across the table.

She wondered why Pasquale would be perusing nursing sites, but decided not to ask, preferring to keep their encounter impersonal. Allison, their married daughter, was also a nurse. She discussed computer-related topics with her tech-savvy father and everything else with her mother. "What did it say?"

"Someone attacked and murdered a young woman. There were pictures, too."

"My God, they didn't have pictures of poor Bethany's body, did they?" Jillian said.

"Nah, the scene. The pictures look like an amateur took them with a cell phone after the police finished. They were grainy, poor quality. You see the crime scene tape and trampled greenery. That's about all."

"Thank heavens for that much. What else did it say?" She had a sinking feeling, and her eyes stung.

"After the cops finished outside, they interviewed students and faculty, then spent at least an hour in your office."

"That's all true."

"There's a couple of links, one to a news channel and a second one to the evening addition of the paper. The writer is posting under a fictitious name by the way. I suspect because he or she writes mostly trash. Anyway, it says you're the prime suspect."

Jillian choked on her wine, sending a spray across the

table, splattering the front of Pasquale's ivory-colored linen shirt. "Why would I kill that young woman? That's ridiculous." A hot flush rose to her face, and a tingle crawled from her lumbar spine all the way to her neck.

"Damn it, Jillian." Pasquale frowned, stretched across the table, dipped the corner of a napkin in her water, and worked on removing the purple stains from his shirt.

"Sorry. Here, use this." She tossed a purse-sized stain remover his direction.

"The blogger claims your test bank's for sale, and the victim had something to do with it."

"When a test bank gets out, we make new questions. We don't murder the student. Expel them if we can prove it, yeah."

"The writer said the girl made an appointment with you yesterday to make a deal." He rubbed at another spot. "This stuff works."

"What kind of deal?" For the second time that day, Jillian felt an oppressive sense of anxiety. Her heart thumped, threatening to explode. She struggled to slow her breathing.

"Check the details on the Web."

She gulped the last of the Merlot, setting the oversized stemware glass on the table with a clunk. "If someone told the police that garbage, they'll think I had a motive to murder the girl. Who would want to do that to me?"

"Let's go." Chantal picked up her pocketbook and nodded toward the exit. She paused, looking thoughtful. "The murderer is trying to frame you. It's obvious. The blog might lead you to the killer."

"Someone in my class would have had to write the damn thing."

"Not necessarily," Pasquale said, raising a gold-braceleted

wrist, index finger extended, to punctuate his point. "They come from different backgrounds and work in a variety of places. You've said so yourself. Somebody had a reason to kill the girl. Could be the blogger is screwing with people's minds, casting doubt, playing around. Or, maybe he or she has a specific reason to want you gone from the picture and wants to push the cops in your direction.

***

After leaving Pasquale in the bar, Jillian insisted on flagging a cab for the short ride home, forgoing their usual walk along the beach.

As they exited, Jillian handed the cabby a ten-dollar bill. "Keep the change."

Chantal reached into her purse. "Let me get half of that."

"No. I'm the one who's spooked."

Chantal held open the entrance door, allowing Jillian to step inside. "The whole point of implicating you is to distract the police from the murderer. If someone is setting you up, why would they attack you? Doesn't make sense to me. They'd want you to stay healthy and remain a viable suspect. I think you're in more danger from the police than anyone else."

"I'll try to relax." Jillian pushed the elevator button for the third floor. "I'll stop at the Evers apartment and see how Eleanor is feeling. She'll be expecting me."

After they stepped off the elevator, Chantal hugged Jillian, lingering a moment, patting her back.

"Thanks. I needed that." She forced a grin. "I feel so alone and vulnerable."

Chantal put the key in the door of apartment 312 while Jillian knocked on the adjacent door. "Anything to help, I'll do. You'll get through this mess."

"I hope so."

"I'm with you, girlfriend," Chantal said, opening their apartment door and smiling.

***

Jillian and Eleanor Evers had become close friends during the few months they'd lived as neighbors. Bonded by comparable grief in the loss of teenage daughters, Eleanor understood and supported Jillian. She, in return, helped to look after Eleanor who coped with the ravages of chronic lung disease.

"Evening, Dewey," Jillian said to Eleanor's husband as he escorted her into the apartment. "How's my friend tonight?"

"Our grandson came earlier and upset her with the details of that poor girl's death. Vincent brought Bethany along a few times when he and Shanna came for dinner. Bethany seemed to be a nice girl." Dewey Evers, a sixty-seven year-old fitness buff with blazing blue eyes and pure white hair and beard, led the way toward the living room. He wore his usual boating clothes, cargo shorts, and an open-to-the-navel white shirt. "I gave Eleanor some oxygen, and she settled down. We were on the boat today. Maybe that was too much, too."

Jillian shrugged. Eleanor liked the boat, tolerated the rides well, and kept a small oxygen tank ready and waiting for the outings. "It's too bad Vincent dwelled on the details about Bethany. He should have realized Eleanor would be disturbed with the news."

"It'll be on every TV station by morning anyway."

The apartment's layout mirrored Jillian's. The kitchen was the first left off the entry foyer. Next came the large living room-dining room combo. A bedroom and bath flanked each side of the main living area.

Eleanor reclined in a tropical-print lounger in front of the window from where she monitored activities both inside and out. She wore baggy, flowered pants and an oversized, brushed-cotton shirt. Wide-toed Birkenstocks covered blue-stockinged feet. The former San Francisco sixties' flower child looked at home in the throwback fashion.

Jillian retrieved a stethoscope and blood pressure cuff from a rattan end table, took the older lady's vital signs, and listened to her heart and lung sounds. "Sounds fine," she said, perching on the edge of Dewey's recliner.

"Vincent said you're a murder suspect."

"When I left Bethany was alive, well, and smiling," Jillian said. "I believe I was on the beach when the attack happened. I should have waited for her to get her soda and walk to the car. Maybe this wouldn't have happened." Jillian wiped a tear. "The whole thing brings my daughter's death back to the surface. It's like it's fresh in my heart again."

"Sweetie, your little girl will always be first in your mind when anyone close to the same age dies. When Vincent gave me the news, the first person I thought of was his mother, and my heart broke all over again. But I've learned over the years, just because death in childbirth is somewhat natural, it still hurts." She patted her friend's hand. "I understand your pain, feel your sadness."

"I feel guilty. I should be feeling grief for Bethany, not my daughter. The poor parents must be devastated." Jillian shook her head, ignoring the tears streaming down. After several moments, she grabbed a tissue and dabbed the moisture from her cheeks, then took a deep breath and exhaled slowly. "I'll get a grip now."

Eleanor appeared thoughtful. "I saw you head toward the beach about eight last night, right before I turned on the TV to watch my program."

"You saw me. Great. I need to tell the detectives. I didn't think anyone saw me except a couple of tourists I'll never find." Jillian leaned forward.

"You might find them. I see the same folks walking toward the beach every evening. Why don't you go and have a look? Can't hurt."

Jillian shuddered. Good sense indicated she wasn't in danger, but she felt uneasy. "I guess I could do that."

"What's the problem? You sound nervous."

Jillian told Eleanor about the Internet site and her notion someone wanted her out of the way. "I can't fathom how I'm a threat to anyone."

"From what Vincent tells me, you're well-liked—except by the ones who are failing."

"Your grandson would know. What else did he tell you?"

Jillian knew Vincent Barrera and his grandmother were close. She raised him when his fifteen-year-old mother died. He wasn't always truthful, however. Jillian recalled several instances when he gave Eleanor a rosy version of the truth, omitting his own near-failing grades and frequent brushes with school disciplinary measures.

Jillian remembered Eleanor commenting that Vincent had trouble with authorities in California, but he was underage and treated as a juvenile. The couple relocated to

Florida with their grandson to change his environment and give him a fresh start. To Jillian's knowledge, he hadn't had any further legal problems since the move and supported himself by working evenings as a bartender at a high-end Cuban restaurant on Oakland Park Boulevard. Eleanor seemed convinced he'd outgrown his youthful rebellion, encouraged him to enroll in school, and helped him with his tuition.

Eleanor squinted, appearing thoughtful. "Vincent didn't tell me anything else about the poor murdered girl that I recall. Shanna came with him, but, as usual, didn't say more than two words." Eleanor shook her head. "I can't warm up to that one, but he's attached, and they get along well since they moved in together."

Jillian shifted the subject to the couple's boat ride, passed a few minutes listening to their comments, then excused herself. It was late, and she wanted to research that blog.

CHAPTER 5

"Hey, Dad." Jillian strolled into her parent's Queen's Court residence early Saturday morning and glanced around. The condominium glowed in soft pastels and rattan. "Where's Mom?"

Ron Grey kissed his daughter on the cheek, then waved to the table-for-two in the kitchen. "Off to the pool for her exercise group." He refilled his coffee cup and poured one for Jillian.

"You should go along. It would be healthy for you."

While in his mid-sixties, he'd suffered a major heart attack, resulting in severe activity limitation. He seldom drove or left the house unaccompanied, except for an occasional solo trip to the store or to the police department to socialize with his old buddies. Insatiable reading of true crime novels—she suspected he got a vicarious kick out of them—and an affinity for crossword puzzles had occupied him for the past ten years.

"I asked the doctor about watercise. He said it's fine as long as there's someone who can help if I get into trouble. The condo board ordered one of those defibrillators for the clubhouse. I'll go along after the machine arrives and the instructors learn to use it."

"Sounds reasonable." Jillian sipped the coffee, recognized the taste as decaf, and wished for caffeine. "Did you happen to talk to the detective?"

"I left a message, but he hasn't called back yet. Should be any minute now." He checked his watch. "Brewer was due in around eight."

"On Saturday?"

"Not unusual with a murder. They need to work while the trail is fresh."

The portable phone on the table came alive and filled the room with a soft electronic-jazz tune Jillian couldn't identify.

"It's Brewer," her father said, pointing to the phone's backlit green screen. "Quiet now." He pushed the speaker button. "Hello, Detective."

"Hey Ron, how's it hangin'?"

"Can't complain. My daughter told me about the young lady's murder and said your man, Zale, treated her like shit."

"That's how he is, my friend. Gets a twitch in his pecker and won't let it go. Keeps banging at the damn thing until he works it out."

Ron glanced at his daughter, then shrugged, mouthing, "Sorry." Then he said, "Yeah, you're right. I remember Zale from years ago. Good cop, tenacious as hell." He paused. "Is there anything you can tell me about the case?"

"Only that the scene was in rough shape, messed up by people and animals. What bugs Zale is why your daughter parked in just that place after she was one of the last people to see the girl. Puts her in a bad light."

Ron said, "Jillian didn't suspect someone was dead in the trees. Then she saw the body."

"The only thing—as a friend, not as a cop—is your

daughter needs to lawyer-up. To Zale, she's a person-of-interest in this investigation and has no alibi. He's going to pursue it until she's one-hundred percent clean in his mind. Okay? Hang on a minute."

Muffled background sounds suggested a hand over the mouthpiece on Brewer's end.

"Catch you later, pal," Brewer said.

After her father broke the connection, Jillian said, "Guess he wanted me to have a crystal ball, too. I told them why I entered the scene. If I knew there was a murder victim there, I wouldn't have gone in. I'm not stupid," she snapped. She raised her hands in apology. "I'm sorry. It's not your fault."

"Nobody thinks you're stupid."

"Zale apparently does. His twenty-twenty retrospectascope is in perfect form. Wonderful hindsight. I should have somehow known not to park in the last available spot yesterday morning."

"Damn, it's just cop talk. Give the man a break."

"There's more." She summarized the information about the blog Pasquale mentioned. "It's obvious someone is trying to make trouble for me, casting blame my way for Bethany's death."

"That kind of information can often lead an investigation astray, albeit temporarily." He paused. "The detectives aren't stupid either. They'll sort through it and arrive at their own conclusions."

"Do you think I'm a suspect?"

"You're a person-of-interest, and you can't prove where you were. You know as well as I do that person-of-interest is a polite way of saying suspect."

"Ah, but I do have a witness that I was on the beach. I

called Brewer's voice mail this morning to tell him." As she filled her father in, she carried her coffee cup to the sink, washed it, and put it in the rack. "I'm going home. I need to check that damned website and see if I can figure out who is defaming me."

After kissing her father, Jillian headed toward the beach, negotiating the sparse weekend traffic with ease. Even so, the trip across the county from Tamarac to east Ft. Lauderdale took the better part of an hour. During the ride, she focused on what she knew about the case, which was precious little.

Jillian parked in her assigned space in the garage and skipped the residents-only elevator, deciding to become more visible to the guards in the lobby. She'd never expected to need witnesses or an alibi and was private, though not secretive, when coming and going. She vowed to change that pattern, at least until police solved Bethany's murder.

Vincent Barrera stepped out of the elevator. "Hi," he mumbled, diverting his eyes. Though average in both height and weight, his mixed-parentage gave him brooding, good looks. He appeared to be Hispanic with Asian overtones, slanted-oval eyes, full lips, and thick, straight black hair.

"How's your grandmother this morning?"

"Okay. They're going out on the boat. Says it relaxes her." He replaced his customary pout with a forced smile that looked more like a grimace.

Jillian let the door close without stepping into the elevator, then touched his arm.

His brow wrinkled, and he frowned.

"Do you know about a nursing student blog on the Net?"

"Sure," he said, "everyone does."

"Guess I'm the last to find out."

"I meant everyone—students. Not everyone—teachers."

"Oh." She forged ahead. "Who's responsible for writing it?"

"Can't say. Only checked it out once or twice." He tugged at the hem of his tee shirt, then smoothed it over his jeans. "It's probably written by some girl with PMS who likes to complain."

"My name's on it. Do you think it's someone in my group now?"

"Who knows? But I heard you're the topic of discussion since you're a suspect in Bethany's murder."

"I'm not a suspect." Jillian's voice sharpened. "I'm concerned the comments will cause the police to think of me that way. That's why I want find out who's writing those lies about me."

"Can't help you there, Ms. Grey. Sorry." He stepped back. "Look, I gotta go. I've got things to do."

"Okay. Thanks for the conversation." Distracted, she watched Vincent walk toward the front entrance, then pushed the elevator button.

***

Jillian grabbed a bottle of water from the fridge and carried it across the living room, past the rose-flowered sofa to the dining table in front of the sliding patio doors. She centered the bottle on a coaster on the polished teak and stared through the glass doors at the shimmering blue of the pool on the deck one level below.

Barrera's attitude was annoying. She thought his comments deliberate barbs. She sat for a few moments, working up the energy to start her research, then moved to the desk in her bedroom.

Jillian settled herself in front of her laptop and searched for the Painful Process blog, clicking a couple of links along the top and learning the server was free of charge. Anyone, anytime, could set up a site. Text ran down the middle of the page, and except for screen names of the participants in the top right corner, there was no identifying information. Both margins flashed with a disorienting array of photographs and links, but again nothing useful.

Four individuals appeared to be involved with authoring the postings—Quick Shot, Pee Turbed, Sleeping Pill, and Cast Off. She smiled at the names and clicked on each one in turn, thinking that at least their names were unique.

As Pasquale suggested, the biographies contained no identifiers, and the email contacts were anonymous Yahoo and Hotmail addresses. All listings stated the writers were single-white-females in their first year of a two-year nursing program in a private college. They gave their location as Florida and provided no useful data, though they listed favorite movies, books, hobbies, and the like. She printed each bio before proceeding. Perhaps some phrase would connect and reveal a clue to a blogger's identity.

Jillian clicked on the link to Quick Shot's comments, wondering if the SWF entries were truthful. If so, the possible candidates narrowed by half.

Quick Shot rambled about lectures, classes, and exams, communicating raw feelings of stress and frustration.

Don't know how long I can keep this shit up. Financial aid hasn't come through. Busting my ass at work. The bitch told me it was my problem *and* she can't help. Sucks...No time to study. She says studying has to be my priority. Those were the b's exact words. What about life? I need some social life, too. Counselor said it may not be a good time for me. I guess the counselor and the b talk. Maybe I'll blow this place. Nobody gives a shit if we pass or not. I'm screwed. For the money we lay out to go to this freaking school, you'd think they'd cut us some slack.

Sleeping Pill's and Cast Off's comments ran along different lines, not mentioning their financial and academic situations. Jillian supposed that meant their lives were okay in those areas, and they were participating in the blog for the social kick. They posted pictures of the beach, the nursing building at Conover College, and a few awful, yet harmless jokes about nursing and medicine.

The last posting by Pee Turbed was another matter. It read:

ms. grey=BITCH. real pain in the ass, someone asked her to review for the exam, b said she tests to the objectives, and we should study that way. all the other teachers reviewed. why can't she? does she think she's friggin special?.

had her test questions for the last exam. during test review last term, that skinny creep stole the friggin test. he put his digital recorder in his pocket and mumbled, but it came out pretty clear. grey thinks she's smart. NEWS FLASH: she's really pretty stupid to give out the exams and let everyone talk.

so bethany bought the exam and then sold it to me-I'm sure I paid extra-she always wanted money. Nothing for free with that girl. i did okay... and i shared it with friends. problem is the b figured it out, and now she'll change the questions for the next test, i mean, she announced it. WHAT THE HELL????!!!! how stupid is that?

bethany was a real ass-kisser, actress type, someone offed her, b should be suspect, i mean, she has to know it was bethany who got the exam from the upperclassman and sold it. actually, i think bethany put-

out to get the exam, she never was above screwing to get her way. bethany told us all that she was going to get b to give her a good grade in exchange for keeping the test bank secret. i figure she pissed off b, and b did her in.

Jillian stared at the computer screen in frank disbelief. True, she knew about the stolen exam. Tanya Li informed her after someone, whom Li declined to name, offered her the opportunity to buy the questions. Jillian then discussed it with the class while explaining a change in the test review policy. Still, she hadn't suspected Bethany was the culprit and wondered if it was true.

Jillian didn't anticipate the students being honest with the police about the cheating. Open admission of dishonesty would jeopardize their nursing careers. She believed the only hope was to discover the bloggers' identities and inform the police. But, she had no clue about how to unmask them.

CHAPTER 6

Outside the Medical Examiner's office, Detective Brewer tapped the car's remote to unlock the passenger side door for his partner, Detective Zale, then took his customary place behind the wheel of the Taurus. Out of necessity, Brewer drove. It was the only way to control his motion sickness.

Brewer reflected on the postmortem exam as he waited for Zale to settle into his seat. "Franklin didn't give us anything we don't already know," he said, referring to the M.E.'s ruling that Bethany Newland died from a broken neck.

Franklin had pointed out extensive bruising on the left side of Newland's jaw and the back of her head, suggesting the assailant grabbed her and twisted her neck until it snapped. There were extensive defensive bruising on the body, indicating Newland fought the assailant and didn't die right away. Franklin estimated the time of death as early evening.

Zale said, "It'll be interesting to see what the scrapings from under the fingernails show. The drop of blood on her collar is interesting, too. It's a different type than the vic's. Probably the perp's. Good DNA source."

Brewer nodded in agreement, then started the car and

put it in reverse. "Athletic girl. A dancer, strong. I'm betting on a male killer."

"Not necessarily," Zale said. "A woman with skills would be plenty strong enough." He paused. "Think she knew her attacker?"

"Possibly. That's where we start," Brewer said, accelerating onto Interstate 95. "He obviously got behind her in the end. Maybe she was worn out, or overpowered. Her wallet was empty except for a few coins, but there was two hundred dollars in the zippered compartment in her purse. No jewelry. Could've been mugged. A guy might not know about the pocket in the lining."

"Doesn't feel right." Zale slipped his notebook out of his pocket. He riffled through the pages, fanning the corners like a deck of cards. "We need to talk to Newland's social group again. Get each one alone and see what they say. And, I want to talk to the family once more. When we informed them yesterday, they didn't seem upset enough to suit me."

"Let's start with the boyfriend, Cooley. What's his address?"

During the drive to the western part of the county, Brewer and Zale set aside the investigation and talked about the Marlins. Zale, a staunch baseball fan, was a Miami native. Brewer hailed from New York City and considered himself a born-again fan, abandoning his birthright loyalty to the Yankees to appease his overzealous partner.

The digital alert on Zale's cell phone interrupted the conversation. He flipped it open, frowned, and answered. "Yeah . . . No, at a crime scene . . . Don't use that. I have plans for it." He listened for a few moments. "Give me some time here. I'll get back to you later."

"What's that about?" Brewer asked.

Zale shrugged. "I'm serious about retirement. I'm setting myself up, seeing if I can pull together enough cash to start a business."

"It's a gamble these days. The economy sucks."

Zale grinned. "I like the odds, and no one is handing me my retirement. I didn't inherit a bunch of dough from a long lost, rich aunt like you did. Lucky bastard. That ring you got for your wife must have set you back a few big ones."

"That it did, my friend."

Cooley's apartment was in a two story, L-shaped building set back from the street. A small pool and a couple of concrete tables filled the common patio area. Brewer parked in the guest space closest to Oliver Cooley's first floor corner apartment. From the brief interviews conducted by patrol officers on Friday, they knew Cooley lived with his older brother, a manager at the Internet research firm, DataNet. Their parents resided in Lakeland and provided support to maintain Cooley's full-time academic status. He didn't have a job.

Though it was almost eleven in the morning, Oliver Cooley answered the door in boxer shorts and tee shirt. He blinked and squinted into the light. The creases in the side of his face suggested the doorbell woke him, and the heavy smell of sleep hovered in the air. "Yeah? Whuz up?"

"Oliver Cooley?" Brewer said, showing his shield. "We'd like to talk with you." He stepped into the apartment, forcing Cooley to backtrack.

"You could have called first and let me get up. I gave the cop-lady my telephone number."

Brewer glanced at the interview report he held. "Yup, it's here."

Cooley waved his hand toward the living room. Text

books, newspapers, and empty beer bottles littered the coffee table, sofa, and floor in between.

Zale pointed to one of the empties. "You old enough to drink, kid?"

"I'm twenty-one, but my older brother is the beer drinker." He cleaned off the sofa and picked up most of the litter, piling the books and papers on the table. "Have a seat. I'm going to take a leak and put on some pants."

Cooley reappeared a few minutes later. He carried a coffee mug and wore baggy jeans, an over-sized shirt, and leather sandals. He pulled a straight-backed chair away from the wall and sat.

"We're interviewing as many of Bethany Newland's associates as possible. We need to establish all we can about her—who she knew, what she did, where she went, how she lived."

"The cop-lady told us yesterday someone mugged her." Cooley's eyes filled with tears, and his pale complexion flushed.

"That's one of the possibilities," Brewer said. "What was your relationship with Bethany?"

"We were going out." Cooley stood and left the room, returning with a hand full of crumpled tissues. He blew his nose before stuffing the tissues in his pocket.

"Dating?"

"Boyfriend, girlfriend."

Brewer smiled. When he interviewed kids, or talked with his own for that matter, the nuances of their language amazed him. He'd learned to take the time to clarify meaning.

"How long were you going out?"

"Six months, maybe. On and off, not steady. Bethany wasn't sure what she wanted. I don't think she wanted me."

"Tough to take."

"No. It's the way women are. Weird, hormonal, flaky." He blew his nose and wiped a tear from his cheek.

Brewer, the father of three girls and four boys ranging in age from seven to twenty-three, nodded his head. He understood.

"How was the relationship lately?"

"Good for the last few weeks, seemed to be settling down."

"I understand she wasn't sure about becoming a nurse either."

"That's true. Bethany wanted to be a dancer. She was awesome. Kept taking classes and didn't tell her parents. That's why her grades were so bad—dancing instead of studying."

"Why didn't she major in dance?"

"Her parents wanted her to be a doctor. Bethany agreed to attend nursing school to shut them up. But they weren't happy. They paid the tuition, but wouldn't pay for dancing, so she got a job as a waitress to get the money to dance. If they paid for that, too, she wouldn't have had to work, and her grades would have been better. I figure it was her parents' fault she had to meet with Professor Grey. It's really their fault she's dead."

"I don't suppose they see it that way." Brewer paused, glancing at Zale.

"How did Bethany explain her time away from home? I'll bet you lied for her." Zale raised a brow.

"I don't know for sure. Sometimes she told them she was with me. They'd call here. I'd say she was in the bathroom, then call her."

"So you did lie. You're a real pal. Makes you a bit hard

to believe now." Zale scowled. "What happened it they called her cell?"

"She'd ignore them. She didn't want the background noises to alert them."

"How did she explain her low grades?"

"She didn't. Bethany is . . . was twenty-four. Even though she lived at home, they never asked. That always seemed strange to me. My parents are on me about my grades every freaking second. They say it's their right since they're footing the bill."

Brewer smiled at the familiar scenario.

Zale pulled out his notebook. "Who were Newland's friends? Other than you, I mean."

Cooley said, "Carrie Kennedy, Tanya Li, Vincent Barrera, and Shanna Albano."

"Did Bethany associate with anyone else on a regular basis?" Brewer said.

"Didn't tell me." Cooley shrugged and frowned. "Sometimes she was vague about where she was going. When I'd call her, she wouldn't say where she was. She blew off my questions. Told me to quit being possessive."

"You think she was getting it on with someone else? Pretty girl. Working in a restaurant. She had to get hit on a lot," Zale said.

Cooley used a tissue to wipe at his eyes. "Bethany was private." He took a sip of coffee and made a face. "She liked to keep people, even me, at a distance. Wanted her own space and own life. That's all."

"So the privacy thing was okay with you? Didn't it make you mad? Maybe make you want to take charge?"

"No. A thousand times no. You had to accept Bethany on her terms, otherwise she'd move on."

Zale scribbled in his notebook. "Besides robbery, can you think of any reason someone would want to kill your girlfriend?"

"No. Bethany was a good person, helped people. Even though she didn't want to be a nurse, she was good with patients. She liked being in the hospital and working with the old folks." Tears streamed over Cooley's cheeks. He made no attempt to dry them. "Can you go now?"

Brewer nodded and stood. "One more thing, for the record. Where were you Thursday evening?"

"Here. I was here with my brother. You can ask him."

"Okay, son," Brewer said. "If you think of anything else, give us a call." He handed Cooley a business card.

***

After checking at the residence and speaking with her mother, the detectives found Carrie Kennedy sitting on a bench at a neighborhood park while her three year-old daughter, Emily, busied herself playing in the sandbox. Kennedy thumbed through a three-inch thick textbook that lay open on her lap. Children laughed and giggled on a nearby jungle gym while women hovered close. An older lady sat in the only tree-shaded area on the far side of the playground.

"Carrie Kennedy?" Brewer said, stopping in front of Kennedy. She reminded him of his daughter's friend—brown-skinned, thin, and pretty, with tiny braids tied together with a blue ribbon.

"Yes?" Kennedy replied in a lilting island accent, her manner polite.

Zale displayed his badge. "Detective Zale." He

55

indicated his partner. "Detective Brewer."

"I recognize you." Kennedy faced the area where her daughter played. She made a sideways motion with her hand. "Can you move so I can see my daughter, please?"

Zale stepped left. Brewer stepped right.

Brewer said, "We understand you were friends with Bethany Newland. You carpooled and studied together."

"Yes."

Zale glanced around the area, then took a half step forward. "Did Miss Newland confide in you about her personal life? Anyone she may have been seeing besides Oliver Cooley? We want to know what she did, who she associated with."

Kennedy looked from one detective to the other. "Gentleman, I have a child, work full-time, and have responsibilities. When I can, I see my daughter and my mother. She is living with me while I finish school, then she wants to go home to Jamaica." She paused. "I'm sorry about Bethany. I mourn her, and I'll miss her. But, I know nothing of her personal life except she went to Conover, dated Oliver, and worked at the same Cuban restaurant as Vincent Barrera."

Zale's eyes widened. "How long did they work together?"

"I don't have any idea, but they acted like they knew each other for a long time."

Brewer handed her a card. "Thank you for your time. Call us if anything more comes to mind."

When the men walked away, Zale waited a beat for Brewer to fall in step. "Interesting. Newland and Barrera worked together."

"Probably nothing. But we need to check it out, talk to

the restaurant owners."

The men settled in the car and headed toward the Li family grocery. Tanya Li said she'd be there all weekend.

Zale skimmed the interview sheet on Barrera. "He said he knew the victim casually. Said he and his girl, ah, Shanna Albano, sometimes hung out with Newland and Cooley. He didn't mention they worked together."

"Wonder why." Brewer turned south onto University Drive.

"So do I," Zale said, making a note. "They seem to be an evasive bunch of kids."

Brewer turned onto a cross street, then made a quick left. He parked in front of Li's Oriental Grocery, which filled three units in the aging strip mall. Through the windows, he saw five or six customers queued for checkout and several more putting items in green plastic baskets as they moved through the narrow aisles. High shelves overflowed with foodstuffs in colorful packaging.

Zale said, "I'll bet the tiny girl behind the register is the one we want."

Brewer exited the Taurus, grunting from the effort. "The only way to find out is to ask. If it's her, I hope there's someone to work the register for a few minutes."

Brewer followed Zale into the store.

Cheryl Li, the woman behind the register, sent them to an office in the rear of the store. "My sister is taking a telephone call." She glanced at the older-style, dual-line phone next to the register. "She is finished now."

Li sat behind the desk in the cramped office with her chair facing the window. Brewer tapped on the doorjamb.

She swiveled to face them. "Detectives Zale and Detective Brewer, I have been expecting you. Carrie

Kennedy called and said you were making your rounds. I am Tanya Li."

Li appeared to be around fourteen-years-old, though Brewer remembered she gave her age as nineteen during the earlier interview. He estimated her to be five feet tall and about ninety pounds. Her demeanor and sense of purpose impressed him. He said, "We have a few questions."

"Have a seat, please." She stood and bent in a hint of a bow, then motioned to two tattered chairs. "I brought those in a few minutes ago."

"Kind of you," Brewer said, noting the difference in the reception between Li and the previous two interviewees. "First, we need to verify your personal information."

As Brewer read the demographic data from the interview sheet, Li verified the accuracy of each statement.

"How long have you lived in this country?"

"Six years. I was born in Taiwan."

Brewer made a note. "What was your relationship with Bethany."

Li maintained her formal manner, nodding to the men, but taking her time before speaking. "Bethany, Oliver, Carrie, and I were a foursome. We were in nursing class together when we started the first time, so we became friendly. We took several subjects together as well—chemistry, psychology, English—then we re-entered the nursing program together this fall."

"Did you all flunk out together?" Zale said, his voice heavy with sarcasm.

Li wrinkled her face, her expression disgusted. After a few seconds, she responded in a slow-paced manner, giving each word its own moment in time. "No. I withdrew because I registered for too heavy a load. My mother became ill, and I needed to work many hours in the store. That is why I slowed my studies. Please ask the others about their reasons."

"Sorry," Brewer said, jumping in. "We didn't mean to offend you."

Li nodded.

"What was your relationship with Bethany?" Brewer asked.

"We studied in the library, and we talked on the telephone. Bethany wasn't serious about learning, and I am. She would come unprepared and expect me to give the information. I liked her, so I helped. She was improving, I believe, doing better than the first time she took the class. Usually, though, I said I needed to work in the store, then I would study on my own."

"You're doing okay in the program?"

"Yes. It's very hard. I work hard, but I earn all high marks. Professor Grey is an excellent teacher. She does everything to help us."

Zale tapped his pen against the bound pad he carried. "Did you see Bethany outside of school?"

"Once or twice we went to the mall. But Bethany was older and had a boyfriend. I have my family and my friends from church."

"So, you're saying Bethany really wasn't your friend. You just helped her study because you're a do-gooder." Zale sneered.

"I do not believe that is what I said."

"Do you know about the Painful Process blog on the Internet?" Brewer said, cutting his eyes in warning at Zale.

"Yes."

"Who's involved?"

Li looked at her hands. "I cannot say."

Brewer sensed her lie and wondered why. He decided she seemed upfront with the rest of her answers, so he wouldn't pursue it. Maybe later. "A student yesterday said to look at the blog to find a motive. We did. One writer said Ms. Grey had a motive for killing Bethany, something about a stolen exam."

"I told the professor about the exam being for sale. Bethany offered it to me for a hundred dollars."

"Did you buy it?" Zale asked, raising an eyebrow.

"No, I do not purchase exams. I am honorable."

"You're saying you could have had the exam questions, but you chose to do it on your own?" Zale looked at Brewer. "Like I said, a real do-gooder."

"Some people are honorable. Perhaps in your line of work you don't meet honorable people. In my culture, people act with honor in all things, I believe."

"Then why do you lie about who wrote the blog? Doesn't seem so honorable to me." Zale rolled his eyes.

"I am not certain, and therefore I cannot say."

"What did Grey say when you talked to her about the exam?" Zale leaned closer to Li.

"I did not tell her it was Bethany. I said a student offered me the exam. She asked me who. I told her I would not tell her. I did not want to be disloyal to my friend, but I did not think what she was doing was right."

"Did anyone tell Ms. Grey it was Bethany?" Brewer said.

Li appeared thoughtful. "No, I do not believe anyone would. Bethany was careful about who she spoke with. Some students do not seem to have ethics. They want to cheat and have it easy, but they have to take a state exam. For that, they will need to have the right answers in their minds."

Brewer smiled at Li's wisdom. "What did Grey say when you told her?"

"She appeared very angry. She could not understand what they were thinking, and said, 'it would be better to spend their energy studying rather than devising ways to cheat.' Then she said—she was still upset—she would have to pull an entirely new exam, and it would take many hours. I felt sorry. The professor works very hard."

"Then what happened?" Brewer said.

"I remember her saying, 'I better get working on it.' She thanked me and promised not to say anything about who told."

"Why'd she say that?"

"I asked her not to tell anyone. My classmates would not understand. I would be ostracized."

"Can you think of anything else about Bethany?" Brewer said.

"There is one thing. I do not know if it matters, but I think she had another boyfriend besides Oliver."

"What gave you that impression?" Brewer said.

"I heard her on her cell one day, talking about meeting someone for dinner. It sounded like a date."

"How so?" Zale asked.

"Bethany said, 'I can't wait to see you again.' Then she said, 'I'll dress nice for you.'"

"You're sure she wasn't talking to Cooley?"

"Yes. Oliver was still finishing his exam, and we were outside waiting for him. She was definitely not talking to him."

Brewer and Zale asked several follow-up questions to clarify the information Li provided. Once satisfied, they thanked her and excused themselves.

"Where to?" Brewer said as he started the car. He adjusted the air-conditioning to accommodate the warm midday.

"Let's hit the family first, then go across town and catch Barrera and Albano. They live together."

"We need to see Evers to verify Grey's alibi." Brewer pulled into the street and stopped at the red light on University.

"Why'd she call it in? Sounds guilty," Zale said.

"You accused her of murder. Remember? What do you expect?"

"Sy, you stricken by her? She was last to see the vic alive."

"You've got a point."

Zale flipped up a finger. "And . . . she found the body. She has scratches on her right arm. The M. E. thinks Newland scratched someone. There's that blood on Newland's collar. Grey took martial arts. If she's a quarter as good as her old man, she has the skill. Quite a list of coincidences if you ask me." He waved four fingers in the air. "Four. That's a lot."

"True," Brewer said, accelerating into the flow of traffic.

"And . . . Newland stole her exam."

"Newland peddled it. We don't know who did the stealing, and we don't know if Grey knew."

"I'm betting she did," Zale said.

"You need to keep your perspective." Brewer shook his head, taking a moment before continuing. "So, on our short list we have Cooley—motive, jealousy."

"Unknown boyfriend—motive, unknown."

"Mugger—motive, money," Brewer said.

"Or Grey, to stop dissemination of her exam."

"Doesn't fly. Needs to be stronger."

"I don't think so. Maybe Grey accused Newland, they fought, and things got out of hand." Zale bit his lower lip.

CHAPTER 7

"Left at the light. Gated community about a half-mile down. Trotter's Run," Zale said, checking his notes.

Bethany Newland's parents resided in an opulent neighborhood. A red brick guardhouse flanked a visitors' lot and welcome center—the source of real estate transactions rather than unconditional welcome. The property management center sat across the driveway.

Brewer stopped behind two cars in the guest lane, awaiting his turn with the guard

"The builder has offices in half the space, and there's community services in the rest." Zale pointed to the administration building. "That department is responsible for the newsletter, social activities, and security. The maintenance fee includes everything, lawn and pool maintenance, exterior upkeep, common grounds, the whole gamut."

"How'd you get so well-versed about how the other half lives?" Brewer asked, reflecting on Zale's constant harping about retiring early and in style.

"Caught a case here when you were on vacation. An embezzlement deal. One of the partners decided to settle the score by shooting his accountant."

"Wasn't that the one with the stupid prick-brain? Smart enough to amass a fortune, but so dumb he did his own killing—with his own gun, no less."

"Yup, short case."

Brewer pulled in front of the guard's window and flashed his badge.

"Who are you visiting, sir?"

"The Newlands."

"I need to call?" The guard reached for the telephone.

"Go ahead. Meanwhile, open the gate," Brewer said.

The guard shrugged and raised the bar blocking the drive.

Huge ficus trees shaded the half-mile drive stretching before them. Brewer hung a left at the end of Canopy Drive, then followed the guard's specific directions through several successive turns before stopping in front of the house.

"Big friggin' joint," Zale said. "Man, I could get off on living in a place like this."

"You and Claudia haven't even bothered to get married, much less have kids. Why would you want to maintain it?" Brewer laughed. "Now, my brood would fit nicely in a place this size."

"Ever figure out what was causing it?"

"What?"

"All the kids."

"Sure did. Got it fixed." Brewer grinned but didn't pursue the familiar banter. Instead, he focused on the property. A BMW, Mercedes, and Jaguar sat in the driveway, each positioned in front of a garage door, leaving the fourth door vacant. Lush greenery framed the two-story entrance, high windows providing a glimpse of the house's circular staircase.

A short, muscular man of about sixty answered the door. In response to Zale's introduction, he said, "I'm Dr. James Newland, Bethany's father. Have you come to tell us who killed our daughter?"

"No sir. May we come in? We have a few questions," Zale said.

Dr. Newland frowned and squinted, shaking his head. "Does it have to be right now? We're in the middle of planning a funeral for our child."

"We'll be brief." Brewer advanced a bit. "But we do need to talk to you and your family today."

Dr. Newland stepped away from the door, waving his hand to usher them into the foyer. "I'll get my wife." He pushed an intercom button on the wall near the door. "Kippy," he said, "the detectives have arrived."

A squat woman of the approximate age of her husband emerged from a side hall. A similar appearing young woman followed.

Nodding to his wife, Dr. Newland said, "Dr. Kippy Brooks, and this is my daughter, Janice," he said, motioning to the younger woman. "We'll talk in the living room."

As they crossed the marble-tiled entry, Brewer observed Bethany was different from the family in every way—looks, body build, and life style—and wondered what kind of stress that created. After settling next to Zale on the crushed-velvet sofa, he saw a group portrait on the mantle. The early-thirties man in the picture, Brewer assumed he was the son, seemed to have been cut from the same mold as the parents.

"Tell us what progress you've made," Dr. Newland said.

Zale said, "Dr. Franklin, the ME, said that the cause of death—"

"I'm aware of the cause of death. Franklin is a friend of mine. I spoke with him earlier." His eyes flashed toward his wife. "Let's spare Bethany's mother the rehashing of the details."

"As you wish," Brewer said, in an effort to head off Zale's rude approach.

"Your daughter waitressed at a restaurant near the school to pay for dance lessons. Friends say she stayed at Conover to please you but preferred to dance." Zale shifted his gaze from one family member to the next. His eyes stopped on the mother.

"My daughter wasn't a waitress," Dr. Brooks said, appearing disgusted. "I would have known if she did something like that." She shook her head.

"Why?" Zale said. "You find honest work a problem?"

Dr. Brooks grimaced. "No. Well, yes. Bethany didn't have to work. We paid for everything. We wanted her to get an education and become self-sufficient."

"You were aware she still danced?"

Dr. Newland frowned. "No."

Janice slid forward in her chair. "I knew. I saw her through the studio window a few months ago. I asked. She said it wasn't my business, so I dropped it. I suppose I agreed." She touched her mother's arm. "Sorry, Mom."

"Miss Newland, where is the studio?"

Zale made a note as she recited the information.

"How about her and Oliver Cooley?" Zale looked from one parent to the other, his eyes wide and brows raised..

"We didn't like it, but she was grown and picked her own friends. The good thing, if there was one, was he's in the nursing program, too. They studied together. I believe it helped her focus," Dr. Brooks said.

"Did she date anyone else?" Brewer said.

Dr. Newland raised his eyebrows. "I have no idea."

Zale and Brewer continued the questioning, learning the family had little to do with Bethany's life, other than providing housing, food, and funding. However, they were aware of the Painful Process blog and thought that Newland was one of the members. She had shown Janice one of her entries a few days prior to her death.

When they were back on Canopy Drive, Zale said, "Strange bunch. Not a wet eye in the place."

"Some people don't let it show in public."

"Crap, man, we're talking about their daughter being murdered."

"I imagine they're crying when nobody's around," Brewer said.

"I'm not so sure. I wonder if they were as estranged from their daughter as they seem. Maybe one of them wanted the kid out of the way. Embarrassment, inheritance, whatever. People kill for less. Every last one is strong enough to break a neck. And their alibis are each other."

"You want to put the family on your short list?" Brewer glared at him. "Come on. Get real. Maybe I'll buy the schoolteacher, but now the family? What's with you?"

"Persons of interest, my man, persons of interest. In case you didn't notice, we don't have a lot to go on." Zale voice had an edge. "I say we cast a broad net and see what we drag in." Zale pulled his notepad from his pocket. "Let's go see Albano and Barrera first, get them while it's early in the day. Then check Grey's alibi." He rattled off the address of the building where Albano and Barrera shared an apartment.

Zale's cell phone vibrated. He put it to his ear. "Hey.

68

I'm on the job . . . Soon, real soon . . . No. Play it cool. I'll handle things like we said." He disconnected and returned the cell phone to his belt.

Brewer said, "Sounds like someone is getting into Claudia's space."

"Nah, not that. Just planning our retirement—mine and Claudia's."

***

Shanna Albano answered the door. A well-worn karate uniform, cinched at the waist with a tattered black belt, did little to hide a curvy figure and full bosom. "Oh, it's you. Vincent, the cops are here." She pushed the door outward.

"We have a few follow-up questions." Brewer grabbed the handle and stepped inside.

"Interesting get up." Zale looked her up and down, thinking she looked good in the gi. He followed Brewer into the small apartment.

"I have a session to teach in a few minutes, and Vincent has to leave for work. It's not a good time."

Zale advanced and flashed his badge. "Talk to us here or talk to us at the station. Your choice."

"Whoa," Barrera said, coming into view. "Let's get it over with." Barrera wore black pants, white shirt, and black sneakers. "I've only got a few minutes, too. I have to get to work."

"If you're cooperative, we'll be done in a few minutes," Brewer said.

The apartment looked threadbare and dingy, though Zale supposed it was clean and tidy for college kids. They walked past a wooden BEACH sign with an arrow pointing east and sat at a small, chipped kitchen table.

"Coffee?" Albano asked, holding the pot.

"Black," both detectives said.

"What do you want?" Barrera sat and pushed the chair away from the table in the same motion.

Zale felt the hair stand up on the back of his neck. The kid needed to learn to control his attitude. "We understand you were friends with Bethany Newland."

"What of it?" Barrera said.

"We're talking to her friends to get background— learning all we can," Brewer said.

"We weren't close," Albano said. "We studied together or had a beer when I went to Vincent's restaurant to meet him after work."

Zale saw Barrera shoot Albano a cautionary glance. "Bethany worked at El Restaurante Cubano with you?" he said, focusing his gaze on Barrera.

"Lots of people work there."

"Why didn't you mention it to the officer yesterday? You sounded like you saw Bethany at school and in study groups on occasion," Brewer said, his voice challenging.

"Just because we work in the same place, doesn't mean I had anything to do with her. I tend bar. She waitressed. What did I do? Hand her a drink now and then, that's all."

Brewer took a sip of his coffee, then leaned forward in his chair. "Let me get this right. You tend bar where she was a waitress, your girlfriend drinks with her and waits for you, and you pass it off. Why was Bethany hanging around drinking with her," he pointed to Albano, "when she could have been home? Odd, don't you think?"

"No, I didn't think about it. Besides, I wasn't assigned to watch her."

Zale glared at Berrara. "Watch your smart mouth, unless you want to continue this conversation downtown."

"Sorry." He didn't sound sorry.

Brewer verified the basic information about the two. They were not forthcoming about their personal lives or their histories. The detectives left the apartment with a promise to return with more questions, unless, of course, the couple chose to volunteer additional information. Neither did.

Brewer said, "You didn't have much to say in there, Nate. Losing your touch?"

"Nah, I wanted to give you a chance to strut your stuff. Figured you'd be better with the kids, given your experience."

"You need to keep an open mind."

"Screw you, Brewer." Zale grinned.

***

Dewey Evers welcomed the detectives into his home. After directing them to the sofa, he sat in the recliner next to his wife. "Now, how can we help you?"

Zale said, "Ms. Grey said you could vouch for her whereabouts on Thursday night."

"I can," Eleanor Evers said. "I was sitting in this chair, and I saw Jillian stroll to the beach."

"Are you sure it was Ms. Grey you saw?" Zale said, thinking the woman was old and ill.

"Certainly. I see her go in that direction almost every night. She's a dear neighbor, helps me a lot. I watch for her. She left later than usual, about eight, right before my favorite program."

"How can you be sure about the day if you see her almost every day? Are you positive?" Brewer said.

"I am." Eleanor Evers raised her chin a bit, then glared at Brewer. "Thursday is the only night that program is on. Also, my grandson came yesterday, on Friday. He told me the poor, sweet girl died, maybe was murdered. So I have a point in time. And," she frowned, "it was two days ago. I'm sick. I'm not senile."

"Who's your grandson?" Zale asked.

"Vincent Barrera."

Zale raised an eyebrow. "I assume you know his girlfriend."

"Of course. Nice girl. A little rough perhaps. She was in the Army. She still acts like that."

Zale tapped his fingers on the arm of the sofa. "Why didn't she tell us about her service record?"

Dewey Evers dropped the footrest on his recliner. "Shanna strikes me as secretive. Vincent told us she served in the Army and had some trouble. Shanna didn't say a word. In fact, when I asked about her background, all she said was she was born and raised in Houston. Her parents were divorced."

"Mrs. Evers," Brewer said. "You said Bethany was a sweet girl. Did you meet her?"

"Oh, yes. She came for dinner with Vincent and Shanna. She wanted so much to be able to dance, but her parents wouldn't permit it. I was the one who suggested she get a job and pay for it herself. The studio is expensive. Vincent didn't tell me where Bethany got the rest of the money."

The detectives left. As they rode the elevator, Zale said, "Grey has an alibi."

"Hell, we're not even sure if the old lady can see." Brewer exhaled through his nose, making a hissing sound. He led the way to the car without commenting further. Once in the street, he turned in the direction of the ballet studio where Newland danced in secret.

CHAPTER 8

After spending most of Saturday on the Internet attempting to determine the authors of the blog, then collapsing into bed for a restless night, Jillian drove to Boynton Beach for a Sunday barbecue. She anticipated spending the afternoon at her daughter and son-in-law's home, playing with her eleven-month old granddaughter, Maggie, and chatting with Allison and her husband, Harold. She headed in the direction of I-95 and avoided the scenic route.

Speeding north on the Interstate, Jillian reviewed what she knew about Bethany's murder, which was damned little, and where her own vulnerability might be. She had three links to the murder—seeing Bethany before her death, finding the body, and the anonymous innuendoes on the Internet. She couldn't do anything about the first two, so discovering who hated her enough to lie was the priority. Whether it helped with the murder investigation or not, she wanted to identify the writers.

During her overdose of blogs on Saturday, Jillian discovered many ordinary contributors concealed their identities while prominent people and managers published their names and electronic contact information. She had emailed the website hosting the Painful Process and received a curt response from the webmaster. The privacy policy included the option for members to register by pen name, email address, and password. He wouldn't give her names. He claimed he didn't have them. He suggested posting a comment on the site, and perhaps someone would contact her. It was a possibility, she supposed, but her first inclination was to avoid a public sparring match with an unethical student—if it were a student.

Cornering onto Allison's street, Jillian put the unpleasantness out of her mind. She intended to enjoy the afternoon.

When she rang the bell, her ex-husband, Pasquale, opened the door. "Jillian," he said, smiling.

Maggie giggled in his arms, squealing in delight each time her grandfather bounced her.

"Thought it might be you," he said.

Jillian stepped into the foyer while thinking well, so much for a stress free afternoon.

Across the spacious living room and through the far window, her son-in-law, Harold, worked on a laptop at the poolside table. The deck chair next to him sat askew. He pointed at a paper laying on the table, then refocused on the computer.

Pasquale reached toward Jillian's purse. "May I?" After she slid the strap off her shoulder and relinquished the bag, he handed over Maggie. "Looks like you need someone to hug."

"True, and this wonderful baby is perfect." She cuddled Maggie for a moment, planted a kiss on her velvety cheek, then settled the tot on a hip.

Maggie smiled and babbled, smearing drool on Jillian's

sleeve.

"I didn't expect to see you today." Jillian resented his annoying ability to read her moods. Too bad he hadn't used his talents to improve their relationship when they were married.

"I came over this morning to help Harold with the computer. He's having problems configuring his wireless router. Luckily, I have the same model. They asked me to stay for lunch. I hope you don't mind."

She sighed. "No, I don't mind. I toyed with the idea of calling you. Maybe we can talk for a few minutes about blogs and such."

He put his arm around Jillian's shoulder, resting his hand on Maggie's back. He gave them both a squeeze. "You're not letting that garbage affect you, I hope."

"How can I not? Some clown accused me of murdering Bethany because she was selling a stolen exam. I'm afraid the police will latch onto that little tidbit and conclude I have motive."

"You're not being realistic. The police won't consider that motive. They were students once themselves. People say terrible things about their professors when things don't go their way."

"But why me and why now?" Footsteps on tile caught Jillian's attention.

"Good, you're here," Allison said.

Jillian kissed her daughter's cheek, then glanced at the slight swelling at her waist. "Honey, how are you?"

"Better than you are, I suspect." Allison held her arms out for the baby, who giggled and nestled deeper into her grandmother's arms. Allison grinned. "I have things to do anyway. You okay with her?"

"Yes, I enjoy holding my grandbaby. I'll give her back when she cries or needs her diaper changed."

"Yeah, right. Like usual you'll give her back when you're heading for home. I'll be lucky to get one hug all day." She looked at her parents. "Don't let me interrupt you. I've got things to do in the kitchen."

A perpetual optimist, Allison often voiced hope for a parental reconciliation. Jillian loved her ex-husband, and she thought he loved her, but the wounds pulling them apart were fresh. After many years of tumultuous marriage, the relationship disintegrated following the death of their eighteen-year-old daughter, Deirdre.

Pasquale led Jillian into the dining room and sat, motioning for her to sit as well.

She pulled Maggie's highchair close to the table, secured the baby in the seat, dug into her purse for house keys, and dropped them onto the tray with a jingle.

"What's on your mind?" he asked.

"Can you help me discover who wrote that entry on the web? The webmaster refused any assistance."

"You've looked around the site for identifying information?"

Allison brought two tall glasses of tea, set them on the table, then dropped a few crackers on the baby's tray.

After thanking her daughter, Jillian said, "Sure. I read all the hogwash entries, way back to the beginning, trying to deduce identities. Some of them may not even be current. Faces change. They come and go."

"I checked the site, too. Nothing came to mind." He shrugged.

"I don't understand why Allison told you about it and not me."

"She didn't know about the nasty entries until I mentioned it this morning. She told me about the site in passing several weeks ago, and I looked it up. I find it somewhat entertaining, so I check it out once or twice a week."

"Must be a boring life you lead as a day trader." Jillian chuckled, forcing herself to lighten the mood.

"When the market isn't moving, the day can be slow."

"How do I find out who the bloggers are?"

"No clue." Again, he raised his shoulders. "You need a subpoena or a hacker."

"Know any hackers?"

Pasquale looked pensive. "Ah . . . no. I'll ask around and call you if I come up with anyone."

"Thanks. I'd appreciate that." Jillian picked up a cracker Maggie dropped and put it on the table well out of the baby's reach. She laughed when the baby flung a second one on the floor.

"I like to hear you laugh. It brings back old times. Makes me wish things were different," Pasquale said.

"We're the way we are because that's how you wanted it. Why pretend regret?" She searched his eyes, hoping to see the truth.

"I'm not pretending. When I asked for the divorce, I thought it was what I wanted. But now, I'm not sure. Maybe we can date again, see where it takes us."

"Now you're sounding like Allison."

He touched her hand. "Things would be different. I'm doing well in the market. I'm not gambling. I'm not drinking." He stroked her arm.

She softened. "I'll give it some thought after this mess is over. Right now, I can't think of anything but this."

"Not even me."

"No, especially not you." She paused, distracted by Maggie rattling the keys and spewing gibberish. "Let's talk about something else. Shall we?"

For a few minutes, Pasquale joined Jillian in entertaining the baby, then he left the room.

Jillian took Maggie from the highchair and lowered her to the floor. After a false start and several teeters, Maggie took a few steps, then plopped onto her diapered bottom. Jillian helped her stand and waddle into the kitchen. Maggie laughed and smiled at Jillian, raising her feet high with each exaggerated step.

"Need an assistant?" Jillian said when Allison looked up from the cutting board.

The step-by-step house renovation had yet to reach the kitchen. Marred counter tops sat atop dreary walnut-laminate cabinets. Jillian had helped select the replacements, which they would order in the near future, the couple's cash flow permitting.

"I'm fine. Keeping Maggie occupied is enough." Allison pulled a second onion from a mesh bag. "Tell me about what's going on. Dad showed me the blog. It's horrible."

Jillian sighed. "I wish you'd told me about the website earlier. Maybe I'd have figured out who was writing it by now. I have to start from scratch, and I'm not sure where to begin."

"I thought you knew. I mean, we never talked about it, but it is at your school."

"I was clueless until your father mentioned it the other evening."

Allison's eyes widened, and a smile crossed her face.

"No, dear. He read about Bethany's death and came to

check on me."

"I was hoping." She touched her mother's hand with cool, wet fingers. "Tell me what's happening with the death of that nursing student. It's terrible."

Jillian gave a quick summary. "It has me in knots. I need to know who's writing those terrible things. I'm so afraid the detectives will believe the accusations. Your grandfather says the police are smarter than that, but I don't believe him. One of the detectives, guy named Zale, Nathan Zale—my heavens he was rude when they questioned me on Friday."

After they'd worn out the topic, Jillian steered the baby in the direction of the patio, letting her toddle for a few steps before offering two fingers for support. She checked the pool gate, then settled Maggie on a padded blanket on the floor.

Jillian joined the men at the table, finding the laptop closed. "Hope I'm not interrupting."

"No," both said at once.

"Tell me about your group this term," Pasquale said.

"There's not much to tell. It's ordinary. Sixty members. Ninety percent female. Fifty-percent under thirty. About a third each, black, white, Hispanic. Oh, and one Asian girl."

"I'd look for the bloggers among the discontented, under-thirty group," Harold said

Jillian bit her lower lip. "There's—maybe—a few more repeaters than usual. The dean welcomes them back as soon as they finish remediation so she can get them through the system and out of her hair."

"How many of them succeed?" Pasquale said.

"Better than seventy percent make it through the beginning courses. I'm not sure what percentage get through the entire curriculum. Half that number perhaps."

Pasquale leaned forward in his chair. "Seems to me, more should pass if they're taking it the second time. Must be stressful for the kids knowing so many flunk."

"Of course, it's stressful," Jillian snapped. His tone was annoying. "But, contrary to common opinion, being a nurse isn't easy. They make the choice to attend and many of them make the choice to do well. They do what's necessary to get the information and succeed." She tapped her fingers on the table and stared at her ex-husband. "For example, several of the those who previously failed got high Bs on the first exam. They're doing what needs to be done. Some of the others, well, they haven't learned their lesson."

"How about Bethany?"

"Smart enough girl. Good family—all physicians. Satisfactory qualifying scores. But, she didn't want nursing. She wanted dance."

"I didn't know the whole family are doctors," Pasquale said.

"How would you? It wasn't in the paper."

"You've got a point." Pasquale scowled and relaxed in his chair. "How about the people she hung out with? Are they doing okay?"

"All the students are bright. They have to have a minimum grade point average to get in, and they need to maintain a specific GPA to stay in the program. The variable is motivation and whatever else they have going in their lives. Those who make the commitment do well. Those who can't, fail. Some on the lower side were Bethany's friends."

"Really?" Pasquale cocked an eyebrow.

"Why all the interest?"

"Looking for a reason for someone to dig at you. That's

all. Trying to help."

Jillian shook her head. While Pasquale was solicitous during their rare social encounters, he made no effort to pursue her otherwise and didn't keep in touch. The sudden concern mystified her.

Deciding she was looking for trouble where none existed, she stood. "Watch the baby, gentlemen. I'll check on Allison." Jillian gestured toward the kitchen.

"Back again?" Allison said when Jillian entered the kitchen.

"What do you need done?"

"Start the salad while I take the chicken to Harold. He's the chef today."

Jillian was washing the lettuce when Allison returned.

Allison said, "If you aren't doing anything tonight, would you mind staying with Maggie? There's a movie at the Plex we want to see. I think there's a seven-o'clock show."

"I'd love to sit with my granddaughter."

"I'm afraid it'll be boring. She's always down for the count by seven, and today she hasn't napped. She's likely to crash long before that."

"You're a lucky mom. She sleeps so much you actually have some time for yourself. Not like you. When you were a baby, you were up at all hours."

"Harold's mother said he slept his babyhood away. Guess it's genetic."

Jillian smiled, planning to use the opportunity to prowl the Internet again. Harold would let her use his laptop, and his wireless network worked, thanks to Pasquale. And if she were lucky, the baby would wake up, and she'd have a chance to rock to sleep.

***

Jillian glanced at Pasquale as they stood in the doorway of Allison's and Harold's house watching the couple back out of the driveway. "You don't have to stay. The baby is asleep. I'm going to hang out for a couple of hours, reread that website. They'll see the movie, have coffee, and be back by ten."

"I don't mind. You've been dwelling on the blog. What else do you expect to learn by spending another three hours poking at it? I'll find someone who can get the information for you. Give me a day or two."

"It would be a big help."

"Let's find a movie on cable." Pasquale made a show of looking at his watch. "There must be something on demand." He closed the door and headed into the Florida room where he picked up the television remote. "Want to watch Goldfinger? That used to be your favorite."

"Sean Connery works for me. Turn it on."

Pasquale retrieved their wineglasses from the patio, refreshed the contents from the white zinfandel jug in the fridge, and handed the one with the apple wine charm to Jillian.

She fiddled with the small pewter ornament. "Clever, these things." Jillian settled onto the far end of the sofa, glass in hand, kicked off her sandals, and rested her feet on the coffee table.

Pasquale sat next to her rather than on the opposite end of the sofa. When she didn't say no, he put his arm around her shoulders.

Now what have I done? Jillian thought. "I'll check the baby. We're at least fourteen commercials away from the start of the movie."

She popped off the sofa, setting her wine on the edge of the kitchen counter, then scooted down the hall, verifying what she already knew. Maggie was asleep. The Goldfinger theme in the distance interrupted her concentration on the baby's breathing—soft, innocent breaths.

"Maggie okay?" Pasquale asked when Jillian returned.

"Um." Jillian sat on the far end of the sofa.

Pasquale moved closer. "I should take your choice of seats as a hint, but I'd rather not." He put an arm around her shoulders again. "Relax. Watch the movie."

Snuggling close to him felt warm and familiar. When he took her drink out of her hand, a drop spilled. When he kissed her, she responded. Just like always. The closeness of being married, the physical contact, didn't exist in her life, so Jillian didn't resist.

He guided Jillian's movements positioning her next to him on the sofa.

The warmth of his hand seared into the skin on her back and expert fingers loosened her bra.

His touch awakened dormant feelings and the urgency of desire.

"I miss you. I've always found you incredibly sexy. I need you," he murmured, running his hand down her abdomen.

Jillian planted her hands against his shoulders and pushed. "Pasquale, I'm sorry, but I don't want to have sex with you. I'm sorry if I led you on."

He moved away and sat. "You didn't lead me on. You only went along. But why not, may I ask? We've always been good together."

"I don't want to want what I can't have. I'm learning to

live life on my own terms. Though we were compatible in the bedroom, we didn't do so well in the rest of the house."

"What difference can one tumble make?"

"That's the point. The next time I make love, if there is a next time, I want it to make a difference."

He picked up the wineglasses and handed one to her. Tapping the rim of her glass with his, he said, "To future differences." He brushed a kiss across her lips, took her hand in his, and turned his head toward the TV.

CHAPTER 9

Jillian was the first faculty member in the office on Monday morning. She wanted to meet with the dean, Marlene Stevenson, and share her concerns before the usual line of appointments formed. After stowing her lunch in the lounge refrigerator, she settled behind her desk, leaving the door open to listen for Marlene's arrival. Jillian booted the desktop computer, opened the test bank, and resumed her revisions.

It wasn't the first time, and it wouldn't be the last, that students acquired test questions. Cheating was a constant source of frustration to teachers, and they revised questions when necessary. Better the cheaters put their efforts into studying, Jillian thought, locating the ending point of her last session—a week earlier. Then they wouldn't have to be dishonest.

"Make a fresh copy first, then more changes," Jillian said, addressing the computer and thinking that a backup could prove to Brewer and Zale that the breach of her materials wasn't a crisis. Plugging her jump drive into the USB port, creating a folder, and copying the entire bank, including the administrative logs, took only a few minutes. While waiting, she pondered her predicament. Paranoid or prepared? Better to be both. After a moment's hesitation, she duplicated her emails, counseling records, grade books, and course materials, then repeated the process on a second drive. Paranoid.

When Jillian heard the dean's door open, she closed her work and stepped into the corridor. "Marlene, can we talk?"

"Grab a couple coffees and bring them along."

Jillian prepared a pot of coffee in the workroom and waited for it to brew, then fixed two cups. Balancing the coffee, a notebook, and a pen slowed her movement to the office at the end of the hall.

Marlene greeted Jillian at the door, taking the coffee and placing it on the desk, and giving her a warm hug before waving her to a chair. Marlene's salt and pepper hair hinted at an approaching sixtieth birthday and gave testament to many years managing problems in academe. At five-six, she was a couple inches taller than Jillian and about the same build, svelte but not too thin. "I've been worried about you. It's a shock to find a body like that. I can't imagine."

"It's every bit as horrible as you imagine. I've been trying to put it out of my mind. Meanwhile, I need to tell you what else is going on."

It took Jillian several minutes to update the dean. "I can't understand why anyone would want to set me up for murder. I've always had a reputation for being fair. The students give me outstanding course evaluations and positive feedback. Graduates come back to give me progress reports and thank me for giving them a good start in nursing."

"First, for your information, several people from your class have called in wanting to help you. I don't see what they can do at this point, but they'll come forward on your behalf if necessary." Marlene appeared thoughtful. "Jillian, we're all standing with you. You have my respect and admiration and the esteem of the rest of the faculty as well. We all think a lot of you. Now, hang on a second." Marlene tapped a few keys on her keyboard. Seconds later, a roster spewed from the printer. "Look at Bethany's class. Lots of repeaters."

Focusing on the printout, Jillian said, "It's nothing unusual. It often takes a restart for the less serious ones to figure out they've entered a demanding program."

"Yes, but the difference is this time you have a bonded group of malcontents. They were with you last fall, socialized together, failed together, and reentered the program together. They asked for another professor when they registered and were vocal about not having a choice."

"You didn't tell me." Jillian raised a hand signaling her frustration.

"No reason to. You shouldn't be concerned. They could have transferred to another school. Awareness could have caused you to do something differently, and that wasn't my intention."

"What I would like to do is figure out who is defaming me. We can talk to them and demand they stop. It's one thing not to love your professor. It's quite another to try to get her arrested for murder."

"If we identify them, I'll be happy to schedule a conference." Marlene hesitated. "Did the police find the blog?"

"If they haven't already, they will soon. One of the kids will tell them. I thought I'd do it myself, reinforce the fact I have nothing to hide."

"Seems reasonable." The dean ran her pen down the list, ticking off several names. "You'll want to pull the files for these. They're the ones who were vocal. Bethany's isn't available. The police have it."

Jillian's face contorted. "I never would have guessed Bethany hated me when we met last week. She was warm, friendly. Seemed sincere and interested in doing well."

"Perhaps Bethany made the appointment to do as the blog suggested, then had second thoughts."

"You read it, too?" Jillian said, leaning forward in her chair, stretching to reach the roster. "I wish you'd told me."

"Sit down, please. I planned on talking with you today. I found out about it yesterday."

Oh, oh, Jillian thought, a feeling of dread welling inside.

"This is very difficult for me. At the moment, I don't need to do anything about your employment status. Announce Bethany's funeral is tomorrow and proceed with your lecture." While handing Jillian a flyer with the information, Marlene continued. "Post this in the hall upstairs and by the elevator."

"Okay, but what did you mean about my job?"

"I have a meeting with the president this morning. He saw the allegations on the Internet as well, and he's already had several calls from concerned parents. Most of them have children on this list." Her fingers made a tapping sound on the roster, highlighting each name. "We'll have to wait and see what he says. You know I support you. I'll do what I can."

Picking up the list, Jillian stood. "I appreciate anything you can do for me. I need my job. I'll never make expenses without it. I only work part-time in the emergency department now." After making brief eye contact with Marlene, Jillian hurried out.

In the storage room, Jillian pulled the files, then hauled them to her desk. She'd speak with as many people on the list as possible over the next couple of days. Several were in her clinical rotation as well as her classroom. Intuition told her the bloggers were among the ten readmits.

The first two records were for older women—known computer-phobes. Jillian set their folders aside. They weren't suspects. Both were performing well, keeping up with the reading, and passing exams. They approached Jillian often with questions about their lessons or with social chitchat.

The remainder of the ten, two men and six women, were in danger of failing again, Bethany among them. Jillian pondered the possibility Bethany was one of the bloggers. Pee Turbed postings appeared after Bethany's death. Quick Shot's comments about financial aid didn't seem to apply to Bethany. Perhaps Sleeping Pill or Cast Off. Without a file to peruse, Jillian made notes about Bethany from memory.

Two more of the remaining seven did not seem to be candidates. While they were discontents and computer savvy, they were loners—arriving alone, leaving alone, and sitting alone in the rear of the room. Jillian reasoned they wouldn't form a four-person site. Their folders expanded the reject pile.

Flipping open the top record on the short stack remaining, Jillian began taking notes. Shanna Albano— Vincent Barrera's girlfriend, 27, receptionist for Carnegie and Watson Investments, born in Texas, four years of service in the Army with a dishonorable discharge, admitted to the nursing program after review of Army records found the situation to be non-relevant.

Grimacing, Jillian wondered what the situation had been and made an entry in the margin to check Albano's background further. While wondering how to go about that task, she picked up the next one.

Vincent Barrera—25, waiter at El Restaurante Cubano,

born in California. Barrera's admission sheet contained scant biographical data. After a moment's hesitation, Jillian included Barrera's history as learned from his grandmother.

Though he was attentive to the older folks, there were many years where Barrera's behavior caused problems in the family, and he had a sealed juvenile record in California. Drawing more detail about Barrera's troubled youth from his grandmother was a priority.

Oliver Cooley—21, Bethany's unemployed boyfriend, withdrew earlier, now readmitted and earning passing grades.

Carrie Kennedy—23, bill collector for American Credit Company, failed previously, borderline now. Picturing her, Jillian saw a tall and thin girl with beautiful dark brown skin and a perpetual frown. She whispered to both Newland and Li during any pause in lecture. On several occasions, Li had rebuked Carrie.

Tanya Li—19, works in parents' oriental market, lives at home, withdrew earlier because of academic overload, readmitted and doing well, computer expertise.

Polite but tending to grumble, Li sent frequent emails to Jillian asking for information about exam questions or complaining that Jillian lectured too fast or made tests too hard.

After studying the data and the roster, Jillian added a couple of additional names to the list. She left room for information from their records, flipped the notebook closed, added it to a pile of materials, and left for lecture.

***

Jillian arrived thirty minutes before class. As usual, several of the high-achieving students arrived early as well, gathering in the seats in front of the podium. "I'm glad to see you all here," she said.

"We've been waiting for you, Professor Grey." Ingrid deHernandez, a middle-aged woman with three grown children, nodded to her friend, a younger lady named Gabriella Alvarez. They approached the podium. "What can we do to help?" Ingrid said in heavily accented English. "We heard about stuff on the Net. We don't want people thinking badly of you,"

"I need the names of the people who are writing about me."

Ingrid stared at the blackboard.

Gabriella took a step back.

Jillian forged ahead, though she knew the students would be reluctant to give names. "Who writes the Painful Process blog? Do you know?"

Ingrid exhaled with a whoosh, then bit her bottom lip. After several seconds, she said, "I don't know, not for sure anyway. I do have a few ideas." Ingrid glanced at her friend, who shook her head. "I don't want to say unless I'm certain. I'll listen to what people say about it. Maybe I can narrow it down for you. It wouldn't be fair if I was wrong."

"It's not fair that I'm being libeled either. They have no identifying information on their site, not even a traceable—at least, not by me—email address. I'm powerless to defend myself." Jillian tapped her pen on her notebook. "Their accusations are not harmless and could cause the police to consider me a suspect."

"I think that's what they want," Gabriella said, her voice almost inaudible above the hum of the projector, computer, and fluorescent lighting. "It's a given they are unhappy and want to put the blame on you. Bethany's murder gave them a way to discredit you. They're failing, and now they have a way to get back at you, for a little while, maybe." She moved side to side, shifting her weight. "My husband is a police officer. He said the detectives will have to include you on their list of suspects, until they rule you out, I mean."

Jillian grimaced, gritting her teeth. It didn't surprise her. She expected as much, but still, it made her angry. "Do you think the bloggers had anything to do with Bethany's death?"

"They're cowards. I overheard some people in the hall. They're taking advantage of the events, twisting things for their own purposes. That's all," Ingrid said, backing away from the podium. "Let's take our seats. People will talk about us being up here for so long. We'll be the next victims."

As others arrived, they formed the customary line in front of Jillian, each with a question about the course or an encouraging word for their professor.

When the line ended, Jillian mulled over Ingrid's comments. Did the writers have the ability to instill fear? It appeared so. How would that affect the willingness of students to cooperate with the investigation? Many of them said they told the police Jillian treated them in a fair manner and was their favorite professor.

Glancing at her watch, Jillian said, "Let's get started. First, I think we should observe a moment of silence for Bethany." While keeping an eye on the activity in the room, she bowed her head.

Most sat with their hands on the top of their desks and their heads bowed. Two or three looked impatient, but remained silent.

Jillian continued. "Bethany's funeral is at the Lombard Chapel tomorrow morning at eleven-fifteen. It's a thirty-minute drive from here, so I suggest, if you're sharing a ride, to meet here at ten. Our clinical day, of course, is cancelled." Jillian wrote the information on the board and included directions, pausing to give note takers time to finish. "We have a lot of material to cover today to get ready for Friday's exam."

In the farthest row, Barrera's hand shot up. "You're not really going to test us this week, are you? I mean, for those of us who know—knew—Bethany, this is very traumatic. Do you understand what I'm saying?"

"I do." Jillian glanced around the room. "How many of you would prefer to wait a week for the exam? We could continue with our material, then test a week from Friday."

A majority voted to delay the test, so Jillian agreed, then reviewed the changes.

"There's something else I want to mention before I start the lecture on wound care." Some students seemed to sink deeper into their chairs. "If anyone has any information about the authors of the Painful Process blog, I would appreciate it if you would share the information with me, the dean, or with the police detectives."

"Ms. Grey, can we get on with the material? You're wasting my time with things that don't concern me," Shanna Albano said, looking around. When no one commented, she shrugged, flipped open her notebook and picked up her pen.

Jillian felt herself flush and turned away, attempting to conceal her anger. She located the lecture folder and sorted her materials, pacing herself and providing opportunity for further comments, even the ones exhibiting bad attitude.

A flurry of activity swept the room—taking out notebooks and pens, setting up laptop computers and plugging them into the nearby outlets, and placing recorders near the lectern.

Omitting her customary side comments and corny jokes, Jillian's lecture was all business. She didn't show the scheduled video at the end. "We'll go ahead and review the last exam. Anyone who wants a look at their bubble sheet and the test booklet can stick around. I'll give the rest of you a moment to gather your things."

Most reviewed their exams and turned them in, smiling or nodding to Jillian, who accepted the booklets.

Barrera made his way to the head of the line, then dominated the proceedings, leaving his peers to wait their turns. "Ms. Grey, how can you say that answer is wrong?" He poked at an open page in his almost new-looking textbook. "It says right here, narcotics are given to control pain."

"The perception of pain." Jillian flipped a page in Barrera's book and pointed to a paragraph that expounded on the topic. "The source of the pain still exists. The pain exists. The central nervous system simply doesn't perceive it any longer."

"I can't see how that makes a difference," Barrera said. Color rose to his face and shifted his normal olive tones to pink.

Barrera had failed another exam, but, given his temperament, Jillian didn't think it was the time or the place to get into it with him. "Reread the material, then we can talk. We can stay a few minutes after class on Friday and meet in my office."

Barrera grabbed Albano's arm and pulled her out of place in the line. "Let's go," he mumbled. "I never get anywhere with the bitch anyway."

Jillian glared at Barrera. "Come back here a minute,

please."

"What for?" Barrera returned to the podium, standing to the side rather than at the front of the line.

Jillian lowered her voice to a whisper, cupping a hand close to Barrera's ear and leaning toward him. "Vincent, I heard your comment. We'll talk about that as well. Be downstairs Friday at two."

Barrera stomped out of the room with Albano following in his wake and tugging her red sweater over snug white pants.

Several students whispered among themselves, some looking embarrassed.

Oliver Cooley stood next in line. Leaning close, he rested his thin forearms on the podium, his tone hushed. "Professor, Vincent's behavior is uncalled for. Bethany and I tried to study with Vincent and Shanna last week, and it was obvious he hadn't read the material. What does he expect?"

"You might think about changing your study group." Jillian paused to allow the comment to sink in.

"Point taken."

"What can I do for you? You seem to have more on your mind."

"Actually, I do." Cooley paused. He was a skinny kid, almost six feet tall with ragged-looking, sun-bleached hair. He leaned further over the podium. "Vincent—well, he's on edge most of the time. I think you should be careful about him." Cooley backed away without giving Jillian a chance to respond.

Jillian dealt with the remainder of the line, answering questions, asking a few, and mixing in advice on learning skills and organizational habits. As beginners in a difficult program, they required a lot of contact and support. Pushed into the program by parents and counselors, or drawn in by the lure of quick employment, many lacked the basic survival skills—math, reading, critical thinking. They struggled to keep up. Jillian referred the neediest for academic counseling.

Finally, Jillian stood alone, packing her notes and supplies together to haul to her office. Vincent Barrera weighed on her mind. His behavior warranted a discussion with the dean.

Conover College administrators often chose to retain students who couldn't survive in the larger public college and university system. Tuition dollars reigned supreme, and the nursing program generated a sizable portion, far outpacing the business, physical science, liberal arts, and criminology revenue. The board had rewarded the school of nursing with the newest, though not the largest, building on the campus.

Jillian hurried downstairs to the dean's office. She tapped on the door jamb and entered the clean, organized work area. Jillian often wondered where the dean stashed all the papers accumulated in the course of the day. The secretaries couldn't possibly keep up. Every encounter required a paper trail.

Jillian settled into a leatherette-upholstered club chair and looked at the dean. "Can we talk about Vincent Barrera for a bit, please? He's a concern."

"Let's have a look at him." Marlene turned to her computer. A few keystrokes later Barrera's academic records flashed onto the monitor. "He's had his problems. He brought a load of credits with him from California—low C average. Barrera spent his first year here getting his average up to the 2.5 requirement for entrance into the program."

"Some things never change. He's almost failing again. More unsettling, though, is he seems to be exhibiting increasingly aggressive behavior." Jillian gave Marlene the details of her morning clash with Barrera. "We're going to meet again on Friday after class. I intend to counsel him on his behavior."

"The Ethics Code will support what you have to say." The dean appeared thoughtful. "Do you think you should have someone else in the room? You said he was threatening."

"More a feeling than an actual threat. I'm sure he's not the first disgruntled person to call me a bitch. I mean, look at that website. I'll get another faculty member to sit in."

"If you want me there, I'll make it a point to be available at two."

"Appreciate the offer, but no. It would be overwhelming. It would make the conversation a bigger issue than it is already. I'll grab another instructor. Keep it low key."

Marlene nodded, but her forehead wrinkled. Her expression was dubious. "Openly disrespecting a faculty member is a serious problem." After making a note on a contact form, she laid down her pen, and settled back in her chair, signaling that Jillian's response would be off the record. "You commented once that you're neighbor to Barrera's family."

"His grandparents, Dewey and Eleanor Evers. When Chantal and I rented the apartment on the beach, they welcomed us into the building and more or less adopted us." Jillian shared some of the less sensitive parts of Barrera's background.

Marlene frowned. "Where there's a whiff of smoke, there's often a spark of fire as well."

Jillian held up both hands and shrugged. "Eh? Eleanor

told me, right after I met the kid, that they came here to give him a fresh start."

"He must have had some issues, or they wouldn't have moved across the continent."

"The thing is Barrera had a rather tough go of it, at least in an emotional sense." Jillian leaned forward. "His mother died in childbirth, then the teenaged father walked out when Barrera was two. His grandparents were happy to continue to raise him, but they're not stereotypical doting grandparents."

"How so?"

Jillian paused, wondering about the propriety of sharing the family history. Eleanor had never asked her to keep the information confidential. After a moment, she continued, hoping the Evers family background wasn't meant to be secret. "Eleanor, Barrera's maternal grandmother, is of mixed parentage, Japanese and American, and was a child when it wasn't acceptable to be part Japanese. The father lived in a camp during the Second World War, and the neighborhood ostracized the mother and her child. I gather Eleanor carried a grudge for years before getting a job at Berkeley as a departmental secretary. She became a sixties' flower child of sorts, had a baby—Barrera's mother—out of wedlock, and partook of the San Francisco lifestyle, all the while continuing to work at the school."

"A closet hippie."

"I suppose. But out of the closet now." Jillian laughed.

"She's a hippie?"

"Philosophically speaking." Jillian ran her fingers through her wavy, collar-length hair. "Barrera has a lot of those qualities, in addition to having a very modern sense of entitlement. He seems to think he can have an anti-establishment attitude and continue to reap the benefits the establishment has to offer. He makes no bones about pursuing nursing because of the employment opportunities. He talks a lot about what specialties are the most lucrative."

"How is he in the hospital with patients?"

"He's in my clinical group. He plays the part, getting it mostly right, though the application of theory is a problem since he's not getting it from his reading." Jillian shifted her weight. "It's touchy. I expect he'll have a rocky road even if he and I come to an agreement about the limits of his behavior. Then I have to hope he doesn't carry his gripes about me to his grandparents' place or out into the public." Jillian grimaced. "It worries me."

"And well it should." Marlene bit her lip, looking thoughtful. "I don't think he exercises much restraint. His girlfriend was in to see me a few days ago about a problem in the library."

"What kind of problem?"

"The librarian complained that Albano was aggressive, demanding, rude, and inappropriate." Marlene wrinkled her brow. "Same loaf, different slice."

"Right you are. Albano and Barrera live down the street. The apartment building with the big Royal Poinciana in front."

"That's a most beautiful tree when it's in bloom."

Jillian studied Marlene's face. "How did your meeting with the president go? Do I have a job?"

"Yes. He doesn't put any stock in the blog or in the comments of the disgruntled students' parents for that matter. You've got a consistent history of excellent feedback and good results. Your kids do well when they move on, and they love you."

"That's a relief. I want to find out who is bashing me and have a chat. Maybe if I confront them, they'll clean up their act."

"Could be, but I wouldn't count on it. Discovery might make their behavior more blatant. If they admit it, we can ask them to stop because it's unprofessional, threaten to expel them. You could even start legal action, I suppose. But, suing a student would be a difficult path for a faculty member to take."

"I want them to stop. It's one thing to complain about me. It's quite another to accuse me of murder."

"Keep me posted." Marlene switched to social mode. "I haven't had lunch yet. Want to get a bite?"

"I'd like to, but I can't today. Chantal and I are meeting on neutral turf to discuss issues."

"Isn't your living arrangement going well? I thought you two divorcees made ideal roommates."

"We usually do. We've shared the apartment for a couple of years already and now have the opportunity to buy it. The building is converting to condo, so we have some details to settle about the business end of our relationship. If it doesn't work out, we need to decide about future housing plans."

"Sounds complex. I wish you luck."

Jillian muttered, "Thanks, we'll need it," and headed out the door in the direction of the School of Physical Sciences.

CHAPTER 10

During the ride across town to Bethany's funeral, Jillian and Chantal continued their discussion from the previous day, rehashing housing options rather than talking about the reason for their journey. The condo conversion was scheduled to take place over the next several months. The intent of the holding company was to convert a few apartments at a time from rentals to condos, giving occupants an opportunity to decide and adjust.

"I don't feel right obligating myself to a mortgage right now," Jillian said. "Marlene said my position is secure for the moment. Whatever that means. But I'm uneasy." She glanced at her friend, welcoming the distraction of Chantal's company, even if the conversation was stressful.

"I can't see that you have anything to worry about."

"I'm dwelling on it, obsessing. That's not like me, but it's nagging like the pending diagnosis of a dreaded disease."

"Understandable." Chantal paused, as if lost in thought. "I remember when Mama got sick. I knew I couldn't do anything but wait. I worried, running all the possibilities through my head, picturing myself without her, seeing the funeral in my mind."

"That's what I'm doing now, envisioning myself convicted of a crime I didn't commit and spending my remaining days in jail or worse. Or maybe I'll have to spend every penny in my savings to clear my name. When Pasquale and I split, I didn't have a cent to my name. He blew it all. Now I have a few dollars set aside."

"Maybe you're worrying for nothing. With Mama, that was the case." Chantal smiled. "She'll be eighty-five next month. Amazing."

"We could ask management to move back our conversion. When I talked to them yesterday, they said the target date for completion was June. They don't mind extending our lease until then. Plenty of the renters have already decided, and they seemed to understand my position."

Chantal frowned. "If things don't go well for you, what am I supposed to do?"

"Move to a place you can afford by yourself, I guess." Jillian paused, checking traffic in the rearview mirror. "When this is over, I may not have the money to live on the beach. What if I lose my job? I can survive for a while, but not for long."

After finding a space toward the back of the lot, the two women hiked a block in the blazing mid-morning sun. A slick-looking man in a dark suit greeted them at the entrance to Lombard Chapel and directed them to a sitting room. Feeling a chill from the penetrating cold of the air-conditioning and the forbidding milieu, Jillian wrapped her sweater tighter. She and Chantal took places at the end of the receiving line where they chatted with teachers and students, while waiting their turn.

The differences between Bethany and the Newland family struck Jillian. The aspiring dancer had been lithe and graceful, favoring trendy styles and, Jillian suspected, an equally free lifestyle. Her parents and siblings looked the part of successful physicians, their blocky physiques attired in tailored clothing, their emotions masked in somber frowns. They spoke a word or two to each participant in the dreary ritual, backing away from cheek kisses and hugs as the line moved past. Their demeanors seemed snooty.

Extending her arm, Jillian approached the group. When no one took her hand, she introduced herself, pulling back as if scalded with hot grease. "I was Bethany's nursing instructor. Your loss saddens me. Bethany was a special person. Please accept my sympathy."

The mother said, "Thank you," before turning away.

When the father, brother, and sister made no comment, Jillian and Chantal moved on, taking seats in the rear of the chapel.

The large room filled and overflowed its near three-hundred capacity. Jillian recognized many students, several faculty members from the science and nursing departments, and the two detectives, Brewer and Zale.

Glancing toward the door, she eyed the back of a tall, thin man with white hair and wondered why her ex-husband came. Pasquale bent close to Shanna Albano, who knitted her brows and spoke. His face reddened and his mouth hardened.

A second later, Pasquale nodded in Jillian's direction, then made his way down the row to squeeze onto the bench between Jillian and Chantal.

"I'm surprised to see you here."

"I thought you might need support." Pasquale sounded sincere.

"Thank you for thinking of me. I appreciate it."

"You seemed distraught on Sunday, and you mentioned you'd be at the funeral. I thought there'd be a chance the police would be here, and you might need someone to stick by you. The time of the service was in the blog."

"Very kind of you. A bit out of character, perhaps, but kind."

"I want to do what's right. Just because we're divorced doesn't mean I don't care."

"I appreciate the effort, Pasquale. Really I do."

"What was that about with Shanna Albano?" Jillian whispered.

"Claimed I pushed in front of her." He shrugged his shoulders.

Jillian glanced past Pasquale to Chantal, who appeared to study the program. The hint of a suppressed smile crinkled her cheek. Chantal had long since gone on record as thinking divorcing Pasquale Pascasio—the most handsome dude in any of her friends' lives—was the smartest thing Jillian ever did.

Jillian touched Pasquale's arm. "Who posted the funeral information?"

"Pee Turbed."

"The prolific one. I hoped when I mentioned it in class, the bloggers would lie low. I didn't have a chance to check the site today."

"If I were you, I'd keep up with it every day. Be a lurker."

"Better than being broadsided, I suppose." Jillian paused, thinking of her list of things to investigate. "Did you find a hacker?"

"I talked to a couple of guys, but they're more into big company sites. Bigger payoff."

"Maybe what I need is a bored college kid of the nerd persuasion."

"I can't help you there."

The minister took his place at the front of the chapel. "Family, friends, we are gathered here today . . ." the reverend intoned, his gaze sweeping the hushed crowd.

Bethany's brother delivered the eulogy, speaking on behalf of the family and reminiscing about Bethany's short life.

An abbreviated graveside ceremony followed the mercifully brief service, during which Jillian saw no demonstrative behavior from Bethany's family. So unlike the emotive Bethany.

The family hailed from the Midwest—Jillian remembered Bethany had mentioned Minnesotan roots—and given their blond hair and sturdy builds, Jillian presumed they were of Norwegian or Swedish stock. Perhaps they were private people, preferring to grieve within the confines of their own home. But she found the lack of visible grief unsettling. Was Bethany the black sheep in this otherwise successful family? Jillian wondered if one of them found Bethany an embarrassment and wanted her out of the way.

Pasquale walked Jillian and Chantal to Jillian's Sentra, then strode to his car, which he'd parked in the grass a few feet away. "I'll be in touch," he said, not making eye contact.

Detectives Brewer and Zale approached, crossing the lot between parked cars rather than using the concrete walk.

"Ms. Grey," Brewer called, "a moment, please?"

"Sure, Detective." Before facing the two men, Jillian looked for Pasquale, but he was gone. "What can I do for you?" Chantal had moved to the front of the car. Out of range, Jillian thought.

"We didn't expect to see you here today," Zale said.

"Why not? Bethany was in my class. Many people from the college came. It's the considerate thing to do."

Zale pointed over his shoulder at the chapel. "I noticed none of your students spoke to you before or after the service, not even at the gravesite."

"Then you're not very observant, sir."

Zale raised a brow. "Touché."

"What can I do for you?" Jillian sought Zale's eyes, then Brewer's.

"Have you been reading the posts on the Internet?" Zale asked.

"I assume you're referring to that inflammatory blog."

"Correct," Zale said.

"Do you have any idea who the writers are?"

"No. Our geeks haven't been able to get that information yet. They will though, never fear. What interests me is why someone is accusing you of murder," Zale said.

Jillian, not hearing a question requiring a response, looked at Brewer. "Did you notice the reserved behavior on the part of the family?"

"Sure did." Brewer nodded to Zale, who stepped back. "Did anything else strike you? You seem to take it all in."

Jillian focused on Brewer and ignored Zale as best she could. "No. Everyone I expected to see was here. All of Bethany's close associates from school. Several of the teachers. The college big shots." She paused, thinking. "Have you talked with my neighbor, Eleanor Evers? She saw me go to the beach last Thursday night."

Zale leaned closer, not moving his feet. "I spoke to her. A friend of yours, right?"

"Yes, and I help her with treatments when I can."

"Anybody else see you?"

"A couple of tourists I spoke with on the beach. I didn't get their names."

"Your husband attended today. Doesn't that strike you as odd?" Zale said, moving forward and stopping within two feet of her.

"He heard what's being said." Jillian stepped back until she bumped against the car door.

"What are you referring to, Ms. Grey?" Zale said, again closing the distance between them.

Jillian rolled her eyes. "The crap on the blog, sir."

"How long have you been aware of that crap, as you put it? Blogging seems to be the thing nowadays, taking the place of coffee houses and underground newspapers."

"I would have guessed Twitter and Facebook were the virtual coffee houses, but maybe you're right." Jillian shrugged.

"The blog? When did you first see it?" Zale's tone had an edge.

"I found out about the site Friday night and have spent some effort since then researching it, trying to figure out who my tormentor is."

"Don't you mean tormentors? Seems several don't like you."

"Detective, I have more than sixty in my course, many of them repeating because of failures. There are four people on the blog. Not a majority," Jillian said, her voice sharper than intended. "Why don't you discuss that very thing with my dean? She'll tell you about my academic reviews and about the current group. I imagine you remember from your own education that students are not always enthralled with a tough teacher. My class is hard. The grading scale is challenging.

Those who are unprepared or don't do the work flunk out. I can't do anything about that. I focus on the majority who want to do well. The failing ones complain. That's how it is."

"Are you finished?"

"Yes. Are you?"

"No."

"Am I a suspect? Am I being arrested?"

"Not at the moment," Zale said. "But I don't like your attitude."

"And I don't like yours. Now, if you'll excuse me." Jillian climbed into the car, waited a second for Chantal to scramble, and drove away, gripping the steering wheel with enough force to turn her knuckles white.

"Wow, that was heavy," Chantal said. "Are you sure you should have shot your mouth off like that?"

"With you as my witness, he provoked me. The bastard. I'd love to cram his agenda down his throat."

As soon as Jillian was out of the parking lot and into the flow of traffic, she called her father. "Dad, I have a feeling I might need a lawyer." She told him about Zale's approach.

"Sweetheart, it sounds like the good cop, bad cop routine. Trying to see what they can find out. Zale has a rep for being a hard-ass, likes to badger people, thinks he gets more information that way. Sy Brewer, on the other hand, is always polite. If he had reason to take you downtown, you'd be in custody."

"Well, ask around and find a criminal defense lawyer. I want one to call if and when . . . . And can you talk to your friends again? See what's really happening?"

"I haven't been to the station for a while. I'll drop by tomorrow and see Mack."

"Isn't he the guy who transferred to Internal Affairs?"

"Yup. But, he has his ears. He'll know who the current legal hotshot is, and he'll have the unofficial line on the investigation, too."

CHAPTER 11

From his vantage point in the front seat of the Taurus, Zale scanned the entire parking lot and the entrance to the funeral home.

"Where to?" Brewer said, sticking the key into the ignition.

"Hang out. See who talks to who and who rode in together. Barrera and Albano weren't at the graveside service. Maybe they had to work." Zale tapped a jazz rhythm on the armrest. "But if they were Newland's good friends, like everyone seems to think, they should have rearranged their schedules."

"Who knows about kids nowadays? Different priorities." Brewer flipped open his notebook, looking thoughtful. "Remember the owner of El Restaurante Cubano said a middle-aged man made a habit of coming in near closing, cuddling it up with Newland, then leaving with Albano, Barrera, and Newland."

Zale reflected on their brief conversation with the restaurateur. "So?"

Brewer turned a page. "Grey's ex-husband, Pasquale Pascasio, fits the description—tall, thin, prematurely gray, handsome."

"That he does, my friend." Zale stroked his chin. "We should talk to him. Do you have an address?"

Brewer glanced at his notes. "Pascasio lives in a high rise by the river. Did you notice he left in a hurry when we approached Grey?"

"Yup. And he spoke for a few seconds with Albano and Barrera in the chapel, right before he took a seat beside his ex. Looked like he passed a pleasantry," Brewer said.

"Not very pleasant. Pascasio frowned, and Albano's face flushed. He looked pissed."

After several minutes, Brewer started the car and pulled out of the almost empty lot.

Zale said, "Let's track down Albano and Barrera first. Ask them a few more questions. Then we should be able to connect with the ballet lady. She's due in the studio at one."

Brewer's trip across town was uneventful, making good time, however Albano and Barrera didn't answer the door or their cell phones.

"Came up dry on that one." Brewer slid behind the wheel with a grunt. "Feeling my age."

"You're not alone, buddy." Zale pointed east. "Give me a minute here." Zale checked a page in his book, then called the work numbers for Albano and Barrera. After brief conversations, he said, "Neither of them are working. Let's head for the dance studio. We'll get there a few minutes earlier than we planned."

While Brewer turned onto the main drag and headed toward the beach, Zale took out his notebook and adjusted his list of people to interview. They rode in silence, as he stared out the window, mind wandering.

"So, I'm thinking," Zale said, "If I can get it together

with the business thing, I can take my twenty and move on, maybe in the spring. If it doesn't work out, I'll be stuck with this shit until I drop dead."

"Doesn't have to be either-or, seems to me," Brewer said, glancing at Zale.

"Man, seems to me you don't have to worry."

"Bullshit, Nate. I have one done with college, Sheri is a sophomore—on the five year plan, looks like—then five more kids left to educate. Aunt Clara's money will only go so far."

"Maybe you shouldn't have gotten that big ring for the wife. That thing could pay for at least one of them."

"She deserves it." Brewer accelerated, avoiding the rising drawbridge over the Intracoastal Waterway, then swung right at the first light and into an open parking spot.

The studio was part of a gym located on a side street abutting A1A, the main street paralleling the ocean. An expansive wall of glass provided an angled view of the water from the second-floor school and a glimpse of dancers for passersby.

When the detectives pulled in front of a fireplug across the street, a session was in progress. The men watched for several moments as slim women and thin, muscular men leapt and twirled in synchrony. Then they badged their way into the facility.

A spiky-haired youth in skin-tight Lycra workout clothes and smelling of sweat escorted them to the second floor by way of a service elevator. Zale thought the kid wanted to keep the clientele from seeing police on the premises.

A dancer, the definition of her sinewy muscles and firm breasts visible under her leotard, met them at the elevator. "I'll take them from here, George." With hand extended she smiled, lines creasing her cheeks and the skin around her eyes. "Gentlemen, my name is Antoinette Fry. I'm the ballet mistress. Can I help you?"

Brewer introduced himself and Zale. "We'd like to ask you some questions about Bethany Newland."

"A lovely girl, talented dancer. A terrible loss." Fry brushed under both eyes with her fingertips. "I'm sorry. I can't stop the tears." She paused. "I've been expecting you. I saw you at the funeral service this morning. How are you doing with the investigation? Have you found out what happened?"

"We're making progress," Zale said, keeping his tone noncommittal. "Is there someplace we can talk?"

"My office." Fry led the way through the studio to a small, glass enclosed space.

They sat around a glass-topped table. The office had a credenza filled with the usual office electronics—combination fax-printer-copier, laptop computer, portable telephone base. Several file cabinets filled the only solid wall. The vertical blinds were stacked to one side of a glass panel, providing an unobstructed view of dancers stretching in front of a wall-to-wall mirror.

"I was concerned about Bethany getting mugged—or worse." Fry clinched her brow.

"Why was that?" Brewer asked."

"Bethany didn't have a strong safety sense."

"How so?"

"She'd leave late, not ask for an escort, not protect her bag. Things like that. Everyone here knew she kept cash in her purse. We spoke about it.

"Probably felt safe," Zale watched the dancers collect their belongings and head toward an open staircase in groups of twos and threes.

"A misplaced feeling. There have been several muggings in the area. Even in here, our members come from a variety of backgrounds, some perhaps a bit unsavory."

Zale held up a hand. "And yet you accepted them into your school?"

Fry exhaled, creating a whooshing sound. "This is a studio. I don't do social rehab or check backgrounds. But I've overheard conversations, and I know some of the dancers have criminal records, drug possession, that sort of thing."

"Who, for example?" Zale leaned forward. "We'd like to talk to a few of them."

"I really can't say. Just non-specific comments overheard. That's all."

"How about a list of your students with their contact information?"

"I don't think so. I ask some of them if they'll talk with you. That I can do."

"We could get a subpoena," Zale said.

"Yes, you could. But you haven't. Can we move this along?"

"Nice place," Brewer said, turning his head toward the dancers. "Elite address for a studio."

"Our dancers appreciate the convenience and environment we provide. Many belong to the gym downstairs, too. The cost of the real estate drives our rates."

"What was Newland paying?"

"Bethany danced here for years. Initially, while attending the magnet school, her parents paid for both her dance tuition and gym membership. She started paying herself a couple years ago after her parents pressured her to quit. I

gave her a break, but the cost was still five-thousand a year.
That didn't include the private lessons. The fees for those are
extra. They usually run fifty an hour, but forty for Bethany.
Her bill last month was almost six-hundred."

"High freight," Brewer said.

"The poor girl worked as a waitress to raise the money.
It was tight for her."

"How did she pay you?" Zale asked.

"Most of our clientele pay with a credit card, but Bethany
was one of the few who paid cash. Tip money, small bills."
Fry stood. "Bethany was an accomplished dancer, with
prospects of a promising career—if her parents allowed her
to dance."

Brewer handed Fry a card. "Call me with the names of
the students who will talk. We'll start there."

Fry took the card. "Good day, gentlemen."

Once back in the car, Brewer tapped his fingers on the
armrest. "Dancing three afternoons a week. Private lessons
two mornings. Working three evenings a week. Not much
time to study nursing. No wonder her grades were in the
crapper."

"It also explains why her parents thought she studied all
the time. Probably told them she was going to study when
she left the house."

"A lie that was supported by at least one friend."

"Cooley. Emotional kid. I wonder if he knew about
Newland's association with the older man," Zale said.

"We'll ask him. But first, I want to stop by the school
and talk with the security guards again."

He retraced his route across the causeway, arriving at the
school a few minutes later. He pulled into a space in the
otherwise empty lot.

Zale smiled, nodding in the direction of the building. "We're in luck."

A four-passenger golf cart with a fringed canopy sat under the portico. An elderly security officer smoked a cigarette at a nearby picnic table.

Brewer approached the man. "Afternoon, Carmichael. We've got a few more questions if you don't mind."

"Sure thing, detective," the old gent replied. "Anything I can do to help. But to tell you the truth, I told you everything when we talked on Friday."

They sat on the bench opposite Carmichael.

"As I understand it," Brewer said, "you were on duty in this area from noon until eight on Thursday."

"That's right. I also cover the student union and the science building after five. We have three men in the lots then."

"Where were you around seven when Professor Grey and Bethany Newland were leaving?"

"I left here about six-thirty. There were, maybe, a two dozen cars total in the lot—a few belonged to the teachers. One was Mrs. Grey's Sentra. Nice lady, Mrs. Grey."

"You said that Friday." Zale pointed to the portion of the lot favored by the beginning nurses. "Any of the vehicles in that area?"

Carmichael appeared thoughtful, knitting his brow and frowning. "As a matter of fact, I did notice a couple. Unusual, too. Normally those kids are long gone a few minutes after they're finished."

"Did you happen to notice whose cars they were?" Brewer asked.

"No. I checked for decals, but didn't note the numbers or anything. No reason to if the decals look legal."

GREGG E. BRICKMAN

"What can you remember about the cars?" Brewer took out his pad and tapped his pen on the cover. "Makes? Models? Colors? Anything?"

"I see a thousand cars a day. I don't pay attention. I watch the students. Check decals. Look for strangers."

"Was there anything else out of the ordinary that evening?" Zale said.

Carmichael closed his eyes and took a long drag from his cigarette before stubbing it out on the table leg, then pocketing the butt. "There was one thing. I didn't think about it Friday. While I was making my rounds in the building about six, I walked by the woman's bathroom. I heard two women yelling. They sounded real angry, but I couldn't make out the words. I don't hear too well sometimes." He pointed to his flesh-colored hearing aids.

"Did you recognize the voices?" Brewer said.

"Can't say I did. Neither were high-pitched. I wouldn't have been able to hear them at all if they were."

"Did you see anyone else around? Someone who might have heard what the argument was about?"

"No. It's rather common. I mean, some of the kids are high strung. They get into jawing at each other. I don't think some of them learned very much at home, if you know what I mean."

Brewer and Zale asked a few follow-up questions, eliciting the same information, thanked the man, and left.

Brewer cornered onto Oakland Park Boulevard. "It wasn't Grey yelling in the bathroom."

"And how exactly can you be so sure?" Zale glanced sideways at his partner.

"I verified her appointments before Newland. After finishing upstairs at five, Grey had a steady flow of

118

appointments until leaving the building at seven."

"Think she could have slipped in a trip to the rest room without anyone paying attention?" Zale said.

"Maybe. But why go to the bathroom to argue with a student in public when she could yell privately in her office? I mean, she was the only teacher left in the suite."

"Who knows?" Zale shrugged. "We need to find out."

CHAPTER 12

Jillian and Chantal opted for a quiet dinner at home. Jillian prepared veal parmigiana, using a recipe from Pasquale's mother. Chantal made the salad and cooked the pasta. They carried their filled plates to the terrace table where they could watch the ocean, eat their meal, and drink the warm Chianti Reserve they purchased on the way home from the funeral.

"You look distraught," Chantal said, sipping her wine.

"That's how I feel. There's a level at which I understand their desperation to pass the courses. But I don't, and probably never will, comprehend why some of them feel so much animosity toward faculty."

Chantal cast a questioning look over the rim of her wineglass.

"I read more of the damned blog." Jillian cut a sliver of veal, then put down her fork.

"I wondered what you were doing in your room while I was starving to death."

"Pee Turbed's comments about me are vicious. Now this person—I presume it's a student—is saying I had a lot of nerve to even attend the funeral, given I'm a suspect in the murder. Pee Turbed claims to have provided information to

the police confirming my guilt and is calling for the college to
fire me and put someone in the class the students trust to not
hurt them. Can you imagine?"

"Did Pee Turbed say what information?"

"No. The only good thing is two of the bloggers, Quick
Shot and Sleeping Pill, posted comments telling Pee Turbed
to back off and implying she—they said she—should be
ignored. Quick Shot wrote that Pee Turbed should be careful
with her wishes, maybe my replacement will be harder."

"That's something anyway. What about the fourth one?"

"Cast Off? Nothing but silence. Maybe that was
Bethany. There haven't been postings since last Thursday."
Jillian picked at the veal, took a small mouthful, then pushed
it away. "I went back through everything again, trying to find
some word or phrase to give away the identities. But the
language is social. When I talk with them, we talk about
nursing, and they keep their comments professional for the
most part."

"Do you suppose all the bloggers are from Bethany's
little clique? I remember when she was in chem one.
Bethany was friendly to everyone, but seemed to gravitate
toward one small group."

"I noticed that, too. But it would be a natural thing.
They are all repeaters, for various reasons, and so they knew
each other coming into the class. I had them before as well.
I don't remember them being so bonded though." Jillian
pushed her chair away from the table. "I'm sorry, but I can't
sit here any longer. I'm going for a walk on the beach."

"Want company?"

"Thanks, but no. I want to be alone. I need to think.
Figure out what I'm going to do. What I'm supposed to do
now." Jillian reached for her plate.

"Leave it. I'll clean up before I go out." Chantal stood, picking up both plates.

"If you're going out, I don't want to make you late. I'll help with the dishes."

"It's not a problem. I'm meeting Kerri Lane to discuss the curriculum project and have a drink. Go ahead. Walk."

Jillian haunted the beach almost every night, setting aside the private moments to remember her lost daughter. She wasn't the type to wallow in problems, but grieved the loss of her family. The wounds gripped her, feeling fresh, raw. Jillian knew of people who suffered similar loss and couldn't get their lives back on track. Eleanor encouraged and supported her, using shared experience as an example. In fact, it was Eleanor who suggested Jillian devote part of each day to the memory of Deirdre, saying the practice would help focus on life rather than death.

So, Jillian allowed herself the luxury of grief and regret for a few minutes every evening and led a near-normal life the rest of the day. Sometimes she dwelled on Deirdre. At other times, her mind drifted to Pasquale and her lost marriage. True, Jillian asked for the divorce after Pasquale chose to cope with Deirdre's death by gambling and drinking, but she missed the positive parts of their lives. She often wondered if accepting Pasquale's oft-proposed reconciliation would prove him a changed man. He claimed it would. Meanwhile, she rejected all masculine overtures, dwelling instead on coming to terms with her emotions.

That evening, however, Jillian focused on her current dilemma. Whether to seek out the bloggers and approach them, perhaps threatening a lawsuit? Or maybe ignore the libel and conduct herself as if nothing were wrong? Even if she decided to confront her tormentor, there was no way of discovering her identity. Her. At least, Jillian thought, I've narrowed it down to one tormentor—a woman. I hope.

Her mind wandered to the funeral and the encounter with the detectives. Zale continued to be obnoxious, while Brewer appeared more open-minded. However, neither seemed to believe her alibi. Eleanor had verified that the two men stopped by and asked numerous questions, including background questions on Barrera and his friends.

Jillian took off her shoes and treaded through the sand. Though the sun had set and the air had cooled, the fine grains warmed her toes. A flea nibbled her ankle. She walked into the surf, stopping when the waves reached mid-calf. If she stood there long enough, the tide would drop the water level, leaving her standing on compact sand.

Looking up and down the beach, Jillian studied each tourist, as she had each evening since Bethany's death. She hoped to see a familiar face, perhaps someone who would remember her walking on Thursday evening. But chances were slim. Many tourists left town on Sunday, making room for a new surge.

Walking away from the water, Jillian stopped to rinse her feet and slip on her shoes before crossing A1A and heading toward a sidewalk café. An empty table and a Coke beckoned.

Despair overtook her, and tears flowed. Could things possibly be any worse? She'd lost her daughter and marriage, was in danger of losing her job and home, and the police seemed keen on her as a suspect in Bethany's death. Helplessness and hopelessness seized her.

Jillian looked up when someone scraped a chair across the concrete. It was Warren Diamond, a long ago friend and business associate of Pasquale's.

"What's the matter, pretty lady?"

Jillian sighed and forced a lame smile. "That's a nice thing to say, Warren. It's nice to see you. Sit. Please."

Before Warren's wife died, Jillian and Pasquale often shared an evening with the couple. They'd lost contact over the years.

"It's good to see you, too." His voice was warm, sincere.

"What have you been up to?" Jillian asked, wiping her eyes with the damp napkin from under her drink.

"I'm living in a condo over there." He pointed to a grouping of tall buildings along the beach. "My mother left me an apartment, so I decided to live in it rather than sell. I'm running my computer consulting business from the spare bedroom."

"Always the techie. I remember when Pasquale called you in a panic because his firewall blocked his Internet access."

"I remember." He paused to order a scotch and soda for himself, offering Jillian another drink in the process. When the waitress left the table, he continued. "Actually, I came looking for you. Pasquale called and said you needed some help with an Internet problem. I called your apartment first. The woman who answered said you'd be down on the beach somewhere, maybe sitting in front of this café." He nodded at the sign.

"Chantal's very supportive," Jillian said, her tone cheerless.

"Pasquale told me about the problem." He patted Jillian's hand. "I might be able to get the information you need."

She looked at him, feeling doubtful.

"There's more than one way to approach the issue. If I

can't get into the site, then we can bait them with an email I can trace and perhaps narrow down your search. What we need to do—that is if you want to start tonight—is get to a computer."

Jillian smiled. "I'm willing to try. At least it's better than drowning in self-pity." Her spirits rose. Warren was a couple of inches under six feet, his brown hair receded to a widow's peak, and his weathered complexion betrayed his love for the sun. His warmth and ordinariness were attractive.

"You okay?" he asked, holding her hand.

"Yes, I believe I am now." Jillian brushed away remaining tears with the back of her hand. "Let's get to it."

Warren stood, then held Jillian's chair. Over her protest, he lay several bills on top of their two checks and set the saltshaker on top. When the waitress glanced in their direction, he pointed to the money and offered an abbreviated wave. He guided Jillian across the street, into the lobby of his apartment building, into the elevator, then through his apartment toward the workroom, as he called it. He pointed into his living and dining areas. "I haven't had the heart to change things yet. I signed my house over to my son and his new wife and left everything but my personal things and computers. Maybe I'll modernize this place. Maybe not."

"Elderly female retiree décor. It's comfortable, homey." Jillian related to his feelings of loss and saw the wisdom in his decision. Family memories surrounded her in her apartment, not only in pictures and mementos, but all of the apartment's furnishings except Chantal's bedroom came from her house. She added new furniture to her mental list of things to buy someday.

Warren's workroom didn't have a hint of his mother's

presence. A huge chrome and glass desk filled two walls, while a shelving unit crammed with computers, external disk drives, and generic black and silver boxes filled a third wall. In the split second before Warren switched on the panel of overhead lights, Jillian had the sensation of walking into the stars. Red, yellow, and green lights twinkled everywhere.

He pulled another chair next to the one in front of the computer and sat, motioning for her to do the same. He tapped the keyboard and three adjacent, oversized monitor screens brightened.

"Now," he said, "what's the blog address?"

As Jillian recited, he typed. Soon the offensive narrative flashed onto the center screen.

The lack of additional postings was pleasing, though she would have been delighted with favorable press. Jillian pointed. "This is the person who seems to be out to get me. The others are just somewhat bitchy. Freedom of speech and all that rot."

Warren scrolled to the bottom of the page and clicked on the webmaster link. "Don't know the guy. That was an outside chance anyway." He displayed the privacy policy. Pointing to the screen, he said, "See, a blogger can register anonymously. They need to provide a name or nickname and an email contact. They ask for additional information to help index the blog, but none of it is identifying."

"Can you hack into the site and get whatever information there is?"

He hit the About Me link, then the email link, and a standard window appeared. Warren wrote down the email address, peeturbed@yahoo.com. "That didn't tell us anything." He typed a series of keystrokes.

Access denied flashed on the monitor.

"This is going to take a while. Let's create an email account and send an email to Pee Turbed. Maybe the person will be cocky enough to respond to the email, then we can trace its source."

"Even from Yahoo or Hotmail?" she said.

"Yup. We can find out where they sent it from and narrow the search."

"Go for it," Jillian said, thinking of the huge banks of open-access computers in the library, cafeteria, and student union.

"Think of a likely name."

She searched her memory for the flavor of the cutesy names the younger generation seemed to prefer. "How about NurseWannabe?"

"Too tame. Something with the attitude Pee Turbed can identify with."

"StickItStudent."

"That's more like it." He registered the email address with gmail, naming the fictitious user Samantha Katz, female, and twenty-two years old. He located a zip code for the Chicago area and inserted it in the appropriate field.

"Samantha Katz?"

"That's what I called my cat—when I had a cat."

"Shall we send the email tonight or wait to see if you can get any information from the site?"

Warren finished the registration and linked to the mail page, where Welcome, Samantha! greeted him. He clicked on the compose button, and an empty email form flashed on the screen. "Now. While I hack around tomorrow, we can be waiting for the fish to take the bait."

Jillian labored over composing the email.

dear pee turbed. my instructor is frickin bitchy. it's like they don't want you to graduete. wish i could get back at her, like you. what do you think i could do? is your blog causing the bitch trouble? maybe i do a blog? answer on the email, not the blog. samantha the stickitstudent

"Interesting grammar and spelling." Warren laughed.

"We have kids from all walks of life. Many are bright, but that doesn't always translate to good English skills. Besides, look at the postings on the blog. These kids write like they talk. It looks pretty realistic to me."

"Off it goes." A click of his mouse sent the message into cyberspace.

She glanced at her watch. "Warren, I'm so sorry. I've already taken too much of your evening. I need to leave."

"First, give me your cell number so I can reach you. Then I'll walk you home."

"I'm fine. It's close."

"I insist."

For the first time since Bethany's murder, Jillian felt hope.

CHAPTER 13

After Jillian left for the beach, Chantal stripped off her jeans, threw them into the corner of her bedroom with the rest of her clothing, and donned sleek black slacks and a lustrous cream sweater. She shook off a modicum of guilt, the same twinges she always experienced when seeing Pasquale Pascasio. Jillian still loved the man. But what the heck, Chantal loved her own ex-husband, Frederick, as well. That didn't mean she was fool enough to reunite with him.

She took the stairs to the garage and hastened its length to her red Camaro. She eased the car over the bump where the driveway met the street and turned in the direction of Oakland Park Boulevard. Pasquale expected her at his condo by nine, and she was late already. Jillian's beach walking habits often gave Chantal the opportunity to slip away without explanation. On the rare occasion that Jillian was awake when Chantal came home, her excuse would be an impromptu drink with Frederick at a local club.

She sped over the causeway, took Federal Highway to Riverfront, and stopped under the canvas canopy in front Pasquale's high-rise. After handing the keys to the doorman and accepting a claim check, she rode the elevator to the fifteenth floor.

Pasquale opened the apartment door and smiled as Chantal walked the short distance down the hall and into the apartment. Her eyes flicked to the pimento-filled olives in the martini glass he held—her favorite. He was so thoughtful.

"I'm happy to see you. It's been a long day. With Jillian upset, I thought you might not make it." He handed her the glass and kissed her.

"Let's not talk about your ex, please. Jillian's the only crack in our beaker. I feel guilty seeing you."

"You're a good friend, but why should you feel that way?" Pasquale cupped her elbow in his palm and directed her through the open balcony doors.

"Because she's my friend." Chantal paused, focusing on his eyes. "You suggested reconciliation again? Is that true?"

"She looked depressed. I thought it would perk her up."

"What if she said yes? She has feelings for you and hasn't had one date since the divorce. Always finds an excuse to refuse."

"Don't let it worry you. She's not the type to back down. Jillian was the one who demanded the divorce. With sound reasoning, I might add." He nuzzled Chantal's neck. "It was hard not to touch you at the funeral today."

"I felt the same way." She set the glass on the high-topped patio table and turned into his arms. "Maybe I should confess about us. What could she say?"

"I can think of any number of things my ex-wife might say before moving out and leaving you stuck with the lease. After, no doubt, telling you to go to hell."

Chantal wiggled free of Pasquale's hug. Picking up her drink and taking a sip, she leaned over the balcony and stared at the murky New River. On the opposite bank, the yacht company's white siding shimmered against the surrounding darker buildings. Several boats motored down the middle of the river, windows and decks awash in bright lights. "Jillian has been my best friend forever. I remember her pointing you out to me in high school. I don't want to have to choose between you two, at least not now."

"It would be premature. But, I'm very attracted to you. I enjoy the time we spend together. You're an exciting woman." Pasquale paused. "I was thinking. Given the situation, you shouldn't purchase the condo with Jillian. When she learns about us, which will happen at some point, things will get uncomfortable. In the long run, your friendship might survive. The lady's fair minded. But, short term, she'll be hurt and angry."

"Don't I know it. In fact, that's why I agreed to wait until the last possible moment to buy the condo. Jillian thought I was being supportive."

Pasquale brushed a light kiss across her lips. "You're beautiful."

"You're a devil." Chantal initiated a deep kiss and felt like the other woman to her best friend's husband.

The ringing doorbell interrupted them.

"Hold that thought," He set down his glass and went to the door. Pasquale admitted Detectives Brewer and Zale to the apartment.

Chantal took a couple of steps to the side, hid behind the half-closed vertical blinds, and peered through the slats.

Pasquale stuck his hand out to Zale. "Nate, it's been awhile."

"Saw you at the funeral today." Zale introduced his partner. "You still playing the ponies?"

"No. Day trading does it for me now. You?"

"Not anymore. Now I'm staying out of trouble."

Brewer raised a brow and glanced at his partner. "We'd like to ask you a couple of questions."

"No problem." Pasquale waved his arm in the direction of the living room, inviting the detectives to the sofa. He sat. "What can I do for you?"

"It's odd you were at Bethany Newland's funeral today," Brewer said.

"Why? My ex-wife is distressed. I went to show support."

"You're on amicable terms then?"

"Very."

Zale leaned forward. "On your way into the funeral home, we saw you stop and speak with Shanna Albano and Vincent Barrera."

"So?"

"Miss Albano looked angry."

"She accused me of cutting in front of her. She stood there, not moving. I stepped past." Pasquale snorted. "I should have excused myself. I was rude. Big deal."

Brewer said, "Seems like an unusual exchange for a couple of people who are well acquainted."

Pasquale grunted.

Zale said, "The proprietor of El Restaurante Cubano claims you are a regular. Said you come in for late dinners. Also said you sat at the bar with Newland and Albano until Barrera got off work. Got all cozy with Newland, snuggled up and touchy like. Even said you left with Newland on occasion."

"Did he now? There's no crime in that." He shrugged. "Bethany was an adult."

"What was your relationship with her?" Brewer said.

"Ah . . ." Pasquale looked in Chantal's direction. "We had a relationship. We met in Cubanos one evening, and she came on strong. She introduced me to the other two."

"You didn't think it irregular to date one of your ex-wife's students?" Zale said, staring at Pasquale.

"Didn't give it any thought."

Zale glanced in Chantal's direction. "Evening, Ms. Rice. I didn't recognize you at first. Looking good. Unteacherlike."

"Thank you. I guess."

"May I ask what you're doing here?"

"Having a drink with a friend?" Chantal waved her glass, stepping into the room from the balcony.

"Interesting." Zale turned back to Pasquale. "It seems you make a habit of having friends among your ex-wife's associates. What does Ms. Grey think of all this? Must be a point of contention."

"I'd appreciate it if you wouldn't mention it. She's had a hard time dealing with our daughter's death and with me for that matter."

Zale said, "Don't know that we can keep it a secret. Seems like an important issue to me . . . especially since everyone we talk to thinks she misses being married to you. Can't understand why myself."

Pasquale's face reddened as he glared at Zale. "You—" He stopped and swallowed. "What else do you want ?"

Zale asked several more questions, focusing on Pasquale's day trading business and obvious financial affluence. Brewer made notes while Pasquale answered.

"That's it for now. We'll let you get back to your guest." Zale frowned. "We'll be in touch."

When Pasquale stood and moved toward the door, Zale said, "Don't bother. We can let ourselves out."

Pasquale shrugged.

"By the way," Zale said, "where were you last Thursday evening between seven and nine?"

"Here, waiting for Chantal."

"Is there anyone who can verify that?"

"Only Chantal. She didn't arrive until nine-thirty."

"Ms. Rice?" Zale looked at her.

"That's about right." Chantal flushed with anger.

"Did you call ahead?"

"No. He called me."

"When?"

Chantal bit her lip. "Maybe around eight, I guess."

Pasquale followed the detectives to the door, locking it behind them. He slipped his cell phone out of his pocket and punched in a few numbers. "Sam, why did you let those two detectives upstairs without calling me?" After a few seconds, he said, "Right. Well, I don't care what they say. Warn me."

With cocktail in hand, Chantal moved to the sofa and sat, sipping her martini. When Pasquale looked at her, she said, "You were having an affair with the murdered girl? How could you do that? I thought we had a relationship." Heat, provoked by betrayal, rose to Chantal's cheeks.

Pasquale sat next to her, touching her the same way he had touched Jillian during the funeral. "Honey, what could I do? I'd had too much to drink, and Bethany came on to me. You know I'm attracted to you, but I'm attracted to other beautiful women, too. That's just how it is."

"Pasquale, ah . . ." Chantal sat with her mouth open. "I'm going home." She set the glass on the table, stood, and walked out of the apartment without looking back.

***

Chantal exited the building, then leaned against the wall while waiting for the valet to bring her car. She glanced in the direction of footsteps.

Brewer approached.

She saw the white Taurus and imagined he'd waited for her. Zale sat in the passenger seat talking on his cell.

"I'm not surprised to see that you cut your visit short," he said.

"I'm shocked he was seeing Bethany Newland."

"Why? You thought he changed his ways? I've been told he's never been a one-woman man."

"I thought . . . it doesn't matter."

"What can you tell us about Pascasio? Anything about his financial affairs?"

"No, we don't talk about our respective jobs much. He day trades and does quite well. I mean, look at where he lives and what he drives."

"Condo's leased. So's the Corvette."

"He talks like he owns them."

"How long have you been seeing him?"

"A couple of months. I've known him for years, since he dated Jillian in high school. He called after we met again at a barbeque at his daughter's house. We chatted. One thing led to another."

"And you don't care what Ms. Grey thinks about it? I got the idea you were best friends."

Chantal slumped. "I have some explaining to do."

"One last question, Mrs. Rice," Brewer said.

"What now?"

"Where were you the night Miss Newland died? I know you came here later, but earlier in the evening."

"I arrived home around six, changed clothes, and headed to the mall. I ate supper in the food court."

"Did you buy anything? Maybe charge it? Speak to anyone?"

"I paid cash for my food." She paused, thinking. "I didn't speak with anyone other than the kid who took my order. The place was busy. I'm sure he won't remember me. Then I wandered and window shopped until Pasquale called."

"So you don't have an alibi for the time of the murder, either."

***

When Jillian walked through the apartment door, she was surprised to see Chantal's nervous behavior and date clothes. "Change of plans? You must have gone out for a drink with Frederick."

"No. Please sit down. We need to talk."

Jillian perched on the edge of the easy chair facing the sofa where Chantal sat. "What's the matter?"

"Everything's the matter." Chantal's eyes brimmed with tears.

"You seem to want to talk about whatever it is."

"There's no way to say it but to say it. I've been seeing Pasquale." Tears ran down her face. "I'm so sorry. I don't know what I was thinking."

"Why? How?"

Without interruption Chantal recounted the short-lived relationship.

"Anything else you need to tell me? I mean, while

Pasquale's trying to get into my pants and asking me to reconcile, he's having an affair with my best friend."

"It gets worse." Chantal told about Pasquale seeing Bethany.

"I can't believe it. All the while he's acting so supportive. He didn't come to the funeral to support me, not even to see you. He came because he was shacking with the dead girl. How sick is that? What did I ever see in that man?" Jillian stopped talking. She thought about their early years, the love she believed they shared. Unbidden, the thought of Warren pushed away her angst.

Chantal sniffled. "What about us being roommates? Can you trust me?"

"Maybe not around my men." Warren popped into her mind again. "But since I don't have any boyfriends, I suppose it doesn't really matter."

Long smudges of eyeliner dirtied Chantal's cheeks. She wiped the tears, making a bigger mess. "That's not what I meant."

"You're my best friend, and I love you. I'm hurt you went behind my back, then let me believe Pasquale had feelings for me. I've been mourning my divorce and the loss of my sweet Deirdre. But we're divorced. He's an attractive man. You're a beautiful woman. You can do what you damn well please."

"You're not mad?"

"I'm furious." Jillian exhaled with a rush. "But frankly, there are more important things for me to worry about now. See Pasquale. I don't give a damn." Jillian stopped, realizing it was true. "In truth, I'm not all that angry. It closes a chapter. I can handle it."

CHAPTER 14

Wednesday morning was a hospital day. Jillian crawled out of bed at four-thirty, a few minutes earlier than necessary. She was due on the nursing unit at five-thirty to prepare the patient assignments for her clinical group. First, however, she wanted to check the Yahoo account and see if Pee Turbed responded to the email.

Jillian booted her PC. After applying a bit of make-up and brushing her hair, she grabbed the next set of white scrubs in the closet and slipped into polished white duty shoes. Glancing in the mirror, she smiled at her miraculous transformation into a clinician. "Image is everything," she said to the reflection.

She logged onto the Internet, accessed Yahoo email, and signed in as Stickitstudent. Jillian was disappointed, though not surprised, to find no response.

She resumed her early morning routine, poured coffee into a travel cup, grabbed a granola bar from the cabinet, and slipped out of the apartment. During the short walk towards the elevator, she dwelled on her last conversation with Chantal and wondered how long the roommate situation could continue.

Chantal hadn't declared her intentions about Pasquale. As Jillian rode the elevator to the first floor, she revalidated her self-illumination of the night before, deciding the affair really didn't matter. Witnessing it did matter, however. When life settled down and she had a clear head, she'd decide about living arrangements.

Breaking routine, Jillian walked through the lobby. "'Morning, Stanley."

The sleepy-looking old man behind the reception desk nodded. A light from a small television flickered under the counter.

Jillian strained to hear the worn soundtrack of a vintage movie. "What are you watching?"

"John Wayne," Stanley said. "What an actor. Those were the days when they knew how to make movies. There was a story, not all special effects and computer animation."

Jillian hated old movies. "You've got a point, Stanley." She paused by the counter.

"Where you off to so early?"

"The hospital with my class."

"Have a nice day," he said, turning back to his movie.

Satisfied the guard would remember their interaction, Jillian exited through the side door into the garage. A few minutes later, she parked in the designated faculty and student section in the back row of the hospital employee parking aisle.

The lot was lit, but only a shadowy hedge and one other car occupied the immediate area. Feeling insecure, Jillian left her car and hurried through the back entrance.

"Hello, Henry." Jillian approached the guard's podium. "I'll have a group of eight arriving in about an hour."

Henry nodded and made a note on his visitor log.

Though Jillian had resolved to have witnesses and alibis whenever possible, the new, more visible persona felt uncomfortable. But the encounter with the detectives in the funeral home parking lot had been unnerving. Being prudent seemed appropriate. Further, their visit to Pasquale's apartment evidenced their continuing interest. Maybe Brewer and Zale considered Pasquale a person of interest, too.

She checked the time, decided there were a few minutes to spare, and stopped at the nursing office to chat with the night-shift supervisor, who assured her the hospital was busy and needed all possible hours from per diem staff. Jillian reviewed the needs list and scheduled herself for shifts in the emergency department on Saturday and Sunday, then climbed the steps to her floor.

After making assignments, Jillian went to meet the students in the cafeteria. They occupied a table on the far side of the large room. Eight total. Only Bethany was missing.

Jillian's rotation was more challenging than usual. Though the entire faculty shared the heavy load of repeaters, Jillian had more since Vincent Barrera, Shanna Albano, Tanya Li, Carrie Kennedy, Oliver Cooley, and Bethany requested the hospital nearest the school. Granting their preferences and those of other students had required extra coordination. She remembered their dismayed looks when they learned of their assignment to her group.

Li and Barrera sat at the north end of the table, their heads together, mouths moving. Albano, scowling, sat three seats away. It wasn't unusual for Albano and Barrera to sit apart. When Jillian learned of their relationship, she had insisted they keep it out of the hospital, asking them to sit apart during conferences and pairing them with other classmates for difficult patient assignments. Li's and Barrera's behavior, however, was out of the ordinary.

As Jillian drew closer—nobody looked her way—she heard the gist of the conversation.

Li said, "The detectives only asked if I knew Bethany and if we studied together."

•"What exactly did you tell them? Don't leave anything out."

Albano stood and nodded in Jillian's direction. "Hold it down, Ms. Grey's here." She walked to the end of the table and bent in close, whispering to Barrera. Her face reddened.

Jillian pulled a chair into the middle of the group. "Good morning." She set her notebook on the table, leaned forward, and lowered her voice. "With all due respect, we need to keep the discussion about Bethany and the police investigation out of the hospital. Most everyone here has read the newspaper accounts. They'll identify you by your uniforms and tune into your conversations. I want you to avoid discussing it with your patients as well."

Li said, "What if the patients ask us questions?"

"Explain that a police investigation is in process, and you've been asked not to say anything."

Several agreed to the request.

Albano said, "I don't see that you have the right to tell us what to talk about with our patients. I mean, like you said, they'll see the uniform and ask. I'm comfortable discussing it. Why can't I?"

"Because it's not appropriate," Jillian said, snapping in anger. "Perhaps you'd rather take the day off. By next week we'll know more. Then you'll be able to say what you please."

"Ah . . . no. I'll stay. I don't want to do make-up days."

"Fine. Your choice. But if you stay, you need to keep

quiet about Bethany."

Jillian distributed assignment slips, asked the group questions about the care they would provide, and ushered them to the elevator. She sighed as the door slid open. In her estimation, it would be a long and stressful day.

After finding their assigned primary nurses, the students waited around for report. Then armed with the current clinical information, they hurried into the rooms, performed physical assessments, set the patients up for breakfast, and started morning care.

Checking her notes, Jillian headed down the north wing to the first room.

Janey Morris, a heavy set, dark-skinned staff nurse with whom Jillian had worked for years, stopped her in the hallway. "I heard you're having problems over at the school. What's going on?"

"Wrong place, wrong time, I guess. I'm sure it will all blow over."

"I hope so. You're the talk of the hospital at the moment. A couple of the kids work here as patient care assistants. They told the regular PCAs that you're a suspect in the murder. Then the regular PCAs told everyone else about it. Even the doctors are talking."

"I'm not surprised. There's nothing I can do about it. I haven't been charged. The detectives don't pay attention to what I say, beyond checking my alibi. They just keep popping up in my life." Jillian glanced at the list in her hand, planning to make an excuse and cut the conversation short. "You working this weekend?"

"Sure am."

"I signed up for a couple of twelves in the emergency department." She referred to the shifts she scheduled for the upcoming weekend.

"Call me for lunch. I'll be on four."

"I'll do that. Now, I have to check my troops." Jillian entered the first room on the left.

Ingrid deHernandez leaned over the patient, stethoscope on his chest, listening to breath sounds.

Jillian approached the bed from the opposite side, noted Ingrid hadn't raised the bed to working height, and put her finger on a button on the side panel. The motor whirred, and the bed moved upward at a slow, steady pace.

"Sit forward, please." Ingrid smiled at Jillian, then placed her stethoscope on the patient's back. "Take a deep breath."

Nodding, Jillian moved the Ingrid's stethoscope a couple of inches to the left. "Try here." She watched the remainder of the chest exam, then left the room, standing in the doorway to organize her thoughts.

"Ms. Grey," Ingrid said in a loud voice as she approached. "I have questions about my patient."

Jillian stepped to the side of the door, leaned against the wall, and turned toward Ingrid. "What can I help you with?"

Speaking in a whisper, Ingrid held out her assignment sheet and pointed. "Before you got here this morning, Vincent was ragging Tanya about talking to the police. He accused her of ratting out Bethany for having the exam questions. He told Tanya it was her fault you killed Bethany."

"Lord, I'm being framed from all angles. First the bloggers and now Barrera." She felt like screaming.

"Not just Vincent, ma'am. Shanna started on Tanya first. Shanna said Bethany thought Tanya told because she was the only one who refused to buy the questions."

"Do you think they're the bloggers?" Jillian rubbed her eyes.

"The younger classmates don't talk to us older ones much. They think we're closer to the faculty than they are, more mature, and it's true. To us, school is like a job. We're goal directed. To them, it's more a social experience."

"Thank you for telling me. Now, I have to decide what to do." Jillian touched Ingrid briefly on the arm and moved on with her rounds.

In Albano's patient's room, she said, "Shanna, meet me in the staff lounge in ten minutes, please. There is something we need to discuss."

Albano glared. "Fine."

Jillian made the same request of Barrera a few minutes later, asking him to follow her to the lounge. When they opened the door, Jillian saw Albano with a cup of coffee.

"Please sit." She looked at Vincent as she settled into a chair. "I understand you two were pressuring Tanya this morning, accusing her of telling me about the stolen exam and saying I killed Bethany for that reason."

"I have a right to say and think whatever I want, and last I checked, teachers don't have the power to stop me. Freedom of speech and all that." Barrera snarled.

"I also have a right to be free of slander and libel. After Bethany's murderer is found, I'll likely sue you both for slander. Meanwhile, I'm going to arrange for you to be transferred to another hospital so your attitudes don't impact the experience for the rest of the group."

"You can't do that," Albano said. "I need to be here. I have to be at work thirty minutes after we finish. I'd never make it from any place else."

"That's the same for me," Barrera said.

"You should have thought of that before you decided to make trouble. You can't really expect me to keep you with me when you accuse me of murder. If you want to bad-mouth me, wait until I'm convicted."

"Ms. Grey, please. I need my job. They'll fire me if I can't get there by two-thirty." Tears pooled in Albano's eyes. She cast an angry glance at Barrera.

"Yes, please. We'll keep our mouths shut." Barrera looked contrite.

"I'll give it some thought." Jillian left the room.

Janey Morris stood next to the doorjamb writing notes on a clipboard. "Thought you needed a few minutes of privacy with those two. I heard them yapping in the hall. Real attitudes."

"Thanks, Janey. I needed someone to bar the door."

Later in the morning, the group assembled in a make-shift charting area at the end of the west wing. Jillian reviewed some of their entries, then noted Barrera, Albano, and Li were absent. She excused herself and went looking.

Hearing angry voices, Jillian opened the door to the stairwell and caught Li saying, ". . . say anything. I haven't even talked to Ms. Grey."

"You did before," Albano said.

"Yes, I did. But I didn't this time." Li's voice trembled.

Jillian coughed. "Vincent, Shanna, I told you to keep it out of the hospital."

They glared at her.

"A staff member overheard your conversations this morning and reported you." Jillian looked at Li. "Go do your charting, please." She squared off against the other two. "Vincent and Shanna, you had the same primary nurse today. Let's find her so you can give report. Then you're dismissed for the day."

Barrera opened his mouth, but Jillian stared him down.

"There is no discussion. I told you a few minutes ago what the expectations were. I've had enough of your behavior."

After directing the remainder of the students to meet at the school for post-conference, she headed to her car while calling her dad on her cell phone.

"How's it going, sweetheart?" Ron Grey said when he answered.

"Not so wonderfully, Dad. Those detectives went to see Pasquale last night, and they're still interested in me. Did you get the name of a lawyer for me?"

"Yup. Just got back from the station. Mack didn't give up much information about the investigation, but he seemed unusually well-informed for an IA officer. He did say Zale and Brewer have you stuck in their sights and agreed that you need help."

Jillian exhaled with a whoosh. "What's the lawyer's name? I'll call right now."

CHAPTER 15

Brewer and Zale stood under the portico outside the entrance to the School of Nursing around eleven that morning.

"Not many here today," Brewer said, looking at the expanse of empty spaces in the parking lot. "Guess we'll talk to Stevenson, then head out. We'll have to catch them at home again."

"I wanted to do it here. Let everyone know we're asking questions. Make them wait their turn. Sweat them a little," Zale said. "I think those kids are holding back on us. I want to find out who made the accusations in that blog and what their ulterior motives are."

"I couldn't agree more. We could take them downtown. Line them up."

"That'll work."

They stepped into the administrative area and made their request. Dean Stevenson's secretary ushered the detectives into the office.

Stevenson looked up. "Gentleman, I'm not surprised to see you again."

"Why is that?" Brewer asked, raising both brows.

"I heard that most murders are solved within the first

forty-eight hours. We're well past that. I thought you'd be around looking for more information."

"Astute." Brewer relaxed into the chair, propping his right ankle on his left knee. "What do Jillian Grey's students think of her in general. We've looked at the Painful Process blog and some of them seem negative. Is that a trend?"

"No, definitely not." Stevenson spun around, opened a file drawer, and extracted a blue folder. She laid a report on the desk for the detectives to read, pointing with her pencil. "Ms. Grey has one of the highest satisfaction rankings of our faculty. High in cultural sensitivity, responsiveness, availability, and respectfulness. We get the results from a confidential survey passed out after the final grades are posted."

"What's the deal with the bloggers then?" Zale asked.

"The current cohort—I mean admission group . . ."

"I know what a cohort is." Zale looked insulted.

"Sorry. This cohort has a high number of repeaters who tend to be dissatisfied with the process. They are people with life responsibilities competing for their attention—jobs, family, lifestyle issues. I suspect that's the case with the bloggers."

"Who are they?" Brewer said.

Stevenson shrugged. "Ms. Grey and I have some ideas. I gave her a list of repeaters to think about."

"She didn't say anything to us," Zale said.

"Frankly, gentlemen, why would she? She feels singled out and harassed as a suspect of convenience. Her father used the expression person of interest rather than a suspect."

A smirk flickered across Zale's face. "I'd say the man is on the right track." He clicked the button on his ballpoint pen a few times then flipped open his notebook. After a few seconds, he continued, "Have you had complaints about Grey?"

"Nothing out of the ordinary. There are always those who complain about faculty, even the best faculty. Because they pay high tuition at a private college, some have the attitude they're buying their education rather than earning it."

"How do you handle that?" Brewer asked, thinking about similar behavior in the School of Criminology.

"We explain expectations to them. Once in a while we invite them to apply to one of the public institutions or to take their tuition dollars somewhere else—anywhere else. It's a tough problem."

After answering a few more questions, Dean Stevenson looked at her watch. "I expect Ms. Grey any time now for her post-conference."

"I thought they stayed at the hospital?" Brewer said.

"Most days, but not today. She called but didn't explain. Perhaps they couldn't find a private space there."

The dean gave them two rooms to use for the interviews, and Brewer and Zale took the outside stairway to the second floor. They stood in the hall waiting for Jillian's group and planning their interviews.

Jillian came down the hall first and stopped in front of the detectives. "Damn."

"We'd like to interview some of your people, individually please," Brewer said.

"Must you interrupt? It's not fair to the ones who aren't involved."

"It would be more disruptive if we called the wagon and hauled them downtown to answer our questions. What's it going to be, Ms. Grey?" Zale said, his tone snide.

"Guess I have no choice." She faced the group. "The

detectives want to see some of you. Go into the lab. You can study or practice your skills while you wait your turn."

They shuffled by in single file.

"Where are Albano and Barrera?" Zale asked, checking his list of names.

"I dismissed them early."

"First you're angry we want to interrupt class. Then you tell me you dismissed them early. Make up your mind, Ms. Grey."

"I asked everyone not to discuss the murder at the hospital. They did anyway."

"Tell me how it happened. You can't really expect people not to talk."

Jillian closed her eyes, then opened them and glared at Zale. "This is what happened. Albano and Barrera badgered Tanya Li for talking to me, then started on her again in the stairwell, voices raised and all. I sent them away, and I'm going to meet with the dean about disciplinary action."

"What's going to happen? Will the dean kick them out?"

"No, but at the very least, I won't have them in the hospital with me again."

"Where are they now?"

"I have no idea. If you want to speak with them, you'll have to find them yourselves. Or, if you persist in using the school as a substation, I expect they'll be here tomorrow morning for lecture."

"Is it customary to refer someone to the dean when they act like assholes?" Zale said.

Jillian grimaced. "In the hospital, yes. We have an ethical code." Jillian glanced toward the open lab doors. "Can you get on with it, please? Many of them have to get to work or to the daycare center to collect their children. I'll be downstairs in my office if you need me. First I'll tell them they're excused when you say they're free to go."

As Jillian walked away, Brewer thought she said, "Wish you had a dean, detective asshole." He laughed.

***

Detective Zale stepped into the lab and surveyed the small group huddled in the corner. Like so many frightened puppies, he thought. "This is the deal. We're going to talk to each of you. When we're finished, you're free to leave. Ingrid deHernandez, I'll start with you. Tanya Li, you can meet with Detective Brewer."

Zale escorted the two women down the hall, opened the door to the classroom where Brewer waited, and showed Li in as he went by. In his room, he positioned two desks to allow close face-to-face contact and sat. "Have a seat." He motioned to deHernandez.

"Tell me about yourself," he said.

In thickly accented speech, she said, "I was born in Columbia. I came to this country when I was nineteen. I'm forty-nine now, married, three grown children. I work as a waitress."

"How long have you been at Conover?"

"Four years. I went part-time to school until my last child graduated college. Now it's my turn. I always wanted to be a nurse. It's my calling, my life's dream."

"Do you like the program here?"

"Oh yes. It's wonderful. I've learned so much." Ingrid looked at her hands, twisting them in her lap.

"What do you think about Mrs. Grey?"

"She is a good teacher. She gives us a lot of attention

and is fair. I shouldn't say, but some of the students aren't very nice to her. They are writing untrue things on the Internet and trying to blame her for Bethany's murder. I don't believe it."

"Why don't you believe it?"

"It is true Bethany had those test questions. The stupid girl offered to sell them to me. Someone told Ms. Grey. She didn't say anything about it in class except a little comment one day about writing more test questions so she couldn't stay long after lecture."

"Did you hear any more about it after that?"

"Only that Bethany was upset and believed someone told. No one would buy the test from her because Ms. Grey was making a new one. I guess Bethany needed the money." Ingrid paused. Her hands stopped moving as well.

***

Tanya Li looked around, then picked a seat two rows away from where Detective Brewer sat. She slid into the chair and slouched down. Her lips trembled, and Brewer felt a pang of sympathy for the young woman.

"Relax, Miss Li. We're only trying to get at the truth here. There is no reason to be afraid."

"There's plenty of reason to be afraid. I was threatened today. I don't want to talk to you anymore. I've said too much already."

"I understand you had a confrontation with Albano and Barrera today."

Li looked at Brewer and began to sob.

"Miss Li, get a grip here." He waited a few moments for her to settle down. "Now, tell me what happened today."

Li blew her nose and swallowed, making a gagging sound. "When Vincent came into the cafeteria he sat next to me. Then he leaned real close and said he knew I told Grey about Bethany having the test. I said I told Grey, but I didn't tell her who was selling it. That's the truth. I knew they'd be mad if I said who. At first I thought Mrs. Grey told them, but then Vincent told Shanna that he had guessed right, that it was me."

"Then what happened?"

"That's when Mrs. Grey came in and made them stop. But later, Shanna grabbed me by the arm and forced me into the stairwell. She told me if I said anything to anyone again, I would be sorry."

"What did Barrera do?"

"Stood by the door and didn't say anything." Li teared up and resumed her sobbing. "You can't tell them I told you what happened. Please."

"I'll do my best, but I can't make any promises." Brewer excused her and watched her walk toward the exit. He brought Oliver Cooley in next.

After the preliminaries, Brewer said, "Mr. Cooley, what I need to know from you is if you knew Bethany had another boyfriend."

"I want to be cooperative. I want to help you find whoever killed Bethany. She was a very special girl."

"Were you aware of the boyfriend?" Brewer repeated, keeping his tone patient.

"I was suspicious. Once or twice her mother called my place and asked for her when I thought she was home. I mean, it was too late to be at the dance studio, and I knew she wasn't working. When I'd call on the cell, I got real quick answers, like trying to get rid of me without being obvious."

"What did you think of that?" Brewer said.

"Honestly, I tried not to think about it. I thought it was a misunderstanding. Reading into things. Maybe she needed time away. You know?" He nodded, then looked at Brewer, as if for confirmation.

"We have reason to believe Bethany was seeing Pasquale Pascasio, Ms. Grey's ex-husband."

"Ah, shit. Man. He's so freaking old. How could that be true? I don't believe you. My Bethany wouldn't go with an old man." Tears welled in his eyes. After a few seconds, he sobbed. "I don't believe it. No. Not for a minute."

Brewer gave Cooley a few moments to calm himself. "When is the last time you saw Bethany?"

"Last Thursday, after lecture. I offered to wait while she met with Ms. Grey, but she told me to leave." He wiped a tear off his cheek. "I waited until her turn with the professor, then I went home. I should have waited and walked her to the parking lot. She'd still be alive. I should have waited." Again, his eyes sought confirmation.

"Was Bethany upset that day?"

"Maybe a little. I heard her argue in the bathroom with another one of the girls. I heard someone yell, 'How could you? That gig was mine.'"

"Did you recognize the voice?"

"Nah, it was kinda muffled. I asked her, but she told me to mind my own business. I thought it was about the thing with the exam questions. Bethany didn't steal the questions. Someone gave them to her, and when she sold some, she shared the money with the thief. I told her not to do it because they would kick her out of school. That didn't matter. She wanted to dance and used the money for dance school."

"Who came out of the bathroom with Bethany?"

"No one that I saw. When she came out, we left the building. We sat outside the double doors to wait for her appointment. I didn't pay any attention after that."

"You stayed until after her meeting. Did you see anyone around?"

"No, I said I left. I didn't hang around. She told me to leave, so I left."

"Where'd you go?"

"Home."

"Anyone see you?"

"No. I doubt it. Our apartment is on the end. I went right inside."

Brewer took a stab in the dark. "Someone said they saw you and Bethany arguing that day."

"Who? It's not true. We never argued. Bethany got enough grief from her family. Once she said if I fought with her or questioned her, we'd be finished."

"Sounds like she had you under control."

"Maybe. I guess you're right." Tear ran from his eyes.

***

Brewer and Zale crossed the parking lot to the Physical Sciences Building.

A young man had called into the station. He saw someone near the trees by the nursing building on the night of the murder. Brewer was curious to hear what the kid had to say.

As promised, they found him waiting in the reception area outside the faculty offices.

He stood. "I'm Steve Abdala. Thanks for not making

me go downtown."

"No problem." Brewer motioned to the door. "Maybe we can find an empty room to talk."

"The chemistry lab is empty. I have the code to get in."

As they walked three-abreast toward the student entrance, Brewer said, "You're a student worker?"

"I'm Rice's lab assistant." Abdala glanced at Brewer, a question in his eyes. He led the way, punched a series of numbers into the digital lock, then dropped into a chair next to the nearest worktable.

"So, man, it's your buck." Zale leaned back in his chair.

"Ah . . . It was last week, the night that girl was killed. We were studying upstairs. The room overlooks the lot. Around seven-forty or maybe a little later, I got up to stretch. I looked out the window. There was a woman by the trees. It looked like she was coming out of them, really."

"Can you describe her?" Zale said.

"Reddish brown hair to here." He held a finger above his collar. "Red shirt."

"Did you see her face?"

"No man. She walked the other way."

Brewer said, "What size was she?"

"Ah, average. Not real tall. Not too short. She was a little thin, maybe."

"Would you recognize her if you saw her again?" Zale said.

"Nah. I said I didn't see her face."

"Why did you take so long to call us?" Zale said.

"I left Friday, went home for a few days. My dad is in the hospital. I found out about the murder this morning."

"Have you discussed what you saw with Professor Rice?" Brewer asked.

"No. Haven't seen her."

The detectives excused themselves. As they walked to the Taurus, Zale said, "Motive, means, opportunity, blood spot, and witness. What more do you want? Grey's our girl."

"Slow down. The blood is not confirmed to be Grey's, and the witness can't identify anyone specifically. An average size lady with short hair. Fits ten percent of the population, including my wife and the dean." Brewer thought Zale might make a strong case, maybe one that would hold up to scrutiny. "You're premature. We need to get the solid evidence, then go for the arrest."

***

Brewer and Zale took a few minutes to compare notes. They hadn't extracted any startling revelations from the nurses. Zale hadn't expected they would, though he found the chemistry student's comments intriguing.

"Newland was party to that rumored bathroom argument," Zale said. "What do you think about Cooley claiming to have overheard it?"

"Cooley could be our man. Even though he was emotional, I got the idea Newland's affair wasn't news. His answers were too solid. I don't think he knew the affair was with Pascasio, though," Brewer said, then pulled his bottom lip into his mouth, biting it.

Zale flipped open his book. "I'll add him to our short list." He scratched through a name. "Carrie Kennedy isn't involved. Solid alibi. Went home after class. She's in another hemisphere."

"Agreed. Take Li off, too. Same deal. Went home. Verified. Too honest for cheating, much less murder. Too small. Couldn't pull off an attack like that on an athletic girl like Newland."

"Let's have another chat with Grey while we're here." Zale led the way down the outside stairs and into the administrative area.

Zale flipped his badge at the receptionist, who muttered a yes, sir and buzzed open the door.

They found Jillian at her desk with a stack of papers spread out next to a laptop computer.

She looked up when Brewer tapped on the doorjamb. "I've been expecting you. You might as well come in." Her voice carried a note of resignation.

They did.

"Now, what can I do for you today?"

Brewer spoke first. "We wanted to tell you we ruled out mugging as a motive for Bethany Newland's homicide. We inventoried the items in her purse. There was nothing missing. In fact, we found two hundred dollars in the zippered compartment."

"Interesting. I thought, maybe, she was mugged."

Zale leaned forward in his chair and rested his forearms on Jillian's desk. He ignored her icy stare, bending further over the desk, invading her personal space. He smirked when she rolled her chair back. "Did you quarrel with Newland before your meeting last Thursday evening?"

"No. I already told you what we discussed."

"Tell us again."

Jillian retrieved a folder from the credenza and took out a piece of paper. "These are the things we discussed." She read the items from the paper.

"Interesting that you took the trouble to write them down. It's as if you have something to hide."

"As I told your partner, I'm in the habit of making counseling notes. A short pencil is better than the longest memory. In this case, my MS Word notes are better. You should have a copy of this in your files already." She handed him the paper. "Here, you can have another one. Perhaps it will jog your memory."

Zale took a minute to skim the paper. "You're a bit snippy."

"With reason."

"Do you have anything to add?" Brewer asked.

"No. I try to be complete when I make notes." Jillian appeared thoughtful. "Have you made any progress uncovering the bloggers who are defaming me?"

"Can't say that we have. I don't see that it matters much myself, and it really isn't police concern. Your dean explained that the class has a few malcontents," Zale said.

"That it does. Don't you think one of them, Pee Turbed especially, might have personal motives? Perhaps that person wants me as a suspect."

"Ms. Grey," Zale said, an edge on his voice. "Why don't you let us run our investigation? Those postings could be written by anyone with an ax to grind. Problem is we can't prove who made the entries, even if we think we know. We have more important things to do."

"Ah-h." Jillian looked frustrated. "How can you say that? Aren't you curious why someone would go to that trouble? I, for one, am."

Zale raised his hand. "What can I tell you?"

Brewer said, "Ms. Grey, we understand Newland had an argument with someone in the lady's room. Did you happen to hear any of it? Your office is quite close to the common wall."

"No. We don't hear conversation or noise from there. Thank Heavens. What time did it happen?"

"We think a little before six."

"I had appointments. I didn't hear anything." She turned to her computer screen and brought up Outlook and printed her schedule for the previous Thursday. "Here are the kids I met with, but you already have this, too."

"Where is the faculty lady's room?"

"There isn't one. We all use the same facilities. Not ideal, but it's how the building was built."

"Perhaps you slipped out to the bathroom and had that argument yourself," Zale said. "A student overhead someone say, 'How dare you? That gig was mine.' We think Newland was there when the comment was made. Perhaps you made it, and the gig in question was your ex-husband."

"I didn't find out that Pasquale had a relationship with Bethany until Chantal told me last night. I can't believe it. I mean, why?" Jillian looked confused and went silent.

"You were saying?" Zale prodded, wanting her to finish the thought.

"I spoke to a lawyer this morning. While I haven't officially retained her services, she did tell me not to talk to you anymore without counsel. Lawyering-up is what my father calls it. So, if you will excuse me, I have a test to prepare."

Detective Zale shrugged and stood. "We'll be talking with you."

Jillian nodded, turned to the computer screen, and gave the detectives her back.

As they walked to their car, Zale said, "Got a lawyer. Guilty conscience."

"I don't see it that way. You've been an asshole. She's

afraid."

"Afraid we'll find her out."

"Scared your mind is made up, and you'll go to any length to prove your point. I agree with her."

"The daughter of a cop wouldn't think like that."

"Buddy, believe me on this one. Her old man, he was old school. Honest. Reliable. When he was sergeant, he didn't put up with any shit. He caught a couple of guys screwing with evidence. He put a stop to it, cost them a suspension. He warned her to be careful. You can bet on it. Ron Grey understands what goes on."

***

Brewer and Zale stopped by Barrera and Albano's apartment, found no one home, then swung by El Restaurante Cubano. The manager told them Barrera wasn't working until later. The next stop was Carnegie and Watson Investments. Brewer itched to show progress in the case.

Brewer pulled to the curb in front of the storefront office, then entered the empty reception area. "Anyone here?" Brewer called, rapping his knuckles on the doorjamb.

A lanky young woman with long brown hair appeared.

"Shanna Albano. I'm surprised to find you here," Zale said, knitting his brow and squeezing his lips together. "When we asked about employment, you said you were full-time at the school."

"I carry twelve credit hours. I didn't lie."

"You didn't tell the truth either." Zale stepped in close. "Is your boss, Watson, here?"

"Yeah. He's in the back." She nodded toward a closed door. "I'll tell him you're here. What should I tell him you want?"

"We'll tell him what we want ourselves." Zale opened the office door and stepped inside.

"Whatever you say." Her voice dripped sass.

"When we're finished with Mr. Watson, we'd like to speak with you. Be sure you're here," Brewer said.

Albano stared at him.

"Will you be here, Miss Albano? Tell me loud and clear. No games."

Albano looked at the floor, the fringes of a smile creasing her cheeks. "I'll be here, detective."

Brewer joined Zale in Watson's office.

Mr. Watson, a small man in his early fifties with receding hair and a too large nose, volunteered no information about Pasquale Pascasio's account. "We sign a confidentiality agreement with our clients. What we provide is an Internet-accessible asset account for the client to use for trading purposes. We also sell trading software, maintain the software if necessary, offer space on our server, and give instruction to new traders. We close the loop by furnishing tax accounting services for those customers who want their taxes done by us."

"Financial records aren't covered by any special privilege."

"That's true, but we do have a contract with our clients. If you want to review the records, get a subpoena. Sorry."

"Okay, fair enough," Brewer said. "We'll arrange it. Tell me, who does the accounting, and what does it entail?"

"We're linked to a national firm, but we're a small office. We have a part-time receptionist and two contracted CPAs besides Carnegie and myself. We all do a portion of the tax work. I specialize in sales. Carnegie is the software geek."

"The receptionist does taxes?" Brewer raised an eyebrow.

"She copies the records from the server and loads them on a secure hard drive for our use."

"Why not look at them on the server?"

"If we did, the client wouldn't have access to the files during our review. The program is more secure when access is limited to one computer address at a time. Shanna works most of her hours after the market is closed. She grabs the files when the client is least apt to need them. Then we can work at leisure."

"What kind of review do you do?" Brewer said.

"Our focus is on taxes, but we look at problems or trends as well. It's part of the service." Watson paused. "What you need to understand is the software keeps track of the trades. It works well. The traders tend to be meticulous with their data. If something slipped by that we caught—I can't imagine what that would be—we'd notify the client to correct the problem."

"Interesting niche market," Zale said.

"It's very productive."

After telling Watson to expect the subpoena, the detectives returned to the outer office. Albano appeared engrossed in the information on the computer monitor.

"Miss Albano, your turn," Zale said, his voice edgy.

"You'll have to wait a few minutes. I need to be sure and download the correct files. It's important I do it right."

They stood at the corner of the desk waiting for Albano to be done. Brewer saw the screen filled with lists of files identified by scrambled alphanumeric codes. She referred to a paper, then selected specific files and copied them to another drive.

After several minutes, she swiveled her chair their direction. "Okay."

Zale hiked his hip onto the side of the desk and leaned within two feet of her face. "Why didn't you tell us you worked here?"

"I didn't think it was any of your business." She rolled her chair closer to Zale. "Close enough for you now, Detective?"

"Works for me." He held his position. "It makes me wonder what you have to hide."

"Hey, think whatever you want. Knock yourself out."

Zale frowned. "We understand you had an altercation with Tanya Li at the hospital this morning."

"We're friends. We had a disagreement."

"That's not how we heard it. Tell us what it was about," Brewer interjected, maintaining his distance. "At the moment, the only version we have is the one where you and Barrera ganged up on the girl because she did the right thing."

"Ratting out your friends is not the right thing."

"Then you admit you ragged Miss Li about the stolen exam?" Brewer said.

"I don't admit a friggin' thing. What I admit is I have work to do. Ask me what you want and then leave before I get fired."

"We understand you knew Pasquale Pascasio, a bit of a four-way friendship with him, Barrera, and Bethany Newland. Want to tell us about that?" Zale said.

"The four of us hung out. What's the big deal?"

"We'll see." Zale tapped his fingers on the top of Albano's monitor. "You and Barrera spoke with Pascasio at the funeral on Tuesday. You looked upset. What was that about?"

"I told him my friend was dead, and he'd better not have had anything to do with it."

"Do you have any reason to think he might have?" Brewer said.

"Hell no. Just needling him. He's an arrogant bastard."

Brewer took a deep breath and exhaled, feeling that Albano was playing it close to the edge. "Miss Albano, where were you last Thursday evening between seven and nine?"

Albano sneered. "What? Am I a suspect now? You two are on some fishing trip."

"Tell us here or tell us at the station. Your choice." Zale said. "If I talk to one more wiseass in this case, I'll take everyone downtown to chat."

"I was home just a-studyin' away. That's what students do."

"Is there anyone to vouch for you?"

"Nope. Vincent was working."

Brewer shook his head in frustration. "Where is Barrera now? We couldn't find him."

She looked at her watch. "He should be at the apartment. He went with his grandfather to take his grandmother to the doctor. She's getting sicker. That's how her disease is."

***

Brewer and Zale found Vincent Barrera at home. In the short, non-productive interview, his attitude and answers mirrored those of his girlfriend. Brewer thought Albano did an admirable job preparing Barrera. Too good, in fact.

His answers were perfect, including his claim to have worked on Thursday evening.

Brewer called the chef at Cubano's, who checked the schedule and said, "Barrera wasn't scheduled to work on Thursday night. Doesn't mean he didn't. Sometimes the bartenders trade off and settle it themselves. They make most of their money on tips anyway. I'll ask around."

CHAPTER 16

Jillian left Conover campus and hurried home to change before speeding across town to meet the lawyer at five.

Xan Xavier met her at the office door, introducing herself and explaining the paralegal was gone for the day.

Though Jillian guessed Xavier's age to be in the mid-thirties, she didn't appear more seasoned than many of Jillian's students. She viewed the younger woman with skepticism. Xavier wore brown slacks and a tailored peach blouse that highlighted tanned skin. Tiny pearls adorned her ears. She wore no other jewelry.

Swearing by the recommendation, Jillian's father claimed the counselor possessed a sterling reputation in criminal defense. Jillian shuddered, having never imagined she'd be visiting a lawyer's office anticipating a murder charge.

"Ms. Grey," Xavier said, "you look troubled. Come on in and sit. Maybe we can get you settled down." She guided Jillian to a roomy office and waited as she sat on an overstuffed ivory-leather sofa. Xavier sank into a matching club chair and reached for an eel skin portfolio.

Neat script filled the top page of the lawyer's legal pad. She needed to believe Xavier grasped the problem and hoped the notes were about her case.

"Miss Xavier, I'm so glad you agreed to represent me. I feel like my world is crashing around me. The detectives were in my office again this afternoon, asking questions, making accusations. One of them is so rude. I want to cry whenever he comes close to me."

"First, please call me Xan." After Jillian reciprocated with a similar request, Xavier said, "Tell me about this afternoon's encounter. Then we'll go to the beginning."

As Jillian began her tale, she handed Xavier copies of all the documents she gave the police. "When the two detectives—"

"Zale and Brewer?"

"Right. When they first interviewed me, I tried to be helpful. It never occurred to me I might have to defend myself. I gave them the documentation of Bethany's counseling then. I even gave Brewer an electronic copy."

"Did you bring one for me?"

"I did. I also brought a copy of everything on my school computer and my personal laptop. Perhaps I've been watching too much television, but I wake every morning expecting them to come in and grab my computers."

"I presume they will." Xavier accepted the flash drive, setting it on the table. "I hope you made a working copy for yourself as well."

"I stashed a copy, and I put one in a safe-deposit box. Too much, I know, but all my materials are on those computers. I'd be out of business without those files." Jillian paused. "The other thing I brought is a set of photographs I took with my iPhone."

Xavier's eyes grew wide. "You took pictures? Of what?"

"Last Friday morning, one of the uniformed officers

crashed through the hedge and over to the body. It didn't look like he made any effort to preserve the scene. I took pictures of him with my phone because . . . I don't know why. It seemed the thing to do."

"Are the police aware you have photos?"

"No. I emailed them to myself then copied them to the disk. I removed them from the computer."

"Did you delete the original from your phone?"

"No. Should I?"

"Don't. If we have to use the photos, we want the police to be able to backtrack to your original files to prove authenticity."

"Did you find out anything about the investigation? My father asked, but no one would give him any real information, just that I should lawyer up, as Dad put it."

Xavier flipped back a page. "I happened to run into Brewer and Zale yesterday after we spoke. Since I knew already that you were Ron Grey's daughter, I took advantage of the situation and talked to them, let them believe I was already representing you. I believe they're considering several suspects."

"How do you know that? Did they tell you?"

"Sy Brewer was vague when I asked him. But if you were the one and only, he would have come on stronger, and you'd have been arrested already. Brewer told me they were getting a lot of pressure from the VIPs to solve the case. Parents are complaining. The mayor is involved. In fact, Brewer called here about an hour ago. He wants me to bring you down to the precinct tomorrow afternoon."

"I'm so confused. I need help to sort this all out." Jillian paused. "Are they going to arrest me?"

"Not right away. They have to rule out the other

suspects first. I don't think they have a case yet. They're hoping taking you downtown will loosen your tongue."

"Will it?"

"No, we'll meet with them, listen to what they have to say, and give little in return. When they ask you a question, look at me before answering. I'll signal if you should answer or not. I suspect it will be a short interview."

"Am I in real trouble?"

"We'll be better informed about your situation tomorrow. Meanwhile, here's what I want you to do."

***

Jillian needed to make one more stop before meeting Warren. Her car waited in the city garage, halfway between Xavier's office near the courthouse and Pasquale's high-rise. There was a matter to discuss with her former spouse.

Though Jillian hadn't called ahead, he acted gracious and poised when he answered his door and admitted Jillian to his apartment.

"Nice to see you," he said, bending to kiss her cheek.

Jillian knew he'd had a few minutes to recover from the unexpectedness of her visit, given the doorman-early-warning-system. She stepped into the apartment and looked around. It looked as anticipated, though it seemed strange to see pieces of furniture that had once been in their home. The coffee table had been a favorite of hers, as was the sofa. When they divorced, she took the family room furniture, and he the living room set. If she went into his bedroom, she'd recognize the dresser and chest there as well.

Jillian motioned to the sofa. "May I sit?"

"You know you don't have to ask."

She sat. "Do I?" Jillian fidgeted with her purse, then set it on the floor. "Pasquale, what were you thinking, getting involved with a kid from my class?"

"I wasn't aware she was your student. Besides, Bethany was no child, believe me. She was old enough and more than willing. In fact, the woman approached me, came on strong." He blushed.

"You always liked the young ones. I'm not surprised about that. Nor do I care anymore."

"Too bad. I hoped you might."

He sounded sincere, but Jillian suspected otherwise.

"I was distressed to learn you were seeing Bethany. I find it humiliating."

"Get off it already, Jillian. I don't recall ever discussing you with her. Perhaps she didn't know."

"Or perhaps she did."

"You didn't come here just to bust my chops about the girl. You've already pointed out you wouldn't care if she wasn't your student. What's your point?"

"I'm a person of interest. Hell, I'm a suspect in Bethany's murder. Not only was the woman selling my exams, she was having an affair with my ex-husband. Someone overheard Bethany arguing with another woman in the bathroom. The cops suggested she and I were fighting over you."

"That's ridiculous."

"I thought so, but the fact remains Zale is adamant I'm involved. Brewer, I think, is less convinced. Tomorrow I find out for sure."

"How so?"

She told him about hiring a lawyer and having to go downtown to talk to the police. "I've talked to them several times already, and they keep coming back for more. That's not a good thing for me."

He nodded. "Did they say anything more about me?"

"No, but my lawyer said you are a person of interest as well."

"Everyone who knew the girl is in that same category. I don't suppose the police have a clue yet."

"Could be. My lawyer wants me to ask about the extent of the connection between you and Bethany."

"Rather personal question, even for you, my dear."

"Getting arrested for murder is damn personal."

"And you think I had something to do with Bethany's murder?"

"Did you?" Jillian stood to leave. "Because, if you did I want to hear it. You owe me that much. I've suffered enough for your transgressions in the past. It's not fair to burden me with them again."

Pasquale took a breath and exhaled through clenched teeth. "I didn't have anything to do with the girl's death. We went out a few times. That's all."

Jillian wanted to believe him, but something in his tone struck her. He was lying, but she didn't know about what.

***

As Jillian walked to her car, she wondered what Pasquale might be hiding. He had a temper, but she didn't believe she could have been married to a man for over twenty years and not know if he was capable of murder.

Perhaps the discussion embarrassed him. That would make sense. There had been similar conversations over the years. He always seemed taken aback by his own behavior, until the final scene, the one where she asked for a divorce. Then he'd been brutal, throwing his affairs at her as weapons.

She envisioned his apartment. It was almost a penthouse and cost far more than her shared rent. Where did he get that kind of money? He was successful at day trading, having finally found his foothold in the business world, but he had massive debt left over from his spending during their marriage.

Jillian forced it all aside. There were other things to accomplish before the day was done.

CHAPTER 17

It was almost seven. Jillian needed to rush to meet Warren on the beach in thirty minutes. She looked up his number, dialed, and left a message for him to wait at the sidewalk café.

Heavy traffic slowed her progress. Warren had implied he had new information. She inspected and repaired her make-up and hair at the traffic light on Federal Highway and Oakland Park Boulevard, then cruised the remainder of the distance to her building, weaving in and out of traffic in a manner that irritated her when done by others.

After parking in the garage, Jillian adhered to her plan to be more visible. She strolled through the lobby of the building, greeted the guard, then left through the front door, picking up speed when she reached the sidewalk. A couple of minutes later, Warren waved from a table outside the same café where they'd met the night before. Could it have been only twenty-four hours ago? So much had happened.

Warren stood and held out his hand, grasping hers as she sat.

"I'm so glad you waited. Sorry I'm late."

"No problem, pretty lady."

Jillian smiled, but didn't feel a lift from the comment.

"How about we have something to eat here, then go to my place and check the email? Pee Turbed responded, but it's best if you read it yourself."

"Fair enough." She squirmed, but didn't want to be rude to the man who helped her. "I've waited this long, another hour won't matter."

He handed her a menu. "I've already ordered you a glass of wine."

Jillian saw a waitress crossing the dining area with a single glass of white wine centered on a tray. This time the smile was sincere.

After they ordered—salmon for her, steak for him—she brought him up to date on her day. "I feel like there's a huge wave threatening to wash me away."

"I understand how you might feel that way. But, the police have to prove their case. They can't ignore the fact your neighbor saw you walk to the beach."

"They can. Eleanor is old and sick. I help take care of her. Zale thinks either she can't see or she's protecting me, or both. In any event, they'd impeach her on the witness stand—if she manages to be in court to testify, that is."

"I didn't know Eleanor was that sick. You didn't say."

"Today the doctor said her condition is worsening. He changed around the medications and ordered additional breathing treatments. I need to give her a hand when we finish the email."

After finishing their dinners, Warren laid a stack of bills on top of the check. "Let's get to it."

He led the way to his apartment. As they walked through the living room, a few touches that weren't his mother's caught her attention. A trendy bookshelf held a selection of current novels—she noted the titles of several she'd read—and a large screen television surrounded by smaller electronics occupied the far wall. She stopped in front of a portrait of Jacqueline, his late wife.

"You must miss her," Jillian said.

"I do. But it's been a long time, and I've started to get my life back together. Moving here was comforting in a way. At least, I don't see reminders everywhere I look."

"Have you started dating again?"

"Some. Nothing serious. In truth, I don't get out much since my home and my work are in the same place." He stepped into the computer room and flipped on the light. "That's the downside of having a home-based business, I suppose."

Jillian pointed toward the window. "Plenty of opportunity out there. Lots of people to meet."

"I suppose." Warren sat in front of the computer monitor and signed onto Yahoo, accessing the stickitstudent account. "You have mail," he said, laughing.

The message flashed on the screen.

samantha, i'm screwin with the bitch's mind, she tryin to figure who i am. if she finds out--she'll kick my ass out of class and probly sue me to. LOL maybe she be in jail then i'm cool. make your own blog, pick a free site where you don't have to give information. WHAT THE HELL?????!!!! keep your comments anonymous sounding so your bitch can't figure you out. the bitch knows i'm at our school, idiot girl on blog gave to much detail. Pee Turbed

"It's not as bad as I thought it would be," Jillian said after rereading the post. "And, Pee Turbed is right. I'll do whatever I can to get her thrown out. The spelling is atrocious."

"Maybe that can help you narrow the field?"

"It's a thought, but many of them don't spell well, and

the ones who can don't edit when they use email. They even send their misspelled missives to faculty. I used to be shocked but not anymore. My daughter's emails look like they were written by a below-average fifth grader."

"Now that you mention it, I've noticed the same thing with my son."

"See?"

"We're starting to sound like a couple of old fogies." Warren chuckled.

"Right, Gramps. Now, how do we trace the message?"

"Already done." He retrieved a sheet of paper and handed it to her. "The sending computer is at the hospital."

"Do you know where at the hospital?" Jillian replayed the day in her mind while staring at the message on the screen. It was sent at eleven-o-five in the morning.

"No, I can't trace it to a specific computer. I'd need the help of their Information Technology people, and I suspect that won't be forthcoming. If you gave the message to the police, they'd have better luck getting the inside channel. I'm not connected to anyone there."

"Too bad. My group gave me all sorts of troubles today." She told him Barrera and Albano ganged up on Li and about sending them home.

"You're a tough one," Warren said, grinning.

"Not tough enough, I'm afraid. I should have shut those two down earlier." Jillian picked up a blank paper from the printer and made notes, recalling the chronology of the day. "I think it was before eleven that we had our last words, and I sent Albano and Barrera away. I went back to the charting area to my other students." Remembering, she wrote down the names of those present, placing them in position around misshapen drawings of a table and counters. "Barrera and

Albano weren't there, neither was Carrie."

"Where was she?"

"Stuck in her patient's room, I think. The woman needed a lot of care, and Carrie didn't finish on time."

"What's the situation with computer access at the hospital?"

"There are computers everywhere. In all the charting areas, including alcoves along the hall, in the main part of the nurses' station, in the physician's dictation room, and in the lounge."

"What you're telling me is any of the three may have gone onto the Internet without your knowledge."

"Yes, providing they had the hospital access code. They could have left the area and gone to another nursing unit. They were dressed in school uniforms. No one would stop them."

"Let's call the detectives and tell them what we found."

"Why? They told me they didn't think the blog had anything to do with the case. They implied they weren't pursuing it. I think it's my problem."

"What are you going to do with the information?"

"I'm going to talk to those three kids tomorrow."

"That's dangerous." Warren touched Jillian's hand. "I wouldn't want to see anything happen to you."

"So much is happening to me now. I need to take control. If I can make the blogger stop, then at least I'll be able to focus on clearing my name with the police. Maybe they'll admit online they know nothing about the crime. Or maybe they know who killed Bethany and are making me the scapegoat. Even though they say otherwise, I know the accusations are one of the reasons the police are focused on me. I don't get why they won't use their resources to find the bloggers. Even Brewer brushes the blog aside."

"Maybe they are looking at it and not telling you."

"Whatever. I'm going to push some buttons at the school."

"Be careful."

Warren walked Jillian home, stopping her before she stepped onto the elevator to kiss her on the cheek. "Can I call you? For dinner, I mean?"

"Please do." The elevator door closed in front of her.

CHAPTER 18

On Thursday morning, Jillian had a list of tasks to accomplish at school before going home to prepare for her two-o'clock appointment with the detectives.

She plugged in her laptop, centered it on the oak laminate desk, and signed in. Responding to a click of the mouse, the grade book opened. All three students, Barrera, Albano, and Carrie, improved on the last test. The other malcontents experienced similar success. The remainder of the class earned the grades she expected. Some scored better, others worse. Pee Turbed's comments about grades would not be useful.

Bethany also improved on the second exam—owing to her possession of the test bank rather than expanded knowledge, Jillian supposed. She wondered why the girl bothered to make an appointment to ask for advice. Maybe there had been another agenda. Perhaps, as Pee Turbed proposed, Bethany wanted to make a deal.

Replaying the last meeting with Bethany, Jillian remembered one long pause when Bethany appeared about to say something. The moment passed when Jillian asked a question to focus the girl on study skills. Now, in retrospect, she regretted her goal directed approach to the meeting. Perhaps she might have learned something that could have saved the girl's life.

Jillian called the financial aid office and asked the receptionist to put her through to the counselor handling the front of the alphabet.

A high-pitched voice came on the line. "Mamie Craig speaking. How may I help you?"

Jillian introduced herself. "I need help assisting my advisees. I have counseling appointments today and need updates with the scholarship and grant programs."

"I can't give specifics—only whether their aid is active or not."

"I understand. The thing is these particular students use their financial aid status as an excuse for not registering promptly, then for not completing assignments because they aren't attending. I want to confront them with the facts and see if I can get them on track."

"Unusual, but I see your point. What are their names?"

"The first is Vincent Barrera."

"Hang on." The sounds of keys clicking came over the line. "He failed to complete his application. That delayed approval of his tuition money."

Jillian wrote Quick Shot next to his name in her notes. "How about Carrie Kennedy?"

Clicking. "Carrie Kennedy's application is complete and her registration current. She is actively receiving financial aid."

Sleeping Pill or possibly Cast Off, Jillian thought, making a note. "Next is Bethany Newland."

"Newland applied for financial aid, but I closed the application," Craig said, answering with no keyboard sounds.

"Why was that?"

"It's not relevant."

Jillian presumed it was because of family finances and the fact she lived at home. Again, Sleeping Pill or Cast Off. "Last, Shanna Albano?"

"Shanna Albano has no application on file."

Jillian wondered why. Most of the students applied for assistance, given the high tuition costs and plentiful scholarships, loans, and grants. "Thank you, Ms. Craig. You've been a big help." She disconnected.

For a moment, Jillian pondered how to poke into Albano's background, then glanced at the rolling cart near her office door. The secretary hadn't taken the files Jillian reviewed on Monday. She retrieved Albano's from the top of the stack, intending to read through it again, looking for more detail and hints about her past. Having second thoughts, she picked up the stack of records, glanced up and down the hallway, and, seeing no one, hurried to the copy room.

Feeling self-conscious, Jillian returned to the office. "If anyone saw me," she muttered, "they'd think I'd lost my mind, or that I had a Nancy Drew complex." She sat with a stapled copy of Albano's record and flipped to the program application. "And I talk to myself, too. Maybe I'm losing it."

The Admissions Committee approved Albano for the program on an appealed decision, which explained why she didn't file for financial aid. While awaiting the decision, she missed the filing deadline. A hand-written comment noted that the coed's explanation of her dishonorable discharge answered all outstanding questions.

Vincent Barrera's admission file looked clean. His original status had been academic probation, given his poor grades in California, but he converted to non-probationary with no stipulations after his first successful term. Jillian reviewed a copy of his transcript, learning his grades at Conover were satisfactory until he failed her class the first time.

She waded through the rest of the files, making notes, but learning nothing extraordinary about the other malcontents. Tanya Li and Oliver Cooley had straightforward admissions with no stipulations and no remediation. Their transcripts indicated withdrawals from their first attempt at the nursing course.

After stowing her laptop under her desk, Jillian slipped the copied records into her binder and headed upstairs. She wanted to ask the pharmacology professor to send Albano, Kennedy, and Barrera to meet with the dean after his lecture.

***

An hour later, while Jillian and Dean Stevenson waited in the cramped, utilitarian conference room in the rear of the department, Jillian brought the dean up to date on her investigation of the bloggers. The dean agreed the Ethics Code applied to the situation, freedom of speech notwithstanding. Libeling a professor and the school was inappropriate.

When the secretary announced over the intercom that the three were in the lobby, the women spent a few moments finishing their conversation before Jillian went to retrieve them. As she stepped into the main corridor, she encountered two uniformed officers blocking her path.

"Ms. Jillian Grey?" the tallest of the two men said, extending a folded paper.

Jillian nodded. "What's this?"

"We have a subpoena to confiscate your computers."

Jillian took the form and opened it. "Who requested this?" Tears stung her eyes, but she refused to cry.

"The requesting officer's name is on the form, ma'am," the shorter, hefty officer said.

"Detective Zale." Jillian wiped an escaped tear. "All he had to do was ask. I would have allowed someone to go through the files. Now I'll have difficulty getting my work done." She paused and considered refusing, then decided against starting a fight she couldn't win. "I'll open the door for you."

"Thank you," the taller man said.

Feeling anger mount, Jillian shook her head and exhaled. "And, you come in when I have students waiting and embarrass me. It's not right. It's not fair." Her eyes burned.

"Sorry, ma'am. We're carrying out the order."

Jillian led them to the office and watched as they hauled out the machines. Then she took a deep breath, wiped her eyes, and dialed the secretary's extension. "Please send them in."

"Okay."

"Did you tell Marlene what the holdup was?"

"Yes, I did. No problem."

Jillian took an extra minute to compose herself, then went to the conference room, slipping in the side door as the students sat.

Dean Stevenson nodded.

While Jillian laid the original email to Pee Turbed and the response on the table, she kept her eyes on the students.

Three sets of eyes dropped to the pages. Kennedy looked up first, made eye contact with Jillian, and shook her head. The other two raised their gazes but showed no response.

"As you can tell, we baited Pee Turbed with an email."

"So?" Albano said, tugging at her red sweater.

"A hospital computer transmitted the reply yesterday morning. I've accounted for everyone in the group except the three of you."

"I was with my patient," Kennedy said. "You can check with the primary nurse. She helped me clean him."

"Shanna, where were you?"

"You sent me home. I left."

"Vincent?"

"I left with her."

"You can be excused." Jillian turned to Kennedy. "Thank you for waiting."

Albano half stood. "Am I excused, too?"

"No. We have two issues here. One of the problems is I believe one of you," she nodded to Albano and Barrera in turn, "wrote the email defaming me. Based on the content of the blog and what's in your files, I believe Shanna uses the pen name Pee Turbed and Vincent uses Quick Shot."

"You can't prove that." Albano spat out the words.

"You're right, I can't. But what I am going to do is turn the emails over to the police this afternoon when I go downtown. I'm also going to give them electronic copies so they have their techs trace the source."

"Whatever. People can write what they want," Albano said.

"If it doesn't include libel." Jillian picked up another piece of paper. "It's true I can't prove which one of you wrote the email, so at this moment, I can't do anything more about it. But, I have additional issues with you." She looked at Barrera. "Vincent, I asked you last Monday to meet with me after your rude behavior."

Barrera glared at Jillian, then glanced at the dean.

Jillian was glad the dean joined the session. "Further," she said, including Albano in her gaze, "I have a problem with both of you, given your conduct in the cafeteria yesterday morning and in the stairwell with Tanya."

"Dean Stevenson," Barrera said. "Can't you see she's picking on us? She thinks we wrote that blog, and now she's out to get us. It's not fair."

Dean Stevenson stood. "I spoke with a staff nurse from the hospital this morning who corroborated Ms. Grey's report, overheard the exchange in the cafeteria, and saw you both enter the stairwell with Tanya Li." She moved to a position across the table from the students. "Further, several of your classmates filed written complaints about your obnoxious comments on Monday. The documentation is solid."

Barrera gulped.

Albano stared straight ahead, seeming to focus on the hem of the dean's pale blue jacket.

"Here's the deal," the dean said. "If you admit to writing the blog and promise to remove it from the Internet, I'll put you on probation with the program—"

"Dean Ste—" Barrera broke in.

"Before you say anything, Mr. Barrera, let me finish." Dean Stevenson held up a hand. "If you choose to deny the obvious, I'll expel you effective today."

"You can't do that," Albano said. "It's not fair. There's freedom of speech. Grey can't control what we say and do."

"Quite wrong, my friends." Dean Stevenson laid two more papers on the table, pushing them close to the students. "Here are copies of the policies you signed. You agreed to maintain a professional demeanor at all times in the hospital, on campus, and in your dealings with the school. I can and will suspend you. In fact, legal counsel approved your expulsions an hour ago, and the president is available and willing to sign. All I need to do is sign my name." She paused. "Now, what will it be?"

Albano and Barrera exchanged glares. Barrera's hand trembled as did Albano's lower lip. Neither spoke.

They caused Jillian immeasurable harm with the spiteful blog, and their insinuations sparked some of the police detectives' interest. Jillian felt no sympathy for their plight.

"Well, people, what will it be?" Dean Stevenson said, her voice soft yet demanding. She clicked a ballpoint, then paused, turning to Jillian. "Let's give them a minute to themselves."

Jillian and Dean Stevenson stepped into the hall and waited by the door.

"I didn't know you talked to the school lawyer about suspending them." Jillian felt like a guard, but didn't want to move, fearing the two might escape.

"I didn't." Dean Stevenson laughed under her breath. "I don't anticipate any difficulty if it comes to that. The president is supportive when we take measures to unload unruly people. He'd rather face an occasional lawsuit than crumble to their demands. They can go down the street to the community college and enroll."

"You were bluffing." Jillian grinned.

"That I was, my dear." She pushed open the door. "Let's go back in." Stevenson returned to the same position at the table. "Well, what will it be?"

Albano spoke first. "I'm sorry. I didn't mean any harm by the blog. Not really."

Jillian opened her mouth to speak, but the dean touched her arm, silencing her.

Keeping her eyes on the dean, Albano said, "When Bethany died, I thought Ms. Grey had reason to get rid of her. I mean, all that stuff I wrote about the stolen exam questions was true, and Bethany did talk about going to meet with Ms. Grey to try and get a better grade."

"She never asked me to change her scores," Jillian said. "We talked about study habits."

"I think she chickened out. Look, I'm sorry. I want to finish this program and change the way my life has gone. I'll take the blog off the Internet and tell everyone we're not doing it anymore."

"Who was who on the blog?" Jillian said.

"I'm Pee Turbed," Albano said.

"I'm Quick Shot," Barrera said. "Bethany was Cast Off, and Carrie is Sleeping Pill, but she doesn't go online often. I'm sorry, too. It got out of hand."

Dean Stevenson slid two printed forms across the table. "These are the conditions for your continuation in the program. One, you will discontinue the blog and institute no similar instrument. You will bring me proof by five-o'clock today. Two, you will refrain from any further disruption in the classroom or in the hospital. Three, you will apologize to Miss Li and to the chief nursing officer at the hospital. Four, you will accept transfer across town to Mrs. Ryan's clinical group. Any further incidents of this sort will result in your immediate dismissal from the program."

"Agreed," Barrera said.

Albano wiped a tear. "Okay. Where do I sign?"

"Here." Stevenson pointed to lines on the bottom of the papers.

CHAPTER 19

Jillian hurried home following the meeting with the students and prepared for the worst—no jewelry except an inexpensive watch, loose jeans and print tee shirt, one credit card, driver's license, cell phone, and a little cash. Remembering a story an old friend told her about being in jail and having her undies stolen after she washed them, Jillian slipped a fresh pair into her pocket. If arrested, she wanted to be as unencumbered as possible.

Jillian planned to meet Xan Xavier in the lobby of the police department fifteen minutes before her two-o'clock appointment. As she drove across town, an overwhelming sense of relief filled her. The incident with the bloggers was over. At least some part of her life would return to normal. All that was left was to get through the afternoon. I have the documents to prove I'm innocent.

The traffic on Broward Boulevard stood still. Jillian glanced at the time, looked around, then checked the dashboard clock. The meeting with the students took longer than planned, given the need to coerce them into confessing. She feared being late.

Taking a deep breath and murmuring a prayer, she

leaned forward and craned to see around the SUV in front of her. An empty car sat in the bus lane, and a Metro bus blocked two lanes of traffic while riders disembarked. The seconds ticked by.

Jillian tapped her fingers against the steering wheel, checked the time, and reached for her iPhone.

Xavier answered on the first ring. "Where are you?"

"Stuck behind a city bus in traffic."

"We only have a few minutes until someone comes looking for us."

"I know. The thing should move any moment."

"We can talk while you wait. First, I need to move outside to be sure I'm not overheard." After a moment, she said, "I'm out."

"Good." Jillian updated Xavier on her morning's successes. "I made copies of all the papers for the police. Maybe they'll get off my back."

"I want to hear what the detectives have to say, then make a decision. We need to hold a couple of trump cards in case we go to trial."

So much for Jillian's feeling of relief. She shuddered. "I understand."

The bus doors closed, and it rolled into the left lane. Jillian crept forward, slipping around the corner as the light changed to red. Sighing, she said, "Moving now. I should be there in five minutes."

"When we get inside, remember to take your cues from me. And, keep your comments as direct and to the point as possible. Don't add any extra explanations." Xavier continued to talk as Jillian scooted through traffic.

After pulling into the huge lot fronting the PD, Jillian zipped into a space in the last row and slammed the transmission into park. She thought they should have front row spots labeled For Suspects Only. A minute later, she ran along the white concrete walk, arriving at the front of the stationhouse breathless and sweating.

Xavier stood at the door. "Okay kid, we're due upstairs. I told them to give us five. Show me the documents."

Jillian handed over the short stack of papers—copies of emails, Warren's research, student files, and the newest counseling reports.

"This is great stuff," Xavier said. "We'll extend them the courtesy of sharing it with them at the proper time."

"The dean threatened Albano and Barrera with expulsion to make them admit to being the bloggers and to agree to take the damn thing off the Internet."

"It could be a problem if they are asked to testify. They might say they admitted to something they didn't do to stay in school."

"If the blog comes off the net today as they promised, the point is made."

"True, but they could claim coincidence. Track it down tonight and print any pages confirming the blog can't be located."

"Will do."

Xavier motioned to the elevator. "Let's not keep the gentlemen in suspense."

A youthful uniformed officer met the women at the elevator and escorted them to a conference room.

Jillian recognized it for what it was, an interrogation room. A narrow table equipped with a tape recorder sat against the far wall, and a video camera hung from the ceiling. The camera pointed at a square table bolted to the floor in the middle of the room. Four straight-backed chairs surrounded the table. Thick, fuzzy material in a drab grey covered the unadorned walls. There were no windows except the small square pane of glass in the door.

"Have a seat," the officer said.

"Thanks, no," Jillian replied, eyeing the chairs. "I'll stand."

The officer left the room, leaving Jillian alone with her lawyer.

"Xan, wh . . ."

"It's best not to talk much in here. The room is not supposed to be bugged." She shrugged. "But, I prefer to speak with my clients outside."

"Oh. Thought that only happened in the movies."

"Sorry." Xavier sat. "You'll need to sit there." She pointed to the chair facing the video camera.

"They're not going to record this, are they?"

"Probably. It has an unsettling effect on people. They use it for that purpose, even if they don't need the tape later."

Jillian sat down and forced a smile. "Let 'em roll." She squirmed in the chair. "Uncomfortable. It doesn't move." She pushed her feet against the floor.

"On purpose as well."

"Well, at least I know the rules."

The door to the interrogation room opened, and Sy Brewer and Nate Zale stepped in. Zale wore a expensive-looking dark blue suit with a white shirt and red print tie. Brewer looked relaxed in striped golf shirt and cotton chinos. The men sat, Zale to Jillian's right, Brewer across the table from her.

"Thank you for coming, ladies," Brewer said. "Hopefully, we can get some things cleared up today." He paused, as if waiting for a response, then made introductions and general comments for the record. "Ms. Grey, tell us again about the morning you found Bethany Newland's body."

Xavier nodded.

Jillian took a deep breath, controlled a long slow exhalation, then retold the week-old story. She had reviewed her notes earlier in the day and hurried through the narrative.

"Almost the same as what you said last Friday."

"It's what happened, sir," Jillian said, her tone flat.

"We expect some variation on the retelling."

"I made notes so I wouldn't forget the details."

"Oh, I see." Brewer removed a small pad from his shirt pocket. "Tell us again about your conference with Bethany last Thursday evening."

Jillian repeated earlier responses. "I've given you a couple copies of the documentation."

Zale stood and moved behind Jillian. "Ms. Grey, the problem I have with all of this is—I think you're lying."

Xavier motioned to keep quiet.

She shuddered, but restrained herself.

"For example, there is the matter of the blog on the Internet. Now, I'm a firm believer where there's a stink, something crapped. One of the bloggers is convinced you're the best suspect. Why would that be?"

Jillian looked at Xavier, who nodded. "Because, as I told you before, we have several malcontents this semester. You spoke with my boss. She gave you information on them and shared my student reviews with you. We can't control all of the students' behavior."

"But you'd like to try, wouldn't you?"

"Those are your words, not mine, sir."

Zale hiked his hip onto the table, blocking Jillian's view

of Xavier. He leaned to within twelve inches of her face. "Tell me, Professor, why were your fingerprints on the victim's pocketbook? In all your many repetitions of your meeting with the girl, you never mentioned touching her belongings."

Xavier shifted left and signaled Jillian to respond.

"I don't know. Bethany sat across the desk from me. I remember her putting some of her things on the corner of my desk. Perhaps I moved them. I did spread out some materials for review."

"What type of materials?" Brewer asked, his voice warm and welcoming by comparison to Zale's.

"Her last test. I drew some illustrations on how to better take notes. I listed those two activities in my counseling record."

"You did." Zale clicked his pen several times. "So, you're telling me you may have touched the purse while she was in your office, but you don't know."

"Yes."

"Why didn't you tell us before?" He turned to Brewer. "Give me the responding officer's report." He tapped the report, holding it for Jillian to read. "Says here you told Morgan you only touched the vic's neck. Which is it, ma'am?"

"I must have touched the handbag. That could have happened in my office on Thursday evening. I didn't touch it when I found her body. I tried to find a carotid pulse. Nothing more." Jillian's insides shook. She tried to push the bolted-down chair away from the table and away from Zale.

"How's that scratch on your arm?"

"Fine." She held it out to show the fine, healed line.

"How did you hurt yourself again?"

Jillian exhaled. "This is exasperating. I told you I got scraped going into the bushes."

"Before or after you touched Newland's neck?"

"Before. Going into the bushes. That was before . . . before I found the body."

"Getting a little upset, here, are you?" Zale said, his voice low and edgy.

Xavier stood. "Detectives, do you have any other questions for Ms. Grey or do you intend to badger her?"

"We have more questions."

"Get to them or this is over."

Zale leaned in on Jillian again. "I understand your alibi for later Thursday evening is you were walking the beach, which you say is attested to by an old woman with severe lung disease."

"Eleanor's eyes are fine," Jillian sassed, then regretted her lapse.

"I don't doubt it," Zale said. "You help take care of her."

"True."

"Did you ask her to give you an alibi?"

"No. I told her about the incident. She volunteered that she saw me heading to the beach and offered to call you with the information."

"How did you say her vision is?"

"As far as I know, it's fine. She's commented before about seeing me walk toward the water. She can see well enough to distinguish me from the other people she sees all the time. I've never found her to be wrong."

"You've tested her then?"

"No. You're twisting what I say. I didn't test her. She comments. She's always right."

"No one else looks like you or walks like you in the building."

"I don't know. What I do know is I went to the beach, and Eleanor said she saw me."

Xavier leaned in, making eye contact with Zale. "Give her a break, would you?"

"Counselor, we are not here to give our prime suspect a break. We're here to get the information," Zale said.

The cold rush of fear shot up Jillian's spine and into her skull. Prime suspect? How can I be the prime suspect?

Zale encroached on Jillian's space again. "We have an eye witness who places you at the scene. Says he saw a woman of your description coming out of the trees at the back of the parking lot."

"Impossible." Jillian's spat out the response and her face reddened. "That witness is mistaken. I left the school and went home to walk the beach."

"Witness saw a woman with short reddish-brown hair and a red shirt."

"He's wrong. I never wear red. Clashes with my hair. Ask my students, ask the other teachers, ask Chantal, you can even ask my ex-husband. He once paid two hundred dollars for a red blouse for me that I refused to wear." Jillian balled her hands into fists, trying to quell their shaking.

Zale sneered. "We'll ask them all." He paused. "One last thing. Why did you erase the hard drive on your PC?"

Jillian opened her mouth but found no words. A full minute later, verging on tears, she said, "I didn't erase the drive. When I used it yesterday, it was fine."

"You were in your office this morning. Why did you erase it?"

"I didn't turn it on this morning." Jillian sat for a

moment. "I plugged in my laptop and looked at the grades. Then I shut it off and put it in the case."

"Why didn't you use the PC?"

"Most times I do, but today I wanted the report from the laptop. I hadn't copied it to the other computer yet. Other than a couple of files, I try to keep the two computers the same, then I have all I need at home or at work."

"But still, you somehow managed to not copy your grades. Sounds like they would be an important part of your work to me."

"There has been a lot going on. I've not been very focused, I guess."

Zale smiled. "Guilty conscience?" He glanced at Brewer, who nodded. "We need a DNA sample. A cheek swab will do."

Xavier shook her head. "Get a court order." She stood and moved toward the door. "Come along. This interview is over." As if having a second thought, she reached into her brief case and extracted some of the papers Jillian had given her. "Gentlemen, here are the students' admissions that the blog was malicious, creative writing. Ms. Grey has a witness to her whereabouts and a total lack of opportunity. I'm sure you'll find your witness is mistaken. It's time you find the killer and leave this woman alone." Ushering Jillian in front of her, she stepped through the door.

CHAPTER 20

Jillian pulled into the garage an hour later than usual. She offered the guard a weak smile and unenthusiastic wave as she scooted through the marble lobby, again making sure she was visible.

After emptying her pockets on the dresser, Jillian headed next door to prepare Eleanor's pills for the next day.

"What kept you?" Eleanor asked when Jillian stepped into the apartment's small kitchen. "You're always on time. I was worried."

"I'm sorry. I should have called. I was distracted. The SOB detectives summoned me to the police station again." Jillian picked up a stethoscope from the counter. As usual, the apartment was hot. Jillian broke into a light sweat. "Let me listen to your lungs, then I'll tell you my troubles."

"Okay, dear." Eleanor planted her feet on the floor and bent forward in the chair.

Jillian warmed the metal chest piece in her hand, lowered the knitted afghan from Eleanor's shoulders, and slipped the stethoscope under her blouse. "Take a deep breath." She moved the instrument. "Again." When finished, she said, "What did the doctor tell you today?"

"He said the same thing as the other day. I'm worse, more congested."

Jillian nodded.

"He said there isn't a lot he can do for me anymore. I'm taking the maximum amount of medication. The home health nurse will give me the IV antibiotics, but otherwise, nothing new. I need to keep on, keepin' on." Eleanor, straining from the effort required to talk, leaned over the table, supporting her weight on her arms, which she extended in front like two legs of a tripod, her butt being the third support. She exhaled long and slow through pursed lips. Her color turned dusky.

While waiting for Eleanor's color to improve, Jillian checked the connection to the portable oxygen tank and adjusted the elastic band holding the plastic prongs in Eleanor's nose. The soft whistle of the gas moving through the system assured Jillian the apparatus worked.

Eleanor relaxed into the chair and looked at Jillian, her expression expectant.

"You listen for a while. I'll talk," Jillian said.

Eleanor nodded.

As Jillian reported on the interrogation at the police station, her unease increased. "I can't figure them out." She wiped a tear from the corner of her eye, then stopped to blow her nose. "They say I'm the prime suspect and act as if I'm hiding something. I've never been treated so rudely in my life—not even by Pasquale. I feel insulted and humiliated . . . degraded."

Motioning with her hand, Eleanor encouraged Jillian to continue.

"It makes me so angry." Jillian shuddered. "I tried to help Bethany with her grades. She used me. The most common opinion is she was intent on extortion—a passing grade for the return of my exam questions. The reward I get for staying to talk with her on my own time is being accused of murder.

"And I feel so lost and alone in my troubles even though people are helping me. My dad called Brewer again. Brewer was nice, but told him to quit calling. I really don't want him involved and upset. He'll have another heart attack. But he insists. He says he's going to go back to the station and talk with his friend Mack. What else can he do except collect rumors? And Mom's in her own world. Tells me not to worry. It'll work out. Good thing I had enough saved to hire Xavier."

"I understand. I felt the same way in California when the police refused to release Vincent into my custody. They said with my hippie past—that's the way they put it, my hippie past—I was a poor choice to monitor him since he was charged with drug possession." She took a few extra breaths. "Imagine that. I was sixty years old and couldn't live down my own police record. They kept him in juvie hall until his trial, then locked him away for two years. It wasn't fair. The cops arrested some of his friends at the same time, but released them to their parents. Every other kid in the world gets a second, third, fourth chance. Vincent went to juvie on his second offense."

It was the first time Eleanor had revealed any details about Barrera's troubled past. Jillian dried her eyes. Drug possession, Jillian thought. She wondered about the details, but wouldn't ask.

"Did their parents have connections that you didn't?"

"I don't think so. I mean they had more money than we did, sure. But we were respectable. Dewey was in retail, and

I was a department secretary at Berkeley."

Eleanor's version of the story seemed to be missing something. However, Barrera's incarceration would, no doubt, impact his present behavior, explaining his aggressiveness. Jillian bit her lip, pondering the information.

Jillian watched the relaxed movement of her friend's chest. When Eleanor was calm, she had fewer breathing difficulties.

"The detectives were here again this morning," Eleanor said.

"What did they want?"

"Asked about my eyesight. Want me to have a test. I told them no. I'm not up to extra doctoring. Getting out is too hard for me right now."

It had only been a few days since Eleanor enjoyed a boat ride with Dewey. The respiratory infection came on fast and set her back. How far? Jillian wondered. She maintained a measured pace to the conversation, allowing Eleanor to rest between responses. "How did the detectives take it?

"They were a little upset, maybe. They said I made a poor witness for the defense."

"Bastards."

"I'll go to the ophthalmologist if I have to. I want to help."

"I appreciate it, but I don't want you putting yourself at any risk. None."

"I think they're chasing phantoms." Eleanor smiled. "They talked to Shanna and Vincent again. He thinks he's a suspect because of his record."

"Could be. The way the cops treat me though, I think Vincent doesn't have a lot to worry about." Or does he? she thought, reflecting on his recent actions.

Eleanor opened her mouth as if to speak, but stopped when the apartment door opened. Barrera and Albano entered the room.

Damn, Jillian thought.

Barrera glared at Jillian, then leaned toward Eleanor. "Hi, Grandma." He kissed her on the cheek, then stepped back and looked her over.

"Hello, Mrs. Evers." Albano maintained a distance, slouching against the kitchen counter.

"How you doing? Feeling a little better?" Barrera said.

"I'm fine, dear. When the medicine works, I'll be back to my old sassy self." Eleanor took a deep breath and exhaled, puckering her lips as if blowing a kiss. "Thanks for taking me to the doctor again today."

"You already thanked me. Besides I told you I don't mind. I'm glad Grandpa has stuff to keep him busy."

"He'd climb the wall stuck here with me all day. Poor man. He appreciated not having to cancel his fishing trip."

Jillian thought Barrera and his grandmother had a warm, positive relationship. Someday he'd let his goodness out for the world to see. She gave herself an imaginary kick in the butt for her Pollyanna attitude.

"What are you doing here?" Barrera glowered at Jillian, his voice conveying contempt.

"Checking. She's congested," Jillian said, annoyed at Barrera's manner. They'd met in his grandmother's apartment on several occasions, and his manner was always the same—insolent.

"Doctor said." Barrera nodded.

Eleanor raised her hand. "Jillian, could you sew a couple buttons on my black sweater? I can't see to sew black on black anymore. There's not enough contrast."

"Happy to." Jillian looked around the kitchen, then glanced into the living room. The cardigan and sewing materials sat on the coffee table. "Let me get started while you three talk."

She left the room, but rather than staying with Eleanor, Barrera followed.

"You didn't tell Grandma about the trouble at school, did you?" Barrera whispered, his tone demanding. "I don't want to upset her."

"Then maybe you should watch how you behave. But, never fear, young man. I know better than to breach your student confidentiality."

"Make damn sure you do."

"Is that a threat?" She raised an eyebrow.

"Take it any damn way you want." Barrera turned and strutted to the kitchen.

She heard Eleanor and Albano talking, their voices strained.

"Remind me," Eleanor said, "what man were you and Bethany discussing the last time you brought her here?"

"Someone she was dating on and off."

"Was it Pasquale Pascasio?"

Jillian shuddered.

"And if it was?" Albano said.

"You encouraged Bethany to chase after him. I think I was in the bedroom, but I heard you telling her to be more forward, to come on real strong, crowd his space."

"She liked him, but he wasn't showing any interest."

"Is that all there was to it?"

"What do you care?" Albano's voice was sharp. "Bethany had the right to chase after any man she wanted."

"Wasn't she dating the nice young man you brought over

to dinner a couple of months ago."

"Bethany and Oliver went out, but she was doing the other guy, too. Cheating, you know. Bethany was like that."

"I had no idea."

"Well, now you do."

"Keep your voices down," Barrera said. "The next thing you know, goody-teacher in there will be repeating the conversation."

Fighting an urge to go to the other room and defend herself, then ask a few questions, Jillian focused on the sewing. Eleanor was doing a good job getting information. She continued to eavesdrop, straining to hear the lowered voices.

Eleanor said, "What is it you have to hide? Your friend was murdered. I'd think you'd want to help. Telling the police Bethany chased after the man could be helpful." Eleanor's breathing became more labored.

Jillian cut the thread on the last button with her teeth, then laid down the sweater, placing the needle and thread on the table next to it. She stood, staring down at the black against black, remembering when her mother began needing help with the same duties. Eleanor wouldn't pass the eye exam, and the police would discount her alibi. Further, she couldn't imagine the two rebellious students volunteering what they knew or coming to her defense.

Stopping in the archway to the kitchen, Jillian said, "I'm going home. Enjoy your visit with the kids." She stepped into the room and kissed Eleanor on the cheek. "I'll stop again tomorrow. Be sure you drink a lot of fluid. It'll help clear your lungs."

"I will, dear." Eleanor held her chest and coughed.

"You'd better stay here until your grandfather gets

home," Jillian said. "Don't leave her alone until she's feeling better."

Barrera nodded, then shoved past Jillian to open the door.

***

On Friday morning, Jillian opened the Fort Lauderdale News where the story about Bethany's murder appeared again on the front page.

The article restated the original information, then pointed out that on the Saturday following the murder, they reported the incident and speculated the motive was robbery. Detective Brewer predicted a rapid solution to the case. Now, they repeated that quote, pointing out that Brewer was wrong. Investigators had ruled out mugging as a motive, and no one was in custody.

The article continued with a quote from Zale.

"There are several scenarios we are considering, and we have, in fact, talked with several witnesses. We brought Jillian Grey, the faculty member who was the last person to see the victim alive, in for questioning. We've questioned other persons of interest as well. I expect an arrest within the next couple of days."

CHAPTER 21

By mid-morning, Jillian sat across from the dean.

Marlene Stevenson stared at the ringing telephone and grimaced. "I hope that's not President McMann again. I've talked to him twice already—since nine. My ear hurts. However, you need to know about how things stand anyway. Maybe we can figure out, together, how to proceed." She pushed the conference button.

The president's voice filled the room. "Marlene, this is the fourteenth complaint from a parent this morning. They all read the article in the News and expect us to do something to protect their children. The last one said her daughter was reluctant to go to school, afraid of talking to the professor, and felt her life endangered if she questioned Ms. Grey in any way. These parents demanded we remove Ms. Grey."

Jillian shifted forward, preparing to stand and leave the room.

Stevenson mouthed, "I'm sorry," and held up her hand, cautioning Jillian to remain quiet. "And what do you think we should do, sir?"

"Suspend Ms. Grey without further delay."

Jillian shrank into her chair, wanting to disappear and

wishing she was anywhere else.

"Without there being charges?" the dean said. "The reporter, and the detective for that matter, are speculating."

"You don't know that."

"But I know Jillian. I've worked with her for years. Not to mention the fact she has a witness. A neighbor saw her go to the beach that evening." Dean Stevenson fiddled with the papers on the desk.

"I talked to the police yesterday. They're not convinced the witness is reliable."

Seeming to ignore the president's comment, Dean Stevenson continued. "The parents are panicking. But, this is an isolated incident, and I think it would be unfair to suspend a faculty member in the midst of all this. There is no proof that she is connected to Bethany's murder."

"We'll talk again later," McMann said before disconnecting the call.

"Damned political animal." Dean Stevenson sighed. "I'm accustomed to dealing with his whims, but he acted supportive at first and was positive this morning. I'm so sorry, if I'd have known he'd do an about-face so fast, I wouldn't have let you hear the conversation."

"I understand. I know what he's like." Jillian shuddered. "I had hoped he would be more reasonable."

Stevenson pushed the intercom button to her assistant. "Please, no interruptions for a few minutes."

"Mrs. Conover-Farnsworth is almost to your door. I couldn't stop her," the assistant said.

A tall woman wearing a beige Armani suit and sporting a huge, glittering diamond on her left hand barged into the room. "Dean Stevenson, I demand to know what you're doing to protect my daughter."

Jillian recognized the woman as Madeleine Conover-Farnsworth, heiress to the fortune of one of the three founding fathers of the college. After contributing the majority of the land necessary for the campus, he insisted the college be named for him.

"I assume you're referring to the unfortunate murder of Bethany Newland." Stevenson locked eyes with the woman.

"Unfortunate is a bit light. Wouldn't you agree?" Uninvited, the woman pulled back one of the side chairs and sat, never offering Jillian a glance.

"Yes, I suppose I do. It's hard to find an adequate word."

"Again, what are you doing to protect my Anna and the other young people?"

"We're cooperating with the police in their investigation. Campus security beefed up their patrols, we're advising students to come and go in groups, and we've discontinued late afternoon office hours to negate the need for individuals to stay late—after their associates have left the campus."

"But that woman continues to work here. Why is that?"

Jillian stood. "Excuse me. I'm that woman. I had nothing to do with Bethany's murder, and I haven't been charged, ma'am."

"I spoke with the police chief this morning. He assured me you're a viable suspect. He said he anticipated your arrest by the end of the week. That's tomorrow." She glanced at her watch.

"It's only because one of the detectives has a blind spot and refuses to investigate. He's looking for a quick solution. At my expense." Jillian stomped out of the room, but lingered in the hall next to the open door where she could hear the conversation.

"The latest information I have is the police have several persons of interest." Dean Stevenson stood. "President McMann is staying informed. He's talking to the police chief on a daily basis as well. Believe me, we've done everything necessary to assure the safety of our students. If and when Professor Grey is charged, we'll decide what we need to do."

"By then, I will have withdrawn my financial support from the college. I will not support a group of academics who coddle a murderer." The woman marched out of the office, sneering at Jillian as she went by. "Did you hear it all? I'll just stop by and see the president."

Stevenson motioned Jillian back into the office. "Sit, please." After waiting a moment, the dean returned to her chair. "I doubt she'll withdraw financial support. After all, Conover-Farnsworth is chairman of the foundation that has the primary purpose of supporting the school. Her threat, however, will carry real weight with McMann. I don't believe he'll risk his job to protect you at this point."

Knowing the political forces would have their way, Jillian nodded, but decided to defend herself. "I saw the article in the newspaper this morning. There isn't any new information in it. Not really. It mentions my name, says the police talked with me yesterday, but it doesn't really imply I'm the one who is likely to be arrested." Jillian's eyes teared.

"I agree. However, you're the only suspect mentioned by name." Dean Stevenson leaned forward and grasped Jillian's hand. "It has caused an uproar among the parents." She repeated some of the comments she'd heard. "And, Conover-Farnsworth wields a lot of power. She may not pull her money, but she will go to McMann. With her, it's not an empty threat. I have no choice but to suspend you."

Jillian's eyes stung.

Dean Stevenson offered Jillian a tissue, who took it, balling it in her hand.

"I'm sorry, but it's without pay. I talked with personnel this morning and tried to get them to make an exception. The faculty contract is specific on the matter. If a faculty member is considered unfit for the job, like being under suspicion of committing a felony, there is no alternative. When you're exonerated, you'll receive your salary retroactively. If you're convicted, well . . . then you won't get it."

"Seems unfair to me. I'm having my salary withheld for something I didn't do and have no control over. How can you . . . they . . . suspend me under a clause that says I'm unfit? What happened to innocent until proven guilty?" Jillian sat for a moment. "I can't believe this is happening. You and McMann said I had the full support of the college. Then because Anna Farnsworth whined to her mother, I'm being suspended. The kid probably doesn't want to take the exam next week."

"I didn't say I agreed." Dean Stevenson frowned. "I have no choice. Either I take action or the president will do it for me. He'll bow to political pressure. He has to."

"First, I had the humiliation of my colleagues and students knowing I'm accused of murder. Then the police searched my office, invaded my space and my privacy. But they were too late. Someone had already erased my computer."

Dean Stevenson looked surprised. "I didn't know that."

"I only found out yesterday when I was at the police station."

"Someone must have broken into your office. It doesn't make sense to me."

"Or to me either. But it did cast further suspicion on me. Now the detectives think I'm hiding information." Jillian flushed. "I can't talk about it anymore. Who's going to teach my class, anyway? Take my clinical?"

"I don't know. I haven't worked that out."

Jillian stood. "What do I care?" She shook her head and squeezed her lips together. "In my opinion, you should cancel the classes until this is straightened out. If they're all so hot to have me out of here, without due process I might add, they should pay the price for their contribution to the decision. At least, they had a say in their situation. I don't." Jillian used the shredded tissue to wipe away the streaming tears as she shuffled, head down, toward her office.

The pediatrics professor, Ursula Tankoff, stepped into the hall and blocked her path. "What's wrong?"

While catching her breath and sobbing, Jillian shoved past her matronly colleague, making it into her office without further interference. She pushed the door tight, stumbled across the space, and collapsed into the chair.

Jillian cried until she ran out of tears. Then, feeling spent, she forced herself to focus on the problem. Crumbling wouldn't help solve anything.

The first priority was securing her income. She cleaned off the desk, locked the file cabinet, picked up her purse, and slipped out the rear exit into the mid-day heat. She'd fill her schedule with shifts from her extra job at the hospital. At every opportunity, the staffing coordinator, Vinette, begged her to work extra. Jillian didn't foresee any problem. The last time she'd was at the hospital, the place overflowed with patients.

CHAPTER 22

"Hey Suzie, I'd like to sign up for as many shifts as possible," Jillian said to the clerk occupying the front desk in the staffing office.

"I don't have the book. I'll get it from Vinette. Have a seat." Suzie stood, walked down the short corridor, and tapped on the staffing coordinator's door.

Jillian sat in one of the worn chairs in the makeshift reception area and picked up a magazine. She thumbed through an American Journal of Nursing and tried to look casual and unconcerned. Voices drifted from behind the closed office door.

"I don't think it's a good idea," Vinette said.

"We need . . . and . . . clinically . . . not charged," a woman said.

Jillian didn't recognize the second voice, but knew it wasn't Suzie's. She strained to hear more, but the conversation was garbled. A moment later, Vinette appeared, straightening her long, white lab coat as she approached.

"I'm sorry. We're all booked up." Vinette seemed to focus on Jillian's chin. "We won't be needing you for the shifts you scheduled for this weekend either. Our recruitment program is a big success."

"How can that be? When I stopped in here two days ago, you pleaded with me to add several more shifts and even offered the seasonal bonus if I could manage it."

"Things change. We have more staff and fewer patients than estimated, I guess." The woman returned to her office and closed the door.

Feeling dirty and dejected, Jillian slunk out of the office. But she was angry as well. It wasn't fair. How would she survive?

The elevator to the same nursing unit she used for the students' clinical experiences beckoned her aboard, then carried her upward.

"Hi, Janey," Jillian said to the first staff nurse she saw. "I hear things are calming down around here."

"Where did you hear that?" Janey Morris said, letting out a huff. "We've got a full census. I wish you were in uniform. I'd put you to work right this minute." She shifted a stack of linen to her other arm. "By the way, did you get the mess straightened out with those students of yours? They were really disruptive on Wednesday. I don't think they're nursing material."

"The dean and I met with them yesterday. We're transferring them to another hospital, splitting them up. Perhaps that will help them behave." Jillian lowered her voice. "Thank you for telling me about their antics the other day. I wouldn't have known they were out of hand in the cafeteria otherwise. And thanks for talking to the dean, too. That really helped."

"You're welcome. Meanwhile, when will you be working again? Vinette was here an hour or so ago begging all of us to work overtime."

"I don't know. She told me to get lost. All booked up. No openings."

"I can't believe that."

"Believe it. Said there were plenty of new hires and no patients."

"Yeah, right. Come with me." Janey stomped into the nurses' station and pointed to the patient board. "Look at that. We're carrying eight patients per RN today and only have one patient care assistant on the whole fricking unit. Can you believe it? The weekend will be worse. Sally Jo invited everyone to her wedding. The few of us who couldn't get the day off will get clobbered."

"I'll bet you will. I'd love to help, but they cancelled my shifts for Saturday and Sunday, too."

"I guess the article in the paper got to them. There has been a lot of talk around the hospital today."

"Seems to be the old story—SSDD." Jillian glanced down the hall into the elevator lobby.

"I hear you. Same shit, different day," Janey said, grimacing.

"I've got to go." Jillian brushed a tear away.

"Wait." Janey touched Jillian's shoulder. "We support you. We all do. We believe you didn't hurt that girl. If there's anything we can do to help, let me know."

"Thanks. I appreciate it. I really do." Jillian turned, thinking Janey made a nice offer. But what could the staff nurses do?

Jillian walked through the other nursing units and found no vacant beds.

Overwhelmed with hopelessness, Jillian wandered out of the hospital, finding herself behind the wheel of the car, unsure of when or how she located the car. Sweat rolled down her face. Her mouth was parched. Waves of nausea assaulted her belly. It was one-fifty in the afternoon. She stared at her watch and calculated she had sat for at least thirty minutes—in the extreme heat.

"I'm losing my mind and talking to myself as well. Isn't that shameful?" Jillian started the car and turned the air-conditioning to maximum.

***

When Jillian let herself into her apartment, the flashing message light on the answering machine caught her attention. Maybe something changed, and I'm not fired from everything. Not believing her own wishful thinking, she retrieved the message.

"Jillian, this is Warren. I've been trying to . . ."

She deleted the message along with three others from Warren and went to bed.

Several hours later, Chantal shook her awake.

"Go away."

"It's almost nine. Warren said he's been leaving messages all day, calling your cell, calling you at work. Nothing. He's worried about you."

"What's to worry about? I have no job, no money, and I'm going to jail." She felt devoid of emotion. "I give up. I give in. I have no more fight in me. Nothing to fight for."

"I don't agree." Chantal pulled the covers off Jillian, who was dressed and damp with perspiration.

"Why not, girl? You're part of the problem." Jillian grabbed the covers and pulled them up to her chin.

"Jillian, please don't feel that way. You're upset that I'm still seeing Pasquale, but you don't want him. You said yourself you didn't care."

"Maybe I don't. It's the idea. Everything is gone. Even the things I don't want."

"I'm going to get you cleaned up, dressed in something decent, then you're going to dinner with Warren."

"Why would I want to do that?"

"Because you need to eat. You need to be with someone who cares about you. And . . . he's standing in the living room, insisting."

CHAPTER 23

Jillian stepped through the bedroom doorway, freshly scrubbed, with damp hair, no jewelry, and wearing black crops and a pale blue tee shirt.

Chantal, maintaining the mothering role, nudged her through the door.

"Hello, Warren," Jillian said in a flat tone.

Warren crossed the living room and put an arm around her shoulder. "Let's take a walk on the beach, and you can tell me all about it. We'll get some dinner when you feel like eating."

Jillian nodded and reached for her keys, slipping them into her pocket. She said a soft goodbye to Chantal and followed Warren out the door, keeping her head down and her eyes on the floor.

They walked the beach in silence for half an hour before Warren said, "Tell me about today." He stopped and took her hand, giving it a gentle squeeze.

Conceding to the urge to unburden, Jillian spilled forth with a chronology of the day's events.

As she talked, Warren held her hand, guiding her among the remnants of sand castles while avoiding the approaching tide. Though it was still eighty degrees, the breeze off the ocean caused Jillian to shiver.

Warren moved to her left side, blocking the salty gusts, and wrapped his arm around her back. She noticed for the first time his pleasant male smell mixing with a light cologne she didn't recognize.

Feeling warmer and more secure, Jillian said, "I've never felt more hopeless, more helpless, or more discouraged in my life, not even when my daughter was killed. Then, people rallied to my support. Now, they shy away as if I'm an E. coli-contaminated hamburger. Present company aside."

"I don't think you're contaminated, and I don't think you're a murderess either. From what you've said, people are doing what they need to do to protect themselves from liability. Their notion, I'm sure, is not that you're guilty, but if anything happens, anything at all, having you teach students or take care of patients puts them at risk."

"I talked to my father today. He's trying to raise money for my defense if I need it. He can come up with a few grand, no more. Allison offered me a room. But I don't think a young couple needs the stress of having a depressed person underfoot, though I would find being with them and my granddaughter comforting."

Warren nodded, tightening his hold on her back.

"If I live with my parents or my daughter, I'll be giving up my whole life. Besides, Chantal can't afford to stay in the apartment alone."

"From what you said about Chantal, that should be the least of your worries." Warren raised a questioning eyebrow.

"I suppose you're right. Truth is, I don't want Pasquale, haven't for a long time. He's asked me to reconcile over and over again, but once a gambler and a cheat, always a gambler and a cheat. His day trading is socially acceptable wagering, nothing more. It would be like flinging myself from the sinking boat into the abyss."

"On an emotional level, how do you feel about Pasquale? If you don't mind my asking, that is."

"I don't mind." Jillian waited a few moments before continuing, giving the question thought. "Funny thing is up until a few days ago I thought I loved him and had made a deliberate, rational choice to keep my distance. When Chantal confessed about their relationship, it made me reconsider." She stopped walking and faced Warren. "I realized I don't love Pasquale and haven't for a long while. It was only a bad habit. One part of me resents Chantal's moving in on what was once mine, on what I believed could be mine again for the asking. But when I told Chantal I didn't care, I was truthful."

He smiled. "That's the bright spot in my day." He slipped his arm around her waist and angled them in the direction of the boardwalk. "I think we'll get dinner at the Italian place by Walgreen's."

"Too expensive. You don't have to do that."

"I want to, and it's no problem." He pointed to a traffic signal a block ahead. "Let's cross there."

Jillian smiled for the first time all day.

They walked to the restaurant in silence. The Friday dinner crowd had thinned, and the maître d' escorted them to an isolated table near the rear of the restaurant.

When they were alone, Jillian said, "Nice place. I've wanted to come in here, and I even stopped and looked at the menu one day. Out of reach on my teacher's pay."

Warren picked up the wine list. "What would you like? I noticed you seem to favor the sweet white varieties."

"That I do. But, I love a good Chianti."

He caught the waiter's attention and placed the order, selecting both the eggplant and mushroom appetizers along with a pricey bottle of Chianti Classico Badia a Passignano.

A few minutes later, while the steward opened the bottle and allowed Warren a taste, the server placed the dishes in front of them. When Warren smiled and nodded, the man poured, half-filling two Tiffany goblets.

"This is too much. You're treating me . . ."

"As you deserve." Raising his glass, Warren said, "To better days."

She touched her glass to his. "So, let it be written. So, let it be done."

"I don't think it'll all happen that easily. I mean, because you wish it so, won't make it be."

"I know that."

"I think you need to take control. Stop being a victim."

"I feel like a victim."

"That could be, but it's not going to help get your life back."

"I told you what happened today. I feel like I'm out of resources."

Warren picked up the mushroom platter and slid a few onto Jillian's plate, repeating the process with a slice of the eggplant. "Eat. You'll think more clearly on a full stomach."

She obeyed. "Yum, good." The succulent crab stuffing in the mushrooms stimulated her appetite. She devoured the mushrooms and dived into the eggplant with gusto.

While Jillian ate, he ordered a salad and an entrée for them to share. "The portions are big here. I hope you don't mind."

"Hope I have room." She pointed to the empty

appetizer plates. "I didn't realize I was so hungry."

"Chantal thought you didn't eat all day."

"I had a slice of toast this morning." She tapped a finger to her temple.

When they'd finished dinner, they sipped the remainder of the wine.

"I don't think I told you, but I got into the blog site," Warren said.

"I checked it. They took it off."

"I mean onto the server. The history is there. What's striking is the blog only turned sour a couple of weeks ago. Prior to that, it was harmless. I checked a few others written by nursing students, and there was no difference. The obvious thing is that the comments by Barrera and Albano were the only ones that turned nasty. The other two bloggers didn't change their tone at all."

"Makes you wonder what stirred up Barrera and Albano. They were always polite to me, business-like but not friendly. I thought they took it personally that they failed my class the first time. Sometimes students do that. They don't want to take responsibility for their problems. It's easier to blame faculty." Jillian paused. "What you're telling me coincides with when they became truly hateful. Were you able to determine who set up the blog? I think the terminology is owner. The name Painful Process doesn't imply a positive outlook."

"From the early entries, I got the idea it was tongue in cheek. They thought they were being cute—or maybe cool. The owner of the blog was Albano. She's the one who discontinued it as well."

"I wonder what changed."

"Whatever it was happened a couple of weeks before

Bethany was murdered."

"That's where I need to start looking." Jillian raised her wineglass and swirled the last of the flavorful liquid. "To success."

They touched glasses.

After Warren settled the tab, he walked her through the side streets to the door of her apartment.

"I'm going to leave you here. Maybe one day, when your mind is clear and this mess is settled, you'll invite me in."

"I'd like that. I appreciate everything you've done for me tonight. You've bolstered my courage, motivated me to continue."

"My pleasure." Warren raised his hand, stopping her before she could say more. "I'm attracted to you, and I want to be with you. Get to know you under normal, boring circumstances."

Jillian smiled.

"The other thing, don't worry about your defense," Warren said. "If it comes to that, I'll pay for the lawyer."

"I can't let you do that. You've done so much already."

"I want to help. I can afford it. You're important to me. Whether anything comes of our relationship or not, you'll still be important to me."

Tears filled her eyes. "I don't know what to say."

He kissed her on the lips. "Good night." He left, casting one last look in her direction before stepping onto the elevator.

***

Feeling energized, Jillian let herself into the apartment, dropped her keys on the dresser, and went to her desk.

She started her personal laptop and accessed her banking program.

Money was the immediate problem. The check to Xavier for six thousand dollars would cover expenses if there wasn't a trial. The lawyer even promised to refund fifty percent of the retainer if the police never filed charges. An extended legal defense would require additional funds, money that didn't exist. Thanks to Warren, she wouldn't need to resort to a public defender, but asking him to finance her defense was an unpleasant last option.

Her living expenses were another matter, one in which Warren could not be involved under any circumstances.

Intent on making a list of her resources, she retrieved a notebook from a pile of school papers, stopping to glance at her notes about the difficult students. At least the blog was no longer an issue.

Contemplating the list, Jillian wondered if any of them had reason to harm Bethany. The girl had proven to be multi-faceted, with many issues and, no doubt, her share of enemies as well. The problem was, Jillian supposed, the police considered her one of them.

And what about Pasquale? Did he have motive?

Maybe someone from Bethany's dancing life hated her? Jillian hadn't considered that option.

Maybe family? They were an uptight bunch, but that didn't mean they were capable of murder.

Pasquale's affair with Bethany distressed Chantal, but how much was the question. When did Chantal find out about it?

The possibilities seemed endless. Why then were the police focused on her? Jillian made notes, thinking she'd give them to Xan.

Jillian flipped to a clean page and began listing financial resources, starting with the balances in her money market and checking accounts—a grand total of four thousand, one hundred, and fifty dollars. Potential sources of loans included her parents—for a few thousand at the most. Pasquale might be convinced to share some of his newfound wealth, given she hadn't requested alimony during the divorce. The new house over extended her daughter, leaving no available cash. And finally Chantal, she had some cash set aside. This evening was the first verbal exchange they'd had since their original conversation about Pasquale.

Jillian had no collateral for a loan and reasoned no bank would lend money to an accused murderer anyway. She listed charge cards and the limits for each, making a note to accept the two credit invitations in recent mail.

After taking a minute to analyze her short list of assets, she figured her financial survival at three months without plunging into debt so deep she'd never recover.

She studied the list, then typed the address for Conover College into her web browser and located the link for personnel, clicked on benefits, and read about how to maintain her health insurance. She adjusted her financial projections to two months, maybe two and a half.

Feeling somewhat better, she said, "Plenty of time to get my life back." Thinking of Warren, she added, "I'd rather have a new life."

CHAPTER 24

The jangling of the telephone roused Jillian from sound slumber. At first the noise was confusing. Then she identified the sound, rolled onto her side, and stretched for the receiver. "Hello." She glanced at the clock—three in the morning.

"This is Dewey. Eleanor's in the emergency room." His voice quivered, the usual mellow tones lost. "They're moving her to the Intensive Care Unit in a few minutes. The doc's trying to decide if they need to put her on a ventilator now, or if they can wait and see how she responds to the medication and treatment."

"My heavens, what happened?" Jillian sat on the side of the bed. "She's been doing so well given the circumstances."

"I don't know why things got worse." He paused. "Around eleven-thirty, I think it was, her breathing got labored. Real noisy, you know. She couldn't get the air out to get more in, and she turned gray. Her head was up on three pillows already—she always sleeps on three pillows lately—so I lifted her out of the bed and carried her to the recliner, which is straighter, but it didn't help. She didn't want me to, but I called 911, and they brought her here.

Didn't want to go—never wants to go to the hospital. I didn't listen. She's sicker than I have ever seen . . . except maybe that time with the flu."

"I'll be there in a few minutes. Do you need anything?"

"No. What could I need? Just my Eleanor home again."

"I might as well go into your place and get her toothbrush, tooth paste, comb. She'll want them in the morning."

"Guess you're right."

"Have you called Vincent yet?"

"No, I'll call him in the morning. Sometimes he gets so edgy when his grandmother is ill that it's better not to have him around until things settle down."

"Your choice. He'll be upset if he doesn't get to see her. You know what I mean."

"You've got a point. I'll call him."

"Hang in there, Dewey."

Jillian pulled on jeans and a tee shirt. Expecting to be on her feet for the rest of the night, she decided to wear sneakers, then grabbed her purse and a light jacket to combat the hospital's air-conditioning before going next door.

After retrieving a small satchel from the closet, she found the necessary items in the master bath. She added clothing for Eleanor to wear home and sturdy sandals and a robe. As an afterthought, she picked up the novel with the lace bookmark midway through from the table next to Eleanor's chair, then stopped in the doorway and looked around the room. There wasn't anything else Eleanor might want right away.

While pulling into a space in the visitors' section of the hospital parking lot, Jillian reflected on her most recent trip there. The memory stung, heralding a resurgence of hopelessness. Eleanor, a good friend and the only person able to give her an alibi for the time of Bethany's murder, was ill. Very ill, if Dewey had his facts right.

Pushing aside the sense of impending doom, Jillian removed her faculty-parking tag from the rear view mirror and the hospital's employee permit from the window. No sense attracting attention by getting a ticket for parking in the wrong lot.

After rushing across the parking lot, she pushed through the doors to the Emergency Department without breaking stride, flashing her hospital ID badge at the uniformed guard near the registration cubicles. "Buzz me back, Mac. Please."

"Yes, ma'am. Didn't expect to see you workin' here just now."

"I'm not. I'm looking for a friend of mine." She stepped toward the door.

He nodded and hit the open button on the wall behind him.

At the nurses' station desk, the unit secretary smiled and pointed. "Your friend's husband said you were coming. You just missed them. We moved the patient to ICU a few minutes ago."

"Thanks. I'm headed that way." Jillian hurried out the back door of the department and stepped into the open door of the service elevator. She stepped off across the hall from the ICU waiting area.

Dewey sat, hunched and forlorn-looking, in the beige-on-beige, claustrophobic room outside the ICU. His disheveled appearance reflected a stressful night.

"What's happening?" She dropped into the chair next to him and scanned the room. All the chairs were either occupied or holding belongings of people who were most likely taking their turns inside the unit.

"Don't know exactly. After I talked to you, they moved her here. They told me they'd be out in a few minutes, but I've been waiting for thirty."

"That's in the right out range for the nurses. They have a lot to do to get her settled."

"I don't remember waiting this long the last time—what? Six months ago?"

"I'll call in and see what's happening."

The directions on a sign posted over the wall-mounted telephone said to dial four, then wait.

Two rings later, a voice said, "ICU."

She recognized the nurse's distinctive, gravely voice. "Marilee, this is Jillian Grey. I'm here with Mr. Evers. What's happening with his wife?"

"Hang on a minute. I'm not assigned to that patient. I'll have to check with Georgia." She paused for a heartbeat. "I heard what Vinette did to you yesterday. I'm sorry. You don't deserve that kind of treatment."

"From your mouth to her pointy little ears."

"I'll be right back." A few moments later, Marilee came back on the line. "They've intubated her. When they transferred her to the bed from the stretcher, she had a respiratory arrest. It'll take another few minutes to get her settled, then you can bring in the mister."

"Damn. Thanks." Jillian returned to Dewey.

"They're putting my wife on the breathing machine?" Dewey said.

"That's already been done. Did you call Vincent?"

"Yes. He's on his way."

They sat in silence for several minutes.

Dewey said, "Eleanor went to the eye doctor today for

an examination."

Jillian motioned for him to continue.

"Doc said she sees fine, even if she is a little more farsighted than she used to be. He told her to get some half-frame reading glasses at the drug store."

"Good news for me. Means she can see well at a distance. It'll make her testimony stronger."

"Eleanor asked the doctor to send a report to Detective Brewer, who, by the way, stopped by the other day and tried to convince Eleanor she couldn't see very well."

"Thank God he isn't right. That good report will help with my troubles."

"That's if Eleanor can testify. They've talked to her a couple of times but didn't take a sworn statement. Suppose they'll have to do that when she gets out."

"I hope they accept the statement, and she doesn't have to go to court. That would be hard on her." Jillian reflected on the nurse's comment and wondered if Eleanor would even make it home.

"You know my El. She'll do whatever it takes to help."

Barrera shuffled in, interrupting the conversation. He glared at Jillian before dropping into a chair next to his grandfather. "What's happening?"

Dewey filled him in.

He pointed his chin in Jillian's direction and raised his voice. "What's she doing here? Everywhere I go, I see her. It's starting to piss me off."

"Shush. Keep you voice low. Our friend is here because I called her. And, by the way, you're here because she suggested I call you now rather than waiting until morning."

Barrera glanced at Jillian, his expression softening.

"What's your problem with Ms. Grey, anyway? Your

grandmother said you and Shanna were rude to her yesterday."

Barrera scowled. "She kicked us out of her clinical group. Now we have to travel across town. I'll lose an hour of work a day and the same for Shanna."

Jillian stood and faced Barrera. "If you're going to tell partial truths, I reserve the right to give your grandfather all the facts of the matter. Do you want me to do that?"

"You can't. Student confidentiality rules, you know." Though quiet, Barrera's voice resounded with threat.

"Actually, young man, I can, and I will. What are they going to do? Suspend me? Tell the whole truth about the situation or close your mouth." She stared him down, then left the waiting room, preferring to stand alone in the corridor next to the double-doored entrance to the ICU.

She strained to hear Dewey questioning Barrera and the cleaned-up but honest responses.

When a nurse came to get them, Jillian asked Dewey if she could go in for a minute first.

His expression relieved, Dewey said, "Thanks, I'd appreciate it. I like to be prepared for what I'm going to see."

Barrera rose but sat again when Dewey put a hand on his forearm. "Okay, Grandpa. It's your show."

"It's not a show. It's my wife's life. If you want to be here and help me, you need to set aside your feelings about Ms. Grey. She helps take care of your grandmother and is entitled to my gratitude and your respect."

"Shanna and I were over after dinner helping Grandma. We come more than you give us credit for."

Dewey continued without acknowledging Barrera's comment. "Ms. Grey's a good friend to both your grandma and me. We depend on her." The mild-mannered man scowled at his grandson. "Sit and wait your turn."

Leaving them to their disagreement, Jillian went into the ICU. Though it was the middle of the night, bright lights, ringing telephones, and scurrying workers mimicked mid-morning. Eleanor was semi-alert. The ventilator gauges indicated the machine did most of the work of breathing for her.

Jillian stood next to the bed, holding Eleanor's hand and listening to the clicks and whishes of the ventilator and the arrhythmic beeping of the cardiac monitor. She eyed the labels on the bags of intravenous medication, then studied the nurses' medication sheet laying open on the overbed table. Indications were that the older woman suffered both respiratory and cardiac complications of the chronic disease. The drugs indicated congestive heart failure. She was sick. Very sick.

"We're here with you."

Eleanor's eyes rolled in Jillian's direction, her expression cloudy.

"I'm going to send Dewey and Vincent in."

Though it was almost imperceptible, Eleanor squeezed her hand.

"Be strong, my friend."

She stopped at the desk and laid out her deductions about Eleanor's condition.

Georgia nodded and said, "You're on the right track. Her output is good and her heart failure is improving. We'll know more about the prognosis in the morning when we get the rest of the testing done." She glanced down at a clipboard. "At this moment, her vital signs are stable, but she's in critical condition. I can't say anything more than that, not without the husband's permission."

Back in the waiting room, Jillian brought Dewey up to date on his wife's condition, omitting nothing, but not making any predictions either. "You'll need to talk with the staff yourself. I only have part of the information. If they're going to talk to me in any detail, they'll need your permission."

Barrera said, "They should talk—"

Dewey interrupted him with a stern look.

***

The nurses asked the visitors to leave so they could attend to change of shift report and morning care for their patients. The filled-to-capacity lounge overflowed into the hall where several people stood with their backs against the wall.

With her head on Dewey's shoulder, Jillian feigned sleep. Worried voices of other patients' family members prevented her from drifting off. But she was more relaxed. Eleanor survived the night, and the physician suggested during a brief six a.m. conversation that she would recover—this time.

Barrera had excused himself after his first trip into the ICU and hadn't returned.

She opened her eyes and glanced at the big-faced wall clock. Eight-twenty. "It'll be another half-hour at least. Let's go downstairs to the cafeteria and get some coffee."

"I'll just sit here. The nurses said I could go in at eight-thirty."

"I'll be back." She stood and shook out the cricks, trying to dispel her exhaustion. The straight-backed chairs prevented comfortable waiting, seemingly by design.

Her cell phone rang in the elevator lobby. "This is Jillian Grey," she said, responding as if on duty.

"It's Xan Xavier. I just got a call from Detective Zale. They want you downtown tomorrow morning at nine. They have more questions."

"Am I going to answer them all this time?"

"That depends on what they ask."

"Should I bring a toothbrush?"

Xavier didn't answer right away. "If they had a warrant for your arrest, they'd probably come to you rather than asking you to come in for questioning. But I've seen them do it both ways." Xavier paused. "If I were you, I'd be prepared. Detective Zale seems as obsessed as a politician in an election year."

Jillian considered the situation and decided she had twenty-four hours to clear her name. Time enough.

"I'm at the hospital now. My neighbor was brought in last night in respiratory failure."

"Not your alibi neighbor, I hope."

"I'm afraid so. Eleanor's more alert this morning, and the doctor says she'll survive. I've seen them be wrong before. By the way, the eye doctor said her vision is fine. In fact, she's farsighted."

"And she's your only alibi. For your sake, I hope the lady lives."

CHAPTER 25

Jillian ran through torrents of rain to hop into the Sentra. Her clothes stuck to her skin, and soaking wet hair clung to her neck. The sudden deluge hadn't cooled the morning or the car's stifling hot interior.

Frustrated, anxious, and impatient, she spun the tires and ripped out of the space. Swerving on the wet pavement, she steered into the skid, straightening the car's path without hitting the parked vehicles lining both sides of the street.

The traffic light at the corner changed from yellow to red, and Jillian braked to a stop, then used the waiting time to calm her nerves and gather her resources. In the rearview mirror, she noticed a dark car stopped about twenty feet away. It was a good thing other drivers were being more careful than she was.

Searching through the clutter in the door pocket, Jillian found the earpiece for her iPhone, which she plugged into the power adaptor. After the light changed to green, she turned the corner, then tapped in Dewey's number.

He answered on the first ring.

"I've left the hospital." She filled him in on Xavier's telephone call. "Got some things I have to do. How's

Eleanor?"

"They sedated her again. Doc said she needed rest, give the antibiotics a chance to work. They'll extubate her later today if all goes well and her blood gasses improve. I don't know, though, she's ashen and hollow looking."

Dewey talked like a pro in Jillian's opinion. He'd been through the drill numerous times and was familiar with the procedure for removing the breathing tube and what the arterial blood test results needed to be before that could happen. "That's what I thought when I was visiting."

"She's a strong old girl," he said.

"Keep those good thoughts."

After they said their goodbyes, Jillian contemplated the next move. Remembering her hurried and irresponsible departure from the hospital's parking lot, she decided to clear her head. She stopped at a coffee house and sloshed through deep puddles and a steady downpour to buy a large cappuccino, then sipped the strong brew and balanced her umbrella for the trek back to the car. The caffeine load would make her jittery, but it would also help her focus and push away the nagging tightness signaling the start of a migraine.

Jillian called Warren and updated him on Eleanor's condition and her night in the hospital. "Do you have some time today?"

"For you, anything."

"I don't want to impose, but I could use help locating information on the Internet. I have to see the police again tomorrow, and I want to be ready."

"What do you need?"

"Can you see what you can find out about Pasquale? And the dance studio? And that investment firm that

Pasquale works with? First, I'll go home, shower, and get into some dry, presentable clothes. Then I want to visit some of the possible suspects myself. Maybe I can find out what the police can't, given they seem motivated to charge me and aren't looking further."

"You don't know that. They wouldn't tell you or your lawyer about other suspects."

"You may be right, but I'm going to check around myself. Take charge. Stop being a victim."

"Somehow I thought I'd hear those words coming back at me. It'll take me an hour or so to run this stuff down. I'll pick you up at your condo at ten-thirty."

"You don't have to spend your day helping me chase people. It's my problem. It should be my risk."

"I'll be there at ten-thirty. Be waiting at the front door."

"Yes, sir." Jillian clicked off, thinking it was nice to have support. She had less than one day to prove her innocence or face jail.

***

The black Toyota Corolla parked near the garage ramp seemed familiar, but the tinted window obscured Jillian's view of the driver. Retailing at around twenty grand, the model was a popular choice for young people at her school. She turned in front of the car and pulled into her parking space.

She pointed and spoke to the guard while crossing the lobby. "Whose car is that?"

"Don't know, ma'am. Some kid going to the beach and not wanting to park in the metered spaces?"

"It's pouring rain."

"Surf's up."

"Suppose there's a level at which that makes sense." Jillian chuckled.

"My son's a surfer. He'd go out in a hurricane if the cops would let him near the water."

Feeling paranoid, Jillian went upstairs and dressed with care, choosing a navy pantsuit with a tailored jacket and matching, high-heeled pumps. She dug into the shelves near the rear of the closet for a leather portfolio. After checking to be sure she had plenty of paper, she grabbed her purse, then gulped the last of the coffee. Even cold, it tasted strong and rich. She shook her head. Her headache was gone, but she dropped a bottle of aspirin with caffeine into her bag anyway.

Warren pulled in front of the building in a new Lexus LS, white with tan leather interior. After Jillian settled into the passenger seat, he handed her a stack of paper. "Here's the info. Where to?"

"Give me a second." She flipped through the pages, putting them in logical order. "There's nothing new here about Pasquale, except, of course, how he's financing his day trading."

"I've kept in touch with him over the years," Warren said. "The last time I helped him with his computer, he mentioned his change of fortune. He didn't go into detail."

"He saves his bragging for the young women he picks up."

"Perhaps you're right, or maybe he didn't think it was my business."

"Let's stop at Pasquale's first. I want to have a private ex-wife to ex-husband talk with him. Then I want to see a few other people and rule them in or out of this mess."

"I don't think they'll talk to you."

"My name has been in the paper, but not my picture." Jillian smiled and tugged at her suit. "I don't intend to tell them who I am. I intend to impersonate a private investigator." She pulled a card out of her folder. "Even printed a few business cards."

"I think you're putting yourself at risk with that. Better to be up front and honest."

"That hasn't worked so far."

"You do have a point there." Warren stopped in front of Pasquale's building, popped the lock, and moved to get out of the car.

"I want to do this one alone."

Warren shook his head, then went around the car and opened her door. "Be careful. I don't think Pasquale killed the girl, but if I'm wrong, you don't want to back him into a corner. I wish you'd let me go up with you."

"Not here. We can decide about the other places as we go along."

"Fair enough."

She entered the building, stopped at the desk, and waited to be cleared and directed to the elevator. Soon Pasquale's door loomed before her.

"This is a pleasant surprise. You look nice," Pasquale said in lieu of a greeting when he opened the door.

"Thanks, you look pretty horrible yourself."

Pasquale was unshaven, uncombed, and dressed in a torn Miami Heat jersey and matching shorts.

His appearance reminded her of the months before the final demise of their marriage when he gambled and drank to excess. He had cleaned up only to slip out to meet one of his lovers.

He looked at his watch. "I've been at the computer since

nine. Overslept. I don't usually do that."

"You're okay then?"

"Yes. Are you?" He stepped back and waved her into his apartment.

"Thing is, when I was talking to my lawyer this morning, I got the idea you may be a suspect, too." She summarized her current situation.

"Says the de-fence. To me, you appear to be the number one candidate."

"I'm hoping to change that. Give Xavier something to work with. Force the police to look beyond me. The parents from school are riled about the lack of progress with the case. That means the money folks will be worrying about enrollment. I don't want to be their convenient solution."

"I see your point. I don't intend to be their patsy either."

"Xavier said you told the police that you gave Bethany money every week to help with her dance lessons."

"Is that so hard to believe? She was a fine dancer."

"Pasquale, you wouldn't know a fine dancer if she did a pirouette on your head. I dragged you to the ballet once, and you had the most miserable night in your life."

"Second most miserable. You forced me to attend the opera, too."

Jillian laughed. "I agree the opera was iffy."

"The review in the paper the next day said the soprano was flat. Everyone in the production was fighting a cold, and the understudy went onstage in spite of an ear infection."

"No choice. The star had laryngitis."

They laughed together at the memory.

After a few moments, Jillian frowned and waved her hand around the apartment. "How are you paying for all this?"

"Day trading. I'm doing well."

"I remember when you were doing well before. Turned out it wasn't so well, and you went dirty-side up. I worked a ka-zillion hours of overtime to pay off your brokerage debt."

"Didn't force you."

"Right. I could have let them come after you and take everything we owned—everything, I might add, that you insisted be in your name alone. I should have let them indict you. The firm was a second away from pressing charges."

He smiled. "You're right."

"The market now is worse than it was. I look at the charts every day. There's no upward movement, not consistent anyway."

"I don't care, as long as there is some action. I study the trends, sell short in the down market. I make money either way."

"You're gambling. That's how you tanked a few years ago." Jillian shook her head and frowned. "And this is how you're earning enough money to support this condo, your hot car, and pay for your girlfriend's dance lessons?"

Pasquale reddened and snorted. "I don't see where it is any of your business."

"It is my business. I'm a murder suspect, and for all I know, you're the guilty one." She took a deep breath, hoping to clear her thoughts and settle her rising anger. "You lost a wonderful job because you were messing around with your clients' portfolios. Most stockbrokers would kill for the job you had and you blew it—and our lifestyle in the process. Now you're living high. I bailed you out of trouble, and I'm scrimping by, worrying about how I'll afford a defense if I need it. I spent most of my savings on the lawyer. Now I can't afford to buy the condo I'm living in, not even if

Chantal and I continue as roommates, which isn't damn likely."

Pasquale grimaced.

"I want to know where you got the money to finance your trading. If you're supporting this lifestyle in the market, you must have had a bankroll to start. When we broke up, we divided the assets and bills. I remember walking away with a ton of debt and two grand in cash."

"Think what you want. You usually do. But I had nothing to do with Bethany's murder. I helped her with dance lessons—her parents wouldn't." He walked to the door and opened it. "I have work to do."

CHAPTER 26

Jillian returned to Warren's car. "Damn that Pasquale. He can be so charming. Then he's such a slime."

"I've always found him to be somewhat self-serving." Warren pulled out of the parking space. "Where to?"

"Only somewhat?"

"I was being polite."

"I want to call my daughter and see what she knows about her father's financial condition." Jillian looked at her watch. "It's almost noon. She'll be home. After that, let's go to Carnegie and Watson Investments and confirm what you learned."

"It should be a good time to find them understaffed, that is if anyone is there."

"The ad in the phonebook said they're open Saturday morning."

"Aren't you afraid of running into Albano? She works there."

"No. I know she teaches karate on Saturday morning. I heard her telling one of her classmates. Maybe you should check first, just in case she cut class."

Jillian dialed Allison on her cell phone. When her

daughter answered, Jillian started with small talk about the baby and her son-in-law.

"Mom, we had this exact discussion yesterday. I have a feeling you called for something specific."

"Because I'm suspended, that's why." She recited a brief version of her miserable Friday. "I don't want to get you in the middle of things, but I have an inkling your father is involved in more ways than having a fling with Bethany."

"He was seeing the girl? Ah, Mom, that's gross," Allison said. "I guess he wouldn't tell me he was seeing someone younger than me."

"The man has his pride."

"He's been seeing Chantal, too. He brought her here for dinner. I was taken aback. He asked me not to say anything to you. He didn't want to mess up your living arrangement. I wanted to tell you. I even started the conversation a couple of times, but then I couldn't bring myself to do it."

"Considerate of you." Jillian worked hard to keep the sarcasm out of her voice, but had limited success.

"Mom, I'm really sorry. I rehearsed in front of the mirror and everything, but it felt so painful."

"That's okay, Honey. I understand, but not to worry. I know all about him and Chantal."

"You don't care?"

"Not beyond the obvious deception on the part of my charming roomie and my ex-husband."

"That's a surprise," Allison said.

"For me, too," Jillian said. "Do you know how your father's financial circumstances improved so much over the last year or so? He was buried in debt, and now he seems to be rolling in cash."

"I asked him. He told me he had a windfall trading. So

far, at least, it looks like he's been able to keep it."

"Can you tell me anything more about it?"

"No. I asked him for details, Harold asked, too, but he wouldn't say anymore. He's so flush, he set up a college fund for Maggie. He said we couldn't afford to do it, so he did."

"At least that's a good thing. I hope it doesn't fall through."

"If it does, she'll never know what she missed. She's only eleven months old, after all." Allison said.

As Jillian concluded the conversation, Warren pulled to the curb a few doors north of the investment firm.

He said, "I'll walk down and have a look around."

"I'll get my head into the role while you're gone."

A few moments later, Warren returned. "I looked in the window. There's a sign on the reception desk directing clients to ring the bell. From what I could see of the back of the suite, someone is using one of the offices. The other door is closed, and there's no light coming through the glass."

"About right for a week-end, I suppose." Jillian slid out of the car. Anxiety tightened her throat. She stood for a minute, focusing on the plan and attempting to calm her nervousness, then nodded, feeling determined. "Alrighty, let's do it. You see what you can find in the outer office, while I keep the man busy and maybe trick him into telling me something I can use." Jillian settled her purse on her shoulder and held her portfolio at her side.

"Why don't you open a button or two? I'd find that very distracting myself."

"Um." She opened two buttons, exposing a healthy hint of cleavage, took a deep breath and exhaled, then strolled into the office and whacked the bell on the front desk.

Warren stood away from the door and windows.

A moment later a short, thin man appeared in the doorway of the back office. "I'm Jack Watson. Can I help you?"

"Sarah Fleming," Jillian said, offering a business card in her extended hand. "I'd like to ask you a few questions."

"Of course." He looked at the card, then pushed back his glasses with one finger on the bridge. "PI. Is there some problem?"

"I need information for a client of mine. Is there somewhere we can talk and not be disturbed?"

"Right this way." Watson led the way to his office, held a chair for Jillian, and dropped into his own chair. He looked at Jillian, blinking rapidly.

Jillian sorted through the papers in her portfolio, taking her time, trying to set the mood. "Here it is." She pretended to read, then pulled out a legal pad.

Watson leaned forward, his eyes riveted to the front of her blouse.

Trying to appear casual, she poised a pen over the clean page. "My client is claiming that with your knowledge and assistance, one of your program users defrauded them."

"What are you talking about? That's not true." Watson's neck and ears reddened.

"From my client's point of view, it's true. Now, we'd like to save everyone all the time and trouble of the complaint my client is talking about filing, so I'm here—at my client's request—to see if we can get to the bottom of the problem."

"I'll do anything I can to help. We don't support our people doing anything illegal with our software. I mean they could, I suppose, if they wanted to." He raised a hand off his desk and the pitch of his voice. "We don't have any control over how our users trade, and we don't help them cover up their activities or anything."

Jillian raised an eyebrow, attempting to look as if she found his statement dubious.

"Who did you say your client is?"

"I didn't say." Jillian wrote a note. "My client prefers to remain anonymous at the moment. If he decides to proceed, he'll file a complaint with Securities and Exchange." She paused.

Watson paled. "We, ah..."

Keeping to her plan, Jillian ignored him. "And he'll file a suit to recover the damages." She looked around the office as if sizing up the worth of the business. "I suppose you'll be bankrupt unless you have adequate insurance coverage."

"We, ah..."

The bell in the outer office rang.

Watson stood. "Let me see who's there. I'll get rid of them, so we can get to the bottom of this mess." Watson went to the door. He tried to turn the knob, failed, dried his hand on his shirt, and opened the door.

Warren said, "I believe Miss Fleming is with you. May I see her for a minute, please?"

"Certainly," Watson said.

Jillian stepped into the outer office.

"I got a call. We need to tend to another matter."

Jillian turned to Watson. "I'm sorry. We'll have to continue this conversation later."

"How can you come in here and raise an issue if you don't have time to finish the job?" Watson's whole body shook.

"I'm sorry. We didn't expect this call until later today. I'll get back to you." Jillian left the office with Warren following close behind.

When they got to the car, she sighed. "I'm glad that's over. I feel sorry for the man. He'll worry himself to death over my little story."

Warren held open the car door for her, then walked around the car and climbed in. "I wouldn't worry about it. I have a suspicion Watson and company are guilty as sin."

"How so?"

"I occupied myself by popping a little backdoor program on their computer."

"What did you find?"

"After I came out here and used my tablet to access the files, I found Pasquale's records." Warren reached over the backseat and grabbed the small computer. "Look at this. He completed a trade for ten grand about a year ago. When the trade cleared, one hundred times that amount was credited to his account."

"Shouldn't he have contacted someone about that? Corrected the mistake?"

"Sure. But he not only kept the money, he moved it from his brokerage account the day after it credited. I checked your ex's tax records, too. Watson did the taxes and reported the transaction for the original amount even though the records are explicit."

"So, Watson is in on the cover-up. What's going to happen when the company discovers the error?"

"I figure they'll discover it during their end of the year audit, and they'll sue Pasquale and maybe Watson. Who knows?" He grinned at Jillian. "With Watson's history of a prior complaint with the commission and your insinuation someone was going to file again, it's easy to understand why you handled him so readily."

"Yeah, right. The information you got off the Net and

Pasquale's larcenous tendencies made it seem plausible." She sat back in the seat. "Pasquale has something to hide. A million somethings."

CHAPTER 27

"Next stop," Jillian said, "Bethany's siblings."

"I tracked down the orthopedic surgeon brother, Jason Newland," Warren said. "His office is near Sample on Federal. He also has Saturday hours."

"Let's do that one first. Did you find the sister?"

"I did. Janice Newland. Medical student at Jackson Memorial Hospital."

"I don't think we have time to drive to Miami to JMH today. And I don't believe we would find her there anyway. The place is huge."

"She's doing a rotation on a medical unit. Working today and the weekend, too. I forget the floor, but it's in the information I gave you earlier."

"My, you are the efficient one."

"I aim to please," Warren said. He held her hand for a moment.

Jillian liked the feel of his hand and wished he hadn't let go, but she felt awkward and said nothing. While flipping down the makeup mirror, the car behind them caught her eye. 'How long has that car been behind us?"

"It followed us around the corner onto Federal."

"I've noticed a black Toyota on three occasions today. I wonder if we're being shadowed."

"That's a dramatic notion. Let's do an maneuver or two." Warren pulled left and turned at the next light.

The black car did likewise.

Warren continued until Andrews Avenue and swung right.

The Toyota did the same, staying about ten lengths behind.

"I'd say you're correct. What do you want to do?"

Jillian puzzled for a minute. "It could be the cops."

"Not likely. What would they gain by following you? You're not selling drugs or laundering money. There's no big fish for them to net."

"Watching a lot of television, huh?"

Warren make a choking sound, caught his breath, and laughed.

"Maybe we should call the police," Jillian said.

"What would we say? A car followed us around the corner."

"Okay. Let's continue with our business. Maybe we can figure out who the driver is. Maybe we can even approach him."

"There's a murderer on the loose, and you want to approach a strange car? Bad idea, babe."

Jillian chuckled, thinking it had been a long while since anyone called her babe. "Yeah, bad idea. We need to stop for something on Andrews. Let the driver believe we came this way on purpose rather than trying to make our tail."

"Now who's talking TV-cop?" He held her hand again, but this time he didn't release it.

"Pull into the Starbucks. I could use a latte, and besides,

we shouldn't get to the brother's office until after one."

Warren parked on the street in front of the coffee shop. Once inside he ordered a couple of coffees and carried them to the table near the window that Jillian selected.

When Jillian tilted her head close to the window, she saw the black car about a half-block south and didn't see the driver get out. She pointed over her shoulder. "How should we handle the visit to the doctor?"

"You go in and talk to the doctor, and I'll keep an eye on our friend, maybe get a plate number."

"That works."

She looked again. "The car is just sitting there. Waiting."

"The problem with this plan is whoever that is in that car will confirm you're checking around. If it's the killer, we may be giving them reason to harm you."

"Or maybe we'll flush them out, which is more than those two detectives are doing. Either way, I can't keep living like this, and I don't want to go to jail for something I didn't do."

"I won't let that happen."

"Maybe you won't get a vote."

Warren grimaced, then checked his watch. "Let's get on our way."

They left the coffee shop in a casual manner, chatting, laughing, and sipping their coffees, then headed north on Andrews again. The tail maintained a polite distance.

Warren stayed with the flow of traffic, signaling turns, and stopping for lights on yellow, making it easy for their shadow. The car kept pace, closing the distance to a couple car lengths.

There were several empty spaces in the back row of the

parking lot. Warren pulled into the one closest to the adjacent street and reached across Jillian to open the door for her.

Jillian hurried into the building, found Newland on the marquee, and poked the elevator button for the fifth floor. She breathed a sigh of relief when the elevator door closed. She wouldn't be sharing an elevator with her shadow.

The doctor's reception area was empty except for a young woman in pink scrubs sitting behind a chest-high counter.

When Jillian approached the counter, the receptionist shoved a clipboard in her direction. "Sign in."

Jillian laid one of the fake business cards on the counter. "I'd like a few minutes of the doctor's time."

"Have a seat. I don't think he has time for you today. You should have called first."

"Ask him, please."

The receptionist rolled her eyes, stood and left, returning several minutes later. "He'll see you. Through that door." She pointed. "Last door on the right."

As Jillian found her way down the hall, she hoped the doctor wouldn't recognize her from his sister's funeral.

Jason Newland, a compact, muscular man, stood when Jillian entered his office. He looked at the card in his hand and motioned to a chair. "Have a seat, Miss Fleming."

Her heart pounded in her chest and a dry, choking sensation gripped her throat. "I'll only take a minute. Thank you for seeing me without an appointment."

"Why are you here?"

Direct and to the point, Jillian thought. "On behalf of my client, I'm looking into your sister's death."

The doctor nodded.

"I'm interested in the relationship Bethany had with the family. I've been led to believe she pursued nursing rather than dancing at your parents' insistence."

"Correct. Bethany was the baby. We all indulged her, but she was on a different wavelength. When it was time to choose a profession, my parents wanted her in medicine. Bethany didn't have the drive to succeed at medicine. Her passion was dance. That's why I helped every month with the tuition for classes."

Jillian knitted her brows, raising a finger to make a point. "I understand she worked as a waitress to pay for the dancing." She feigned looking at her notes. "Also, Pasquale Pascasio claims to have given her money for dance."

He snorted. "That'd be my sister—would have been my sister. She was somewhat of an operator as well. Looking for the easy way." He tapped his pen on his desk. "Don't get me wrong. I adored Bethany. She was fresh, unusual, exciting, qualities the rest of us in the family lack. And, Bethany was an astounding dancer. That's the best word to describe her. Dancing was the only thing she ever worked at. My folks would be angry if they knew I circumvented their desires and paid for dance school. They paid her routine expenses and tuition at Conover. I think that's why she worked as a waitress, so she could account for the dance money if our parents ever got wise."

"Uh huh. You're painting a rather mixed picture here, one of a young lady willing to work, but who is also unscrupulous."

"Not my choice of words. Let's say my little sister was an opportunist."

"How did your family feel about that part of her personality?" Jillian said.

"We accepted her. I think Mom and Dad expected she'd end up dancing, but they wanted her to have something to fall back on. I suppose we all did. Her biggest problem with dance was that she was too tall. Her preference was ballet, and shorter young women comprise the majority of the troupes. Her height limited her marketability."

Jillian took a moment to consider his comments. She thought of the few ballets she had attended, remembering the females, like so many matchsticks, standing next to taller males, all of similar heights. "Do you think Bethany may have been involved in anything else? Blackmail, for instance? The police suggest she was blackmailing her instructor for grades."

"If she was blackmailing someone, which I don't believe, it would have been for money. She didn't care enough about grades to bother."

"Would you be willing to testify to that opinion?"

"I would. I don't believe you killed my sister, Ms. Grey."

Jillian gulped and felt her face redden. "Busted."

"I remember you from the funeral."

Feeling embarrassed, Jillian bowed her head. "I'm sorry."

"I suspect you're sorry I caught you, but no matter. I'm aware the police are stuck on you as a suspect. My parents don't believe you killed Bethany either. No motive. I don't blame you for trying to defend yourself. I assure you my parents, my sister, and I all want the murderer caught—not you framed. We'll all testify to Bethany's personality, her frame of mind, and her activities. The other thing you need to know is Bethany had expensive tastes. Designer clothing. Designer travel. Designer drugs. Designer men. Two personalities in one energetic body. My parents knew about the clothes, of course, but not the rest of it."

The intercom crackled and the receptionist's voice filled the room. "Doctor, your next patient is here."

He stood. "I need to see my patients. If you want to talk to me again, please call ahead."

Jillian repeated her apologies and left the office feeling chastised but successful.

After sliding into the Lexus next to Warren, she motioned the wagons-ho sign, then gave him a rundown on the meeting with Newland. She looked in the rear view mirror. "Car's still there. Patient person. We need to get the tag number and find out who it is."

Warren smiled and glanced her way. "I accomplished that task while you were with the good doctor."

"How?"

"I walked down the street to the convenience store and got the number on the way back."

"Did you see who was in the car?"

"No. Dark windows. Besides, I didn't even glance inside."

"You can track the plate, I assume?"

"Yup."

"I think it's time we get rid of the tail then. Can we do that without letting on we know we're being followed?"

"I think so. We'll have to drive a few extra miles in the process."

Warren turned onto Sample Road and headed west in the heavy mid-day traffic. He changed lanes, settling in behind a slower car, then moved one more lane to the right, slipping through the traffic light at Military Trail on yellow. At the next light, he turned right.

Jillian looked back and saw the Toyota cross the

intersection and continue west. "That was easy."

"Guess it wasn't the cops tailing us. We wouldn't have lost them with that elementary move."

"Do you think there was more than one car? I've seen that on TV a lot."

Warren laughed. "Give me a break." He found a place and turned around. "I'll keep checking in the mirror and take an indirect route. I assume we're going to the dance studio."

"Right you are." Jillian settled into the soft leather seat. "I don't think anyone in Bethany's family had anything to do with her death. What would they have to gain?"

"Maybe one of the kids wanted her share of the inheritance. I could see where they would believe they were more deserving."

"Nah." Jillian shook her head. "The brother is making a ton of money as a surgeon. You should see his office—roomy, expensive furnishings, all sorts of video equipment in the waiting room. The sister will have the same setup. And, why would he give her money if he wanted her share of the estate?"

"Maybe they found her to be an embarrassment," Warren said.

"Again, why support her? Why not send her on her way out into the mean, unforgiving world?"

"I think we need to keep an open mind on the subject. He knew who you were. He wouldn't give himself away if he was the murderer. Did you ask about alibis?"

"I didn't. After he made me, how could I?"

CHAPTER 28

Warren took the causeway over the Intracoastal Waterway at Commercial Boulevard, rechecked the address, found the dance studio, and pulled into a metered slot in front of the building.

"High-priced real estate. Designer dance classes to go with her other high-dollar tastes," Jillian said, studying the location.

"First floor gym." Warren pointed at the floor to ceiling windows on the second floor. "Dance is upstairs."

Jillian lowered the window and stuck her head out, checked both ways in the street, then leaned back in the seat and raised the window. "The black Toyota hasn't reappeared. I'd like to wait until the class breaks and stop a couple of people to ask questions."

"You're not going inside?"

"Maybe after. My charade hasn't worked very well. I don't want to blow it and have someone call Brewer and Zale. Maybe you can give me a hand."

"Let's be reporters. That's a lot less threatening than a private investigator."

"We can stand near the door and stop the dancers when

257

they leave."

"Very reporter-like."

She pointed to the glass door and the steps beyond. "Looks like people are coming down now."

Warren and Jillian got out of the car and approached the first person, a man of about thirty.

"Excuse me, can we ask you some questions?" Jillian said.

"Who are you?"

"Reporters," Warren said. "We're doing a follow-up piece on the Bethany Newland murder."

"Sorry." The man left.

"That didn't work," Warren said.

"I think it's a good plan though. Let's try it again."

The reporter persona worked on the next departees, a group of four who appeared to be in their late teens or early twenties.

"What do you want to know?" A petite twenty-something woman wearing a big shirt over a leotard moved a half step closer.

Jillian made a show of noting the dancer's name and address before asking about her relationship to Bethany.

"We were in several of the same sessions. She rushed in, danced, rushed out. Didn't socialize much, but she was friendly, you know, when we took a break."

A man with intense blue eyes and a fine-boned face said, "She was weird, if you ask me. Had some gig going. Told me things were going to change, that she wasn't going to have to go to school or work. She'd be able to just dance."

"Anything more specific?" Jillian said.

"Not to me."

"I overheard her on the phone," the petite dancer said.

"Talking all soft and sexy. Then she said, 'That'll cost you more.' Jeffy told me about what she'd said to him. I thought her gig might be that she was selling it."

"Define it. I want to be sure I understand what you mean," Warren said.

"Are you going to put this in the paper?" the girl asked.

"No, not like you're telling us anyway. We have to get corroborating sources before our editor lets us print anything you tell us."

The dancer glanced at her friends, then at Warren and Jillian. "I thought she was a prostitute. You know, like to earn money to dance or maybe for drugs. Some people do that. Sometimes she'd be high when she came in. It'd take her a while to settle in."

"I'm surprised they let her come in high," Jillian said.

"I don't think the instructor, like, knew it. And it wasn't like it was all the time, you know. Just now and then, you know."

Jillian thanked the group, watched them walk away, and turned to the next group, who politely refused to stop. A couple of stragglers agreed to talk, but added nothing new.

Jillian touched Warren's arm. "What the talkative group said agreed with the brother's comments in a loose sort of way."

"Yup." His forehead furrowed as he stared into the distance. "We've got company."

"The black Toyota?"

"Driver's smarter than I thought."

Jillian shuddered, feeling a cold spike of fear. "Maybe looking in the obvious places. I think we should leave. It seems to me the only way we're going to find out what Bethany was doing and who killed her is to get to my students." Her hands shook. She clasped them together. "I have to finish this. This whole mess has to be over soon."

Warren touched her face. "I'm with you all the way."

"Sometimes I think it's only you who is."

"You can't run from house to house. Someone is bound to call the detectives if you do. Then you'll never get the rest to talk," Warren said.

"Asking questions isn't illegal."

"No, it's not. But Zale and Brewer won't appreciate the static it'll cause. They'll tell the kids to keep quiet and charge you with interfering with an ongoing investigation."

"I suppose you're right. Okay, it's Saturday night. I know Bethany's study group met every Saturday night at a bookstore on University Drive. We could stop there later and see if the rest of them are meeting."

"Maybe you should see if they had class yesterday. If they did, they might maintain their habits."

Jillian extracted her iPhone, found Ursula Tankoff's number, and pressed send.

Her former colleague answered on the first ring. "Jillian, is that you? I recognized your number. What's going on? Where are you? I tried to call you at home and on your cell."

"I turned it off in the hospital and forgot to put it on. Sorry. Now, I'm running around town trying to find some way to get the police off my back. Why were you looking for me? What did you want?"

"Stevenson asked me to cover your schedule."

"What about your own class?"

"I moved it to later in the day. I'm doing both until we know what's going to happen. She doesn't want to hire an adjunct yet."

"Thank God."

"I let myself into your office with the passkey and found next Friday's exam. Attendance was poor, so I sent a group email and reminded them the test had been moved to Friday, and I would give it as scheduled."

"Good. Nice to know. In fact, the reason I called was to ask about the class. Did any of the kids mention study groups meeting?"

"There was a lot of mumbling. Nothing specific."

After Jillian fielded a dozen more questions from Tankoff, she excused herself and disconnected. Once they were settled and the car was in motion, she said, "Can you go online and investigate the students?"

"I'll check the plate on that Toyota as well." Warren's eyes turned toward the rearview mirror. "I'm not convinced Pasquale isn't involved. From what you said, he wasn't forthcoming."

"Stonewalled me would be more like it."

They drove in silence for several minutes, then Warren turned down the street towards Jillian's condo.

"I'll walk you upstairs, make sure you're safe, then head home for some quality hacking time."

Warren parked his car in the fifteen-minute loading-unloading zone and escorted her upstairs. "I'll pick you up— when?"

"Around eight. It's their habit to study, then some of them go out after." She stepped forward and gave him a big hug. It felt good when he returned the embrace, adding a gentle kiss. "Thanks so much for helping. I don't know what I'd do without you."

CHAPTER 29

Chantal met Jillian at the door. "Where have you been? Dewey called. He said Eleanor is staying on the ventilator."

"Did he say why?"

"You know how he is, trying to take everything in stride. From what I gathered, the doctors gave her a trial of breathing on her own, and she didn't do well. So they'll try again tomorrow. She's sedated, and he's heading home for the night."

"She must be stable, considering the situation. He'd never leave otherwise. Translates to some improvement." Jillian pictured Eleanor in the ICU bed. "She looked rough when I was there."

Chantal nodded. "I made chicken for dinner. There's enough for two."

"If you made it, there's enough for a week."

"I'm getting better," Chantal said. "Eat with me. Please."

Jillian glanced at the time. "It's only five, but okay. I am hungry."

While Jillian changed into jeans and a button-down blouse, Chantal set another place at the small table in the kitchen.

"We celebrating something?" Jillian stepped into the room and looked around, then pointed to the filled wine glasses and the bottle on ice. In her estimation, she didn't have cause for rejoicing on any front.

"The return of my good sense." Chantal handed Jillian a glass of chilled Pinot Grigio. "I told your ex-husband to go to hell. Well, in truth, I gave him a set of biologically impossible instructions." She grinned.

"Salut." Jillian raised her glass, feeling more relieved than celebratory. They both sat. "Tell me."

"There isn't much to tell." Chantal sipped. "He called and wanted to get together. Said he'd had a stressful day."

"I'll bet he did." Jillian forced a weak smile.

"Did you have something to do with it?"

"I did. Finish your story."

"It came over me. What was I doing? You're more important to me than that man. Any man. Besides which, he'd already cheated on me, and the girl is dead, and maybe he had something to do with that, too. So I told him to take his sweet ass down the street."

"You did, did you? But, what exactly did you tell him? To go to hell, or to F himself, or to haul his sweet ass down the street?"

"All of the above."

Jillian's laugh rolled up from her toes, lightening her mood. "I'd have liked to see his face."

"Me, too."

As Chantal dished up her famous roast chicken, parsley potatoes, and sautéed green beans, Jillian served the salad.

"What's happening with your problems?"

"The best thing in my life right now, other than my

daughter, is Warren. He's been a jewel. The worst thing is that if I don't go to jail, I'll be out in the street. I'm almost out of money, and this has only just begun. Right now I'm trying to get together enough money for a defense."

Chantal nibbled a piece of chicken. "I can't help much with your defense fund, but I can afford the rent and apartment expenses on my own for a while. In fact, I went down to the office and paid the rent this afternoon."

"I'll write you a check."

"No. It can wait until you're back to work. You won't starve. I promise you. And, you won't be out of a home either. I did you wrong and for that I'm sorry. I want to make it up to you. If you'll allow me."

"Thanks, girlfriend." Jillian raised her glass and drank.

Over dinner, Jillian filled her friend in on the progress of her investigation and the likelihood of her imminent arrest.

Together they cleared the dishes and loaded the dishwasher.

As Jillian returned the vase of pink silk tulips to the table, Chantal said, "I need to run. I have an appointment with my personal trainer at seven." She looked at her watch. "I don't want to be late. It'll be my last session for a while."

"You'd better hurry then."

Chantal hurried out, waving goodbye as she pulled the door closed behind her.

Jillian had almost an hour and a half before Warren would arrive. She spread her notes in the dining area, intent on finding some clue, some common relationships in the mess of information. There were so many holes. Hopefully, Warren's latest foray onto the Internet would fill in the missing pieces.

Bethany's brother was a believable sort, lacking in

motive, and upfront in his manner. The family didn't play as possible suspects. There was no reason for them to kill Bethany. The few dancers who stopped to talk didn't seem to have any connection with Bethany outside of the studio. Again, she couldn't envision a possible reason, but couldn't rule out the connection either.

Pasquale was a viable suspect though without a clear motive. She summarized her thoughts, then moved on to considering the social group—Oliver Cooley, Vincent Barrera, and Shanna Albano, all of whom she hoped to see in a couple of hours. Again, what reason would any of them have to hurt Bethany? Cooley, jealousy perhaps. The other two, though she found them to be difficult, unprofessional, and unethical, didn't appear to have reason to kill the girl.

The doorbell rang. Thinking it was Warren, and wondering how he got past the guard, Jillian threw open the door.

Pasquale charged into the living room. He was dressed in pressed jeans and a golf shirt—a major improvement over his appearance earlier in the day. His face, lined with tension, looked harsh and ugly.

"Chantal isn't here," Jillian said, staying near the open door.

"What in the hell do you think you're doing, woman?"

"Meaning?"

"I got a call from Watson. He said you and some man were in his office. It took him a while to place you, then he remembered seeing your picture in my apartment. While you kept him busy playing private eye and threatening a lawsuit, the man, Warren—I presume, since he knows the program—went onto Watson's system and tapped into my trading records. The system tracks all entries, even back door ones."

"What did you want me to do? I came to see you and asked you first. You refused to give me any information. I've spent the last twenty-five years enduring the worst of your irresponsible, despicable behavior. I'm not going to take a murder rap for you, too."

"You think I killed Bethany? Why would I do that? I could just walk away from that little flirt anytime I chose."

"But you didn't choose, or you couldn't. Which was it? I've got a couple of thoughts to share with my lawyer and the police when I see them tomorrow."

"I didn't kill Bethany."

"I think you might have. You have a million dollars that doesn't belong to you. Shanna Albano works for your buddy Watson, does records or something for him. Was she wise to your windfall? Maybe those kids were blackmailing you. That's what the money you gave Bethany was for, wasn't it?"

"Meddling bitch. You have no idea what you're talking about."

"Don't I? Why didn't you tell the police about the money and the blackmail? Bethany's brother was giving her money for dance. Her parents paid her living expenses. I figure she was bleeding you for all the expensive extras she wanted."

Pasquale dropped onto the sofa. He bowed his head and sat for a moment tracing one of the roses on the cushion cover with his index finger. When he looked back at Jillian, he said, "You've got it mostly right, but I didn't kill her."

"Tell me, Pasquale. The police think I killed the kid, and I didn't."

"Yeah, I know that."

"You'd better tell me—and the police—your role in this mess. Tomorrow I'm going to turn over the information I have to them and hope it keeps me out of jail. They'll be after you next. Blackmailing for big bucks is a lot more potent motive than for grades, especially when we're talking about a student who didn't give a flying rip about school."

Pasquale sprung off the sofa and stormed across the room. His face flushed deep purple. He drew his right fist back.

Jillian stepped in the direction of the open door while looking for something with which to defend herself. Pasquale had never struck her, not even in their worst moments. A hand touched her shoulder. She shuddered.

"Back off, Pascasio." Warren said. "Touch her, and you're a dead man."

Jillian glanced at Warren. "Thank God, you're here."

"Just in time, too." He pointed to the sofa. "Sit."

"And you're going to make me?" Pasquale snarled. "How do you plan on doing that, computer boy?"

Warren raised a brow, stepped out from behind Jillian, and pointed a small pistol at him.

Anger, then defeat, crossed Pasquale's face. He sank onto the sofa.

"A gun? Has it come to that?" Jillian said.

"I was concerned about the car following us all day, so I thought I'd bring a little extra protection. I know how to use it, even have a permit."

Jillian shook her head.

"To be on the safe side. Don't worry, I won't shoot the son of a bitch." Warren nodded in the direction of a chair across the room from Pasquale. "Sit for a minute."

She sat.

Warren pushed the apartment door shut, then lowered himself onto a dining room chair, laying the gun on the glass table top in front of him. "Now, my friend, tell all. Don't leave anything out. I'll be checking the details."

"You're right about the money. I made a trade and when the credit posted, there were extra zeros. I figured why tell them? Their mistake. So I moved the money out of the brokerage account into an offshore account I opened years ago." His smile was nasty. "Even before we divorced."

"I'm not surprised. I always knew you were a son of a bitch. They'll find out. How will you pay it back?" Jillian said.

"It's been almost a year, and they haven't found it yet. But I haven't spent it either, none of it. I'm taking the interest. That's how I fund my trading and expenses."

"So why was Albano searching your account?" Warren asked.

"I was a regular at Cubano's. Met Barrera at the bar. Chatted. Got acquainted with Shanna when she came in to meet him. Then Bethany started as a waitress there. We went out a few times. No big deal."

"Seems like it became one," Warren said.

"Yeah, well, Shanna found out I did business with her boss. She went into the records and found the million-dollar error. The next thing I knew, Bethany wanted money. Our little romance was defunct, and it became a business relationship."

"So you killed her?" Jillian said, feeling nauseated.

"No, I swear, I didn't kill her. I'm not sorry she's dead, mind you, but I didn't kill her."

"Who did?"

"Beats me," Pasquale said.

"I think we need to call Brewer and Zale. They need to hear this. The sooner the better," Warren said.

Pasquale stood.

Warren picked up the gun and waved it in his direction.

Pasquale collapsed back onto the sofa. "I said I didn't kill her, and I'm willing to talk to the police. First, I'd like to find out who did kill her. Maybe we can clear both of our names."

"Pasquale Pascasio, why should I give you a moment's consideration?" Jillian said. "You were prepared to let me fry. You lied to the cops. You lied to me. Hell, you probably lied to your mother, too," Jillian shook her fist.

"No doubt," Pasquale said, his voice calm. "We should talk to the kids. You didn't kill her. I didn't kill her."

"You say," Jillian said.

"That leaves Albano and Barrera as big candidates in my opinion. Let's check it out before we go to the cops."

Jillian looked at Warren, who nodded.

"We're planning to go to the bookstore and see if we can talk to Bethany's whole study group at one time."

Warren jerked his gun, pointing at the door, then back at Pasquale. "You come along. That way you won't call anyone and warn them we're coming."

Pasquale focused on Warren's gun. "You won't be needing that."

"I'll keep it handy, if you don't mind." Warren slipped his hand and the gun into his jacket pocket. "Let's go." He stood back, allowing Pasquale to exit the apartment first.

CHAPTER 30

Jillian drove the Lexus with Pasquale in the front and Warren behind him. No one spoke during the tense ride across town.

Warren's appearance with weapon in hand had come as a surprise to Jillian, though it was also a relief. She wasn't sure what to make of it. Asking him about it would have to wait until later. It didn't jibe with Warren's computer nerd persona.

She wanted to believe Pasquale's story. Keeping someone else's million dollars suited his something-for-nothing personality and would also make him a target for blackmail. That meant her field of possible suspects had narrowed to the students. She couldn't think of anyone else who would want Bethany dead. Maybe the police had other viable candidates, but Jillian doubted it. They wouldn't be stuck on her if they did.

Jillian drove up and down the rows in front of the bookstore, around the side of the building, then across the street, looking for a space and the black Toyota. When a red Porsche Boxster backed out, she parked in front of Starbucks.

"Hot car. Maybe I'll go that way next," Pasquale said,

turning his head to watch the tail lights disappear down the street.

"You need to return the money," Jillian said. "You'll be clear of murder and charged with theft."

"Very wifely concern coming from you." His voice rang with scorn.

"Whatever. Do what you like."

On the stroll to the store, Jillian studied every black car. The black Toyota was not there.

"You know these kids. What's your idea for the approach?" Warren said, keeping his hand in his gun pocket with the barrel directed at Pasquale.

"I've heard the kids mention gathering toward the rear by the cookbooks. It's close enough to the nursing texts to be convenient. Let's join the group and have a chat," Jillian said.

"I don't think you'll find out anything that way. No one will talk in front of the whole group," Warren said.

"True, but it will put the guilty person on notice and maybe force the killer to do something stupid."

"I don't like this at all." Warren shook his head. "We could be forcing the killer to come after you."

"Why? As I see it, if the killer does nothing, then I swing in his or her place."

"Desperate people do desperate things. Forcing their hand could change their plans. You're the one they've been focused on all along. You'll be in danger."

"I'm in danger of going to jail now. Might as well fight back." She looked from one man to the other. "You with me? Warren, please take your gun off Pasquale. He can't call them now. Let's fan out and come at them from different directions."

Warren opened the door, allowing Jillian and Pasquale to

precede him into the bright interior.

Pasquale wandered off to the right. He glanced over his shoulder in Jillian's direction and disappeared in the stacks.

"I'm going to stay a row or two over from you." Warren hung back for a minute.

"Fine." She grasped his hand for a second before heading down the center row, sidestepping the displays and a tantrum-throwing two-year-old. She smiled at the child, then frowned when the child screamed louder.

Jillian turned left at the coffee counter, glanced down the row to the cookbooks, and noted the study group members. Tanya Li. Carrie Kennedy. Oliver Cooley. Oliver, as the boyfriend Bethany cheated on, was a suspect in Jillian's opinion. The two girls had no motive. It might be possible to get something out of Tanya or Carrie if she got them alone.

Jillian circled around to the back of the nursing and medical section, looking around, hoping for a glimpse of Pasquale. Warren was keeping her in sight, so she didn't look for him.

Jillian heard voices on the other side of the rack and stopped to listen.

"You don't own me, Vincent."

Jillian recognized Shanna Albano's voice.

"I figure as long as I'm paying the rent, I've got a right to know where you are and what you're doing."

"Screw you, Barrera. I'll get my stuff and move tomorrow."

"Tonight would be better."

"Fine."

There was a long pause and stomping footsteps. Albano spoke again. "I don't get it."

"What's not to get? You said you were home last Thursday night. You weren't home. I called. I checked on my break. Today, you said you'd see me at class, but you never showed. What are you into? I don't like secrets. Maybe you didn't break it off with that cop boyfriend of yours after all."

"Whoa," Jillian mouthed in amazement. She wished for another witness or a tape recorder to document that Albano didn't have an alibi for the evening Bethany died and to attest to the comment about the cop. She slipped closer to the end of the bookcase, wanting to sneak a peak around the corner. She did and glimpsed Warren a row over.

She flicked her thumb in the direction of the quarreling couple and pointed to her ear.

Warren nodded.

"You bastard. You know very well I don't answer the phone when I study," Albano said, her voice loud and distinct. "Today I had things to do, errands to run."

Jillian heard a scuffle. She and Warren converged at the end of the row.

Albano directed a knife-hand jab toward Barrera's face. In an instant, Warren grabbed her by the arms from behind. Barrera backed off.

Albano yelled, "Who the hell are you?" She wiggled and turned in his grasp. "Let me go, asshole."

Jillian looked at Barrera. "Pretty feisty. This is my friend Warren." She pointed at him.

"I've had enough of the bitch," Barrera said. "She's freaking crazy."

Albano shook loose of Warren's grip. "Look who's talking." She took a step back, then smoothed her red sweater over white slacks. "I'm outta here. Give me a couple of hours. I'll be out of your place."

Barrera shook his head, looking embarrassed, then wandered off in the opposite direction from Shanna.

"Ms. Grey, what are you doing here?" Tanya Li asked. She stood between Kennedy and Cooley at the end of the row.

"I came to find you. Can we talk a bit? I've got some problems, and I hope you'll help me with them."

The students looked from one to another, then backed up a few steps and whispered together. Tanya pushed Carrie forward, as if directing her to be the spokesperson.

"Okay," Carrie Kennedy said. "We'll talk."

Jillian pointed to the seating area with the students' books and notes scattered about. "Let's sit there for a minute." She waited for everyone but Warren to precede her. "Where's Pasquale?"

"Don't know. He skipped. Doesn't matter anyway." Warren shrugged.

"Son of a bitch." She joined the students.

Two tweed upholstered loveseats and two matching chairs circled a large coffee table. Jillian and Warren sat, and Jillian introduced Warren to the group.

"Like I said," Jillian began, "I need your help. I don't know all that's being said about me, so I'm going to tell you what's happened first."

The three nodded.

Jillian started with her meeting with Bethany, then talked about finding her body, the blog, and what she knew about the police investigation. "I can't tell you the details about the meeting with Shanna and Vincent at the school, but I can tell you Shanna admitted to putting the blog on the Internet and promised to remove it."

Jillian looked at Cooley when he squirmed in his seat. "You have something to add?"

"She took the Painful Process blog off, like she promised, then set up another one on a different server the same day. She's not talking about the school or classes, but she's trashing you pretty bad."

Jillian's face flushed red. She clenched her fists. "It just doesn't stop." She took a deep breath, closed her eyes and exhaled. "Thanks for telling me. We'll come back to that. Please don't think I'm disrespectful of Bethany's memory, but I need to tell you the rest of the story." Jillian talked about being suspended from both jobs, Eleanor's illness, Barrera's behavior, and Pasquale's accusation that Bethany was blackmailing him.

"Wow," Li said. "I knew something was going on. I overhead Bethany and Shanna fighting in the bathroom the day Bethany was killed. I was in another stall."

"Why didn't you tell the police?"

"I was going to. Really, I was, but Shanna knew I was there and heard the fight. On Wednesday, when those two were picking on me in the stairway, before you came, they threatened me. Shanna said she'd hurt me if I told the police. She said it would give them the wrong idea."

"Or maybe the right idea." Jillian shook her head. "Why are you telling us now?"

Li bowed her head. "We all talked about it." She looked around at the others. "We know you're getting framed, so we've decided to help. We just don't know what to do."

"Start by calling Brewer and Zale," Warren said.

"Are they going to give us a problem about not telling earlier?" Li said.

"Just explain things to them," Warren said.

Jillian slid forward on her chair, getting closer to Cooley. "Tell me what happened before you left Bethany at my office on Thursday."

"Nothing happened. She went into the lady's room. When she and Shanna came out, she seemed angry. I asked her what was going on, and she said Shanna was a bitch. She told me to go on home."

"Did you?"

"Sure. Bethany got touchy if I tried to stay close. So I left."

Jillian paused, thinking about that evening. "I left the office with Bethany, but she stopped to get a soda, and I went to my car. I didn't pay any attention to the student parking area. When you left, whose cars were there?"

Cooley squeezed his eyes closed. When he opened them he said, "I parked next to Bethany. She got to school a second before me. Shanna's car was in the row behind us. Tanya and Carrie drove together. They were leaving when I got to my car. When I got onto Oakland, I saw Shanna turn around and head back to campus, like she'd forgotten something."

"What does Shanna drive?" Jillian asked.

"Black Toyota," Cooley said.

"Corolla?" Jillian asked.

"That's one of the things I didn't want to tell you with Pasquale around," Warren said. "The car following us all day is registered to Shanna Albano."

"Guess I was the errand she had to run today." She slid back in her chair. "You kids would have saved me a mess of grief if you told the police all of this last Friday."

Kennedy said, "We know. We were scared. We knew Bethany was involved. But we didn't see her with Vincent and Shanna very much, just at study group, then they'd sometimes be in their own little side conversations, away from us so we couldn't hear."

"Do you have any idea what they were doing?"

"No, they kept it quiet. I mean, Oliver was always right there. They wouldn't talk about Bethany having another man with him sitting there."

"I suppose you're right," Jillian said. "Tell us about the new blog."

"I'm not involved with it," Kennedy said. "I'm sorry I joined the first one."

"Why did you?"

"I have a baby, so I'm home a lot. I have no social life, only on the Internet. I did it to be social, talk to people."

"I understand."

Carrie had her straightened hair tied at the nape of her neck. She fiddled with the rubber band for a moment. "Oliver can tell you more."

Cooley opened his notebook and read the address for the new blog. "Shanna moved the pictures of the crime scene to the site. She's mostly talking about the investigation, what's been in the paper. She said the police are going to charge you with the murder tomorrow. Said she knows a cop downtown who's in the know. What else? Oh yeah. She said the school and the hospital fired you. Now you said that's not true either."

"She may be right about the arrest. The detectives want me downtown with my lawyer in the morning. I need to tell them about this conversation. They'll be talking with all of you again, I'm sure."

"We're ready," Li said. "I'm so ashamed for not helping more to begin with. The students who flunked the first time convinced us we'd get someone easier if we kept our mouths shut."

"It's not too late. I appreciate your change of heart." Jillian stood. "We'll leave you to your studying. Please be careful when you go home. I don't want anything to happen to any of you."

Kennedy said, "Wait a minute. Remember when we were with the dean and you asked if we saw someone hiding behind the blinds right after Bethany's body was found."

"I remember," Jillian said.

"Well, it was Shanna hiding. The rest of us stood out in the open, but not her. When I asked her about it, she left the room. Didn't even answer me."

CHAPTER 31

When Jillian and Warren stopped at the hospital, they learned Eleanor was sedated, intubated, and on a ventilator. In the morning, the physicians planned to remove the equipment and allow her to breathe on her own, providing the oxygen level in her blood remained adequate.

As they left in the Lexus, Jillian said, "Even if Eleanor recovers from this episode, there will be another in the near future. Closer hospitalizations. More serious symptoms."

"It's a sad situation. That's how it was with my wife. Dewey has my sympathy."

"Mine as well. I still fight a battle with myself because of my daughter's death."

Traffic was light, and they rode in silence for two blocks.

"Have you heard from your dad?" Warren glanced in her direction. "Didn't he intend to make contact with his buddy at the station again?"

"He hasn't called. Besides, I know what will happen."

"Call him anyway."

"Okay. They won't be in bed yet." Jillian pulled out her cell and punched the speed dial. "Hey, Dad?"

"I've been trying to get you all day. Don't you ever stay

home?"

"Sorry. I've had a lot going on." She updated him.

"I still don't think you should be poking around alone. You don't know what you're getting into. You're not prepared to handle what you might stir up."

"I'm not alone. Warren is helping me."

"Big comfort." He sounded disgusted. "Some computer nerd is protecting you."

"He's not just that, Dad. It'll be okay." She waited for him to continue.

"I ran into Mack, my friend from IA, at breakfast yesterday morning."

Jillian laughed. "What a coincidence."

"I decided to have a bite down the street from the station."

"And?" Jillian said.

"Mack told me he's involved in an investigation of a detective. That's why he couldn't get back to me."

"Did he say who?"

"No, of course not. He can't be giving details to a civilian. He probably said too much anyway. But, he acted like he wanted me to have the information. Called me right over. You know, like he was waiting to tell me. Then he made a big deal about it being an unusual case that I would be interested in. He said there might be more against you than the facts."

"Or, maybe they're using you for a patsy. You know, by trying to make me relax and let my guard down," Jillian said. "

"Jillian, that's not true. In fact, it's wrong thinking. I think he just wanted me to know there is more going on than meets the eye. The IA guys don't get involved at the level you're implying."

Hearing tension in her father's voice, she decided to back off and not aggravate him further or stress his heart. "What do you think I should do?"

"Be careful. Remember, I told you Zale is a good cop, even though he acts like a bastard most of the time."

"Yeah. Right."

Jillian ended the conversation as Warren pulled into his assigned space in the garage under his condominium. She repeated her dad's comments as they rode the elevator upward. "I couldn't argue with Dad anymore, but I can't get my mind around Zale as a good cop."

"Why not? Zale's behavior reflects his personality rather than his ethics. Mention it to Xavier before your meeting in the morning. At least she'll be on notice that something unusual is going on."

"But we can't be sure it's Zale who's the target of the IA investigation. Can we?"

"No, but . . ." Warren said.

"I'll tell her first thing. Though it doesn't explain why Zale is trying to frame me."

"It doesn't." Warren paused in the entryway. "Let's have a glass of wine before we get back to work. Relax a bit and change our perspective."

"It would go down easy." Jillian preceded Warren into the apartment and settled on the sofa. "Homey."

"It's comfortable, but a bit old lady-ish. It's time I get rid of some of the old and bring in new things."

Jillian shrugged. "I suppose you're right. Me, too."

"White Zin okay with you? I've got a half-empty bottle of Pinot Grigio, too, but I can't vouch for it."

"Let's try the Pinot since it's already open. I don't think I can handle more than a glass."

While Warren was in the kitchen, Jillian took the opportunity to inspect his living space. The only additions to his mother's décor appeared to be an entertainment unit supporting a digital television and several pictures of his son and late wife. Jillian and Warren had both been touched by personal tragedy—his wife, her daughter, both their marriages. His son looked like him, except younger, with a full head of sandy brown hair. His wife had been a petite woman, coming to Warren's shoulder. She died of breast cancer before her thirty-fifth birthday.

Warren touched Jillian's hand with the stem of the wineglass, breaking her reverie.

"Losing the people we love is so difficult." She sipped the wine and continued to look at the family photos.

"It is. I focus on the good times. Now I find myself wanting to be in a relationship again. For years, I wasn't interested. I compared everyone to my wife. Not fair. No one can compete with the dead."

Jillian's laugh rang sad. "Sometimes no one can compete with the living either."

"Is there a message in that statement?"

"No." She turned to him. "Not anymore there isn't. This mess and your kindness and concern pulled me from the pity pit I dug for myself. My daughter wouldn't want me to give my life to grief. And Pasquale—damn him—isn't worth the trouble."

Warren brushed a kiss across her lips. "Nice to hear." He kissed her again.

Desire tingled through her. It was a feeling she once believed could be aroused by Pasquale alone. Giving herself to the kiss, she parted her lips and accepted his warm explorations.

After the kiss, he held her in his arms, nuzzling his face into her hair. "I'd like to know you better. A lot better."

"I'd like that." Feeling relaxed and secure, Jillian settled against him, closing her eyes, enjoying the feeling of strength. After several moments, she said, "This feels nice, but if we're going to make any progress, we'd better get to it."

"I, um, you're right." He released her, then brushed a light kiss across her lips.

Remembering the gun Warren flashed at Pasquale, she pushed away a bit. "What was with the gun? That was a shocker."

He brushed his lips across her forehead. "I retired after twenty with the FBI. Learned a lot of interesting skills working there."

"I thought you were a computer geek."

"I worked with computers for many years with the Bureau. Started out in Intelligence, moved into the Cyber Division, and stayed there."

She realized Pasquale hadn't seemed surprised by the sight of Warren carrying a gun. "That explains a lot. I wonder why Pasquale never mentioned you were with the FBI, back when the four of us went out to dinner."

"To be honest, I don't think Pasquale knew about my background until a few months ago. It never came up. When I connected with him, I'd just started my consulting business."

"I half expected Pasquale to run out on us." She thought about it. "But now, FBI and all, I wonder why you didn't stop him."

"No reason to. I dragged him along to stop him from warning the kids. We planned to talk to them alone anyway.

If Pasquale disappears, the cops can track him down." He kissed her again, lingering in the embrace.

"I think we need to see what information appeared online while we were busy. If we don't move, I may not be able to think about anything but you."

"Um—" Warren initiated the next kiss, then broke the embrace. "My inclination is to take your mind off the situation, but you're right. We'd better get to work."

Jillian followed Warren into his workroom and pulled a rolling chair next to him, resting her arm against his shoulder as she leaned close to see the computer screen.

The first document was the registration for Albano's Toyota.

Warren said, "This was easy. The background checks on Albano and Barrera were more troublesome."

"Can you find out anything?"

"I expect so. I called a couple of buddies. In Vincent Barrera's case, the thing about sealed records is that they aren't really sealed. The history isn't destroyed and agencies like the FBI can get it. If my guess is right, we should have something by now." Warren clicked on his email, found what he was looking for, and opened it. "Here we go." He printed the attachment.

"Wow," she said. "I had no clue. Eleanor told me Vincent had a problem with drugs, but . . . man, she didn't let on." Jillian pointed to the paper. "He was arrested and convicted three times before he was sixteen. Breaking and entering. Assault and battery. Possession with intent to sell. He got probation, then they locked him up. He was off the street from ages sixteen to eighteen. I've seen his transcript. He took remedial classes—I guess to make up for what he missed, then got a GED. He went to a community college for a couple of years in San Francisco and almost flunked out." She tapped the next line. "He was arrested again for drugs when he was twenty. No conviction. Again a year later. No conviction. Eleanor told me they moved here from California about three years ago to get their grandson out of the environment, give him chance to start over."

"How does she think that's working?"

"Eleanor told me it worked like a skillfully rolled joint— her words, not mine. He settled down, got serious. It was his idea to repeat the reading remediation before starting at Conover. That's when he got his reading skills up to the twelfth grade level."

"It sounds like he smartened up—maybe enough to keep his grandmother in the dark about his activities." He clicked on another email. "Let me show you what I found out about Albano."

"Shanna is turning out to be a scary young woman." Jillian slid closer to Warren. The email on the screen contained an attachment.

"This is Albano's service record. I looked at it earlier."

"Your friend sent it on the Internet?"

"Not a problem. Secure server."

The file opened and filled the screen.

"How'd he get it?"

"He's an accomplished fisherman."

"Would you look at that?" Jillian said. "That's a record of the dishonorable discharge from the army. I knew about that. She put it on her school application and had to get clearance from the admissions committee to get into the nursing program."

"The problem is we can't find out the reason this way." He went back to his email program. "I contacted a former associate. She's a hacker par excellence. Way better than I am. That's her job with the Bureau." He clicked. "Here it is already." He opened the email and scrolled down the lines of text. "Albano makes Barrera look like a cream puff."

"How so?"

"Look at this. An affair with her commanding officer. Stalked him and his wife. She got the wife alone and attacked her. By the way, her records show excellence in hand-to-hand combat and martial arts. After she pounded the wife, the MPs arrested her and charged her with attempted murder. She got off with aggravated assault on a plea bargain. She served her sentence, and the Army discharged her."

"I can't imagine why she wanted to be a nurse."

"It begs a bigger question. How could the authorities at your school let these two into a nursing program? I can't fathom their reasoning."

"The admissions department refuses to screen with stricter criteria for specialty programs like ours. They say it's the student's responsibility to know the requirements of the profession, and the state board's job to keep them out."

"Unbelievable." He shrugged. "What I do believe is the personalities of those two people. The fact Albano followed us around all day, and her link to Pasquale's windfall and Bethany's blackmail, give some very strong links to the murder."

"Stronger than protecting a test bank, that's for sure. All I have to do is get the police to believe me."

"I don't see it as a problem." Warren opened his browser, then dug a scrap of paper from his shirt pocket. "Let's see if we can find Albano's new blog." He entered a few keystrokes and waited. "I think this is the one." He paused while he read the screen. "Being careful to be an observer."

"Can you verify who wrote it?"

His fingers moved over the keyboard. "No. As expected, anonymous."

"Why is she bothering?"

"Beats me. Ego. Because she can. Give me a minute here." Warren hacked into the site. "I'm getting good at finding the back door to these blogs. New skill. Maybe I'll add it to my list of services."

"I don't think it's advisable to advertise you're a hacker."

"It's all in the wording, my dear." He clicked around, bringing up one screen after another. "I don't think there is anything here that will help you."

He tapped the back arrow, scrolled through several inches of rambling text, clicked on links, and looked at a smattering of posted replies. Many of the links led to photos in the Ft. Lauderdale News.

Jillian saw a picture of herself from the college identification system. Either the newspaper reporter or the blogger could have clipped it from the college website. Based on student comments, Jillian thought the posting was Albano's, but anyone who wanted to maintain the pressure could have done it—Barrera, perhaps.

One picture in particular caught her attention. "What can you find out about that picture?"

Warren hovered over it with his mouse. "The blogger posted it."

The grainy frame showed the crime scene from a distance. The angle suggested the photographer was on the second floor of the college's nursing building. The cadre of faculty onlookers created a border between the police vehicles and the woods. Jillian saw herself at the end of the line. She guessed Albano took it while hiding behind the blinds. The angle seemed right.

"Let's read this," Warren said as he centered the most recent comment on the screen.

Friday morning:

The nice thing about all of this is that I'm likely to be rid of two pests at the same time. The little bitch is gone for good, and the cops will arrest the other one—won't she be surprised. It's nice to have connections. She deserves it too. This all is going to work out well. Students should have a way to take care of teachers who get on their backs. It's only right.

"The style doesn't look like what we identified as Albano on the first site. The grammar is decent, and the author used capital letters and punctuation. But it feels like Albano all the same." Jillian smiled. "Nice to learn I'm a pest."

"For what it's worth, I'm going to print this out so you can take it with you in the morning."

"I'd like to send it to the dean, too. It will tell her the topic is still on the Internet."

"Problem is, with no names and no specifics, there is no libel. Nothing the dean can do about it."

With few other comments on the blog, they concluded it wasn't getting much attention and wasn't a problem they could deal with anyway.

After Jillian provided the email address, Warren sent the blog's link to the dean. He slipped all the reports—Barrera's police record, Albano's service history and the explanation, and the text of the blog—into a large envelope.

"Here you go. I hope it all helps." He stood. "Let's polish off the wine, then I'll walk you home. Tomorrow will be another long day for you."

They retrieved the bottle from the kitchen and went out

on the balcony. The southern view included a wedge of ocean, a slice of street, and the next condominium.

Jillian sipped and thought about their encounter with the students at the bookstore. "I remember seeing a scrap of red fabric at the murder scene. I thought, perhaps, a bird carried it in for nesting material. But maybe it tore off the assailant's clothing. Earlier tonight, when we saw Albano, I remembered she wears a lot of red. Not at the hospital of course, but any time I've seen her in street clothes, she's wearing something red. Usually it's a sweater. And that would make her fit the description of the woman coming out of the trees. The one the detectives think was me."

"Something else to tell them tomorrow."

CHAPTER 32

Jillian proceeded Warren through the glass entry doors into her apartment building lobby where Detectives Brewer and Zale stood talking with the elderly guard.

Deciding to be proactive, Jillian walked into Brewer's line of vision. "I presume you two aren't making the rounds chatting up retired police officers."

Zale grunted, then stepped forward. "You're under arrest for the murder of Bethany Newland."

As he read the Miranda warning, he grabbed her arm and turned her around.

"Wait a minute," she said. "Let me talk to Warren."

"You've had all day to talk to him," Zale said.

"Give Ms. Grey some time," Brewer said.

The officers stood back.

Jillian handed Warren her purse, apartment keys, and the envelope with the information about Albano and Barrera. "You'll find Xavier's number on the desk in my bedroom."

"Your room is on the right?"

"Yes. Please let her know what's happened." Jillian leaned close and kissed him on the lips. "Get this information to her. There's another envelope in the side pocket of my laptop case. Take that along. There's information in there we'll need at the police station."

"I'm on it. Don't answer any questions until Xavier gets there."

"I won't." She kissed him again, then joined the detectives, putting her hands behind her back.

Cold metal encircled her wrists and pinched.

"That hurts. Is it really necessary? I'm not fighting you."

"Procedure," Zale said, scowling. He put a hand on Jillian's shoulder, pushing toward the exit.

As Warren looked on, Zale ushered Jillian into the waiting squad car by pressing her head forward, forcing her to duck. She looked into the lobby as the officer eased the vehicle away from the curb. Warren was stepping into the elevator. She glanced back. Brewer and Zale followed in the white Taurus.

They're treating me like a criminal, she thought, believing she'd be in jail for murder before the night was through. She vowed not to cry.

After the young patrol officer parked toward the front of the police station lot, he assisted Jillian from the vehicle. "Ma'am, they'll take off those cuffs as soon as we get inside. I know it's uncomfortable, but I can't remove them out here."

"It's not your fault." Jillian tried to wipe a tear on her shoulder but failed. The effort dug the cuffs deeper into both wrists.

To Jillian's surprise, Xavier stood near the entrance to the police station, wearing blue jeans and a peach-colored pullover. A dark jacket draped over her left arm covered the handle of a briefcase. She had tied her hair at the nape of the neck, giving her an austere appearance.

Xavier's presence buoyed Jillian. "I'm glad to see you."

Xavier nodded.

Jillian knitted her brows, started to speak, then put on a passive expression in response to Xavier's warning stare.

Brewer and Zale had parked in the second row of the parking lot. As they approached, Xavier stepped into their path.

"What's the meaning of this outrage?" Xavier said.

"You think it's an outrage?" Zale said. "I think it's about time."

"We had an appointment to talk in the morning."

Zale tilted his head toward a single, shrugged shoulder. "We had probable cause. You're welcome to wait until the morning to talk. I'm sure she'll enjoy her first night as our guest."

"I'll talk to Ms. Grey now." Xavier's voice was demanding.

"That can be arranged," Brewer said.

"Let's book her first," Zale said.

"What's the rush? Let them talk. We have all night."

"Fine." Zale, scowling, plodded through the station doors.

Brewer escorted the two women to a drab-green interrogation room. The ever-present video recorder hung on the wall. He removed Jillian's cuffs and motioned to a chair. "We'll be waiting outside."

Once they were alone, Jillian said, "How'd you get here so fast?"

"Your friend called. I live nearby so I came right over. He'll be here in a few minutes with whatever it was you wanted me to see. Meanwhile, tell me what's going on."

Jillian recited the events of the day, sparing no details.

Xavier frowned when Jillian confessed to impersonating

a private investigator, but said nothing.

"Warren has proof of everything I've told you."

The door opened, and Brewer stepped into the room. He handed Xavier two envelopes. "Some guy dropped these at the sergeant's desk, said to bring them right up." He left, pulling the door closed behind him.

Xavier reviewed the materials, pausing to clarify a point or to look back in the pile. "There's enough here to cast real doubt on the charges against you and enough to get you acquitted if they elect to play this thing out, which I don't think they will. I recommend we call the detectives in, show them everything, and see if we can get them to drop the charges. We can still use the material at trial if need be."

"Whatever you think is best."

Xavier left the room.

Jillian heard muted voices outside the door and knew Xavier was engaged in conversation with the detectives.

A few minutes later, she reappeared, sat in a chair across the corner from Jillian, and leaned close. "Brewer said they moved on arresting you because he got a tip you were leaving town."

"That's pure BS. Someone is setting me up. You know that." Jillian wiped a tear.

Zale entered the room, selecting the chair nearest the recording equipment.

A moment later Brewer came in and sat.

"We'd like to see the proof you have that someone else murdered Miss Newman."

"I said we have proof other people had not only the means, but the motive and opportunity. Solving the murder is your job." Xavier leaned back in the metal chair. "Why should we give you what we have now? You seem intent on putting my client in jail no matter what the evidence. Maybe we should wait and spring it in court." Xavier sounded insolent.

"Working with us is in your client's best interest." Brewer removed a small notebook from his pocket, flipped through the pages, then laid his pen inside before placing it on the table in front of him. He glanced at Zale. "Make the intro comments."

Zale stood, took a moment to turn on the recorder, returned to his seat, and made introductions for the record.

Xavier said, "I take it you think you have enough evidence to charge my client with the murder."

"True enough. That's why we moved on the arrest," Brewer said.

Xavier sucked air through clenched teeth and closed lips, making a high-pitched hissing sound. "You wanted to get your chief and the mayor off your backs. The morning paper quoted the mayor as saying a suspect would be in custody before Monday."

Zale shifted his weight. "Let's get started here."

Warren had encouraged Jillian to stop being a victim. She took several deep breaths, thinking extra oxygen to her brain would help her concentrate. "Would it be possible to get a cup of coffee? It's been a long day."

"We can manage that." Brewer left the room and returned two minutes later with four cups of coffee and the necessary accompaniments. He helped himself from the tray, slid it towards the women, and waited for Jillian to serve herself. "We have proof Pasquale Pascasio gave Bethany Newland money."

Jillian kept quiet.

"And what is the proof?" Xavier said.

Brewer pulled the chair out and sat. "Bank records show regular withdrawals from Pascasio's bank account over the last two months and deposits on the same day and in the same amount into Newland's account."

"So?" Xavier raised an eyebrow. "What could the banking habits of my client's former husband have to do with her? I don't get the connection."

Zale said, "Maybe a whole lot. We talked to Pascasio. He didn't deny giving money to Newland. He said the money was a gift. He said the girl had real talent, and he wanted to help with dancing lessons."

Jillian stifled a laugh, choked on a mouthful of coffee, and managed to get a hand to her mouth to avert a spray on the table and her lawyer. "Excuse me. Wrong pipe," she croaked.

Xavier shook her head, while Jillian resumed a complacent, albeit forced, demeanor.

"School records indicate Newland made payments of about the same amount within the next couple of days. Those payments were in cash."

"Again, I don't get the connection. You believe his story about the dancing?"

"No," Brewer said. "We had two theories. One is that Newland was blackmailing Pascasio, he got sick of it, and did her in. But the fact remains, we can't put him anywhere near Conover College on the night of the murder. We also haven't uncovered anything worth paying to hide."

Xavier glanced in Jillian's direction, then turned back to Brewer. "Sounds like you have a problem. What's your other theory?"

"We think we can prove Pascasio paid Newland as a gift, perhaps in consideration of her ongoing sexual favors."

Jillian shuddered.

Xavier motioned for Brewer to continue.

Zale said, "Newland visited Ms. Grey to discuss a grade in exchange for returning the test bank. Ms. Grey, angered by the audacity of the demand and incensed over Newland's affair with her ex, murdered Bethany."

"And what? Dragged the body out of the office in broad daylight, struck Newland's head on the concrete near the student parking, then carried her back to the trees and dumped her?" Xavier's pitch rose, suggesting she was incredulous.

"Grey killed the girl in her office, then waited there until the campus area emptied," Brewer said. "We have a witness who saw someone matching Mrs. Grey's description dragging something heavy across the lot."

"Again a witness? Who is it? Is the description as vague as the science student's?" Xavier said.

"You can request that information from the State Attorney during discovery." Brewer waved his hand as if brushing away a gnat.

"Gentlemen, you have to do better than that. You take this into court, and you'll be the laughing stock of law enforcement." She stood. "I want the charges dropped. Your whole case is preposterous."

"Whoa. Have a seat." When Xavier didn't sit, Brewer said. "We've got more things to air out. Please sit."

Xavier sat, looking perturbed.

"We're going to lay our cards on the table here. If Mrs. Grey helps us, we'll discuss reducing the charge with the State Attorney."

Xavier rolled her brown eyes toward the ceiling.

"Ms. Grey claimed she touched only Newland's neck,

then she remembered touching Newland's purse."

Jillian opened her mouth to speak.

Xavier frowned, shaking her head.

"No, I'm sorry Xan, but they keep harping at incorrect information, and I'm sick of it. Detectives, you asked me about it before. Bethany put her things on my desk while she was going through her backpack looking for her class notes. I moved them to the corner of the desk so I could put the note-taking example in front of her."

"Suddenly, you're positive?" Zale said. "When we talked about it, you thought maybe."

"I remember telling the first-responding officer that I'd touched Bethany's neck and nothing else, but I was referring to Friday morning. I wasn't thinking of the night before."

"Why didn't you mention it when we were in your office questioning you about your meeting with the girl?" Brewer asked.

"You didn't ask, and I wasn't focused on that point. Later when you told me about the fingerprints, I remembered. Why are you asking me about it again?"

Xavier smiled at Jillian. "Seems like a reasonable question to me, gentlemen, and the counseling records prove that Bethany was in Ms. Grey's office." She looked from one detective to the other.

"Eleanor Evers, if she survives . . ." Brewer paused.

Jillian cringed.

"She isn't a reliable alibi witness. She's elderly, flaky, in poor health, and has questionable vision, given her age," Brewer said.

Jillian said, "Eleanor had an eye exam right before she went into the hospital. She's farsighted. Being farsighted increases the likelihood seeing me at a distance. Don't you think?"

Zale nodded.

"Anything else?" Xavier said.

Zale glared at Xavier. "Our crime scene technicians went over the area surrounding the victim's body with great care. They didn't find evidence, none at all, of anyone being in the area other than the victim and your client. Do you have a pat explanation for that as well?"

"I can prove the obvious inaccuracy in the statement." Xavier lifted her briefcase to the table and clicked it open.

"What do you mean by that?" Zale huffed.

"I mean this." She slid a copy of a grainy photograph of Officer Goetz stomping into the crime scene across the table to each detective. Then she laid a CD on the table. "Here's an electronic copy of the file as well. You'll see the photos were taken Friday morning, right after the 911 call." Xavier stood and signaled to Jillian to do the same. She looked at Zale. "You have no case against my client. You never had a case against my client. You're just peeing into a headwind, but you went ahead and implied she was guilty in the newspaper. As a result, both employers suspended her "

"That's how it is sometimes," Zale said. "Our priority is solving the case,"

"You'd better go ahead and solve it, but leave my client alone. There are more holes in your case than in a shot-up car in a B-grade gangster movie. Let me lay it out for you." Xavier spread out the documentation of Pascasio's windfall stock profit and summarized the comments made by the students, including Cooley's sighting of Shanna Albano on campus before the murder. "Here's the latest blog someone is writing about the case. Whoever wrote it all but confesses, stupid as it may sound." She flopped it on the table. "Here's

Vincent Barrera's record." She spread the papers. "This is
Shanna Albano's military file. They both have criminal
records."

"You've been busy," Zale said. "Why didn't you give us
this information sooner?"

"My client was preparing for tomorrow's scheduled
meeting. Someone in a black Toyota Corolla followed Ms.
Grey and Mr. Diamond around town today. Albano owns
the car." Xavier paused. "How can you charge my client
with murder?"

Zale flushed.

"Let's talk outside for a minute," Brewer said, looking at
Zale.

"Wait a minute," Xavier said. "I want the charges
dropped. I want you to contact the newspapers—no, I'll do
that for you. When they call you, I want you to tell them she
is no longer a suspect. I want you to insist they print it. And,
I want you to notify both the college and the hospital that
Ms. Grey is not a suspect."

"And if we don't?" Zale sneered.

"Then I'll file a motion with the court on Monday
morning. I'll follow it with a civil suit charging false arrest
and harassment. I'll send copies of both filings to the press,
along with photos of Goetz contaminating the scene. Then,
Detective Zale, I'll find out why you're so intent on framing
my client."

"I'm not trying to frame your client. The evidence was
strong. And, you can't threaten us."

"Why not? You've been threatening this poor woman all
along, destroying her life in the process." She pointed to the
door. "Is she excused?"

"Yes," said Brewer. "We'll be in touch. Don't leave

town."

***

Jillian and Xavier found Warren waiting in the lobby of the police station.

"I thought you'd be released," he said in response to her tired smile.

"You should have gone home. You could have sat here all night."

He leaned in and kissed Jillian, then grinned at Xavier.

"I suspect they'll leave you alone now," Xavier said as they stepped out into the cool, clear night. "Even if Zale still believes you had something to do with the girl's death, he knows he'll never prove it in court. The evidence is circumstantial, and we can create reasonable doubt. I'll clean up the mess on Monday, make sure the charges are dropped. You need to put your life back together."

"How do I get my credibility and my reputation restored?"

"That's a bigger problem, I'm afraid. Until the murderer is caught and convicted, some people will have doubts about you."

"Which means the college may not be willing to give me my job back. The students' parents have a big say in my future."

"I expect that's true, but it doesn't change the fact you need to distance yourself from the problem. No more private detecting. Focus on what you can control."

"I'll try," Jillian said, extending a hand. "Thanks again for coming to my rescue. I was certain I'd spend the rest of my life in jail."

Xavier's hand was warm, her grasp reassuring. "I'll be in touch on Monday."

Jillian and Warren watched Xavier climb into an SUV and pull out of the lot. They walked hand-in-hand to Warren's car.

Jillian leaned against the seat and closed her eyes, drifting off to sleep as soon as the car was in motion.

He woke her when he stopped in front of her building. "I'll walk you upstairs," he said and opened his car door. "I don't want you out and about alone until the murderer is caught. I think you may be at risk."

"I suppose you're right," Jillian said, suppressing a yawn. When Warren opened her car door, she stood, grabbing the top of the frame for support. "I feel disoriented."

"I can tell." Warren guided her through the lobby, nodding to the guard on the way past.

At her apartment door, Jillian grasped the knob then stopped. "It's only been eight days, but it seems like my world disintegrated a lifetime ago. I need to get on track, find my bearings. I need to call the dean tomorrow and make sure she knows it's just a matter of days before I'm in the clear. I need my job. I need to call my daughter. I need my life back."

CHAPTER 33

Exhausted, Jillian slept until almost ten, then flipped on the television in the feeble hope of hearing the local news clearing her name. After listening awhile, she switched off the TV, deciding to spend some time attending to business.

First on the to do list was a call to her parents. Multiple answering machine messages were testament to their worry.

When her father answered, he said, "Where in the hell have you been. We've been worried sick."

"The son of a bitch, Zale, wanted to put me in jail. He convinced himself I was guilty of murder, then arranged the facts to prove his opinion. Luckily, we were prepared for him." She gave an abbreviated rendition of the scene in the interrogation room. "Xavier says they'll give me some space."

"I told you to ease up on Zale. For some reason he thought he had the facts."

Jillian decided on a conciliatory approach, not wanting to upset him again. "Xavier thinks Zale is a good cop at heart. She said circumstances misled him—last to see Bethany alive and first to see her dead, plus all the allegations about stolen exam questions. Then, when they found my prints on the purse, he was convinced. Xavier also thinks pressure from the higher-ups to solve the case blinded him." Jillian heard an exasperated sigh but continued anyway. "Sorry. Xavier also mentioned Zale is having personal problems. She didn't go into detail, but implied that if they pressed charges, she had ammunition to discredit him on the witness stand."

Ron Grey grunted. "Everyone downtown knows Zale had an expensive gambling habit. Dogs. Horses. Cards. You name it, he'd bet on it. His wife left him over it. Took him for everything. He joined Gamblers Anonymous. The information I have is he stayed clean. I don't see there's anything to use against him."

Her dad always sided with the detectives in any disagreement with defense attorneys. He sometimes entertained a different point of view, but she doubted he believed what he said. Jillian changed the subject. "Daddy, I'm going to try to unearth who killed Bethany. I don't think it was Pasquale. I don't want it to be Pasquale. But I can't get it out of my mind. Something doesn't make sense. Something everyone is missing. I also want to find out why Zale tried to frame me. Why would a supposedly good cop ignore the obvious?"

"Now, Jillian, you don't know that's true. And you shouldn't get in the way of the investigation. You'll find yourself in trouble again. You and Xavier withholding those photographs and springing them at the last moment couldn't have set well with Zale. He'll be looking for a bit of revenge."

"I have to see what I can find out. I won't have a normal life until the murderer is found."

"Be careful. You're no longer a suspect, so there's a murderer out there who will feel the need to take action."

"You're right, Dad. I hadn't thought of that."

They said their goodbyes, then Jillian signed onto the Internet to catch up on the new blog. After locating the site, she created a bookmark and read the latest entries.

Friday night:

The bitch was arrested, just like I said, but then I saw her leave the police station a couple of hours later. I need to find out what's going on.

I'm not sorry the little blond bitch is dead. She deserved to die.

Sunday morning:

No comments posted from anyone. It's odd. Also, I expected a visit from the police, but I guess they didn't have enough to keep her in jail but didn't think to look at me either. I'll have to see what I can do about that. I'm tired of this game already.

Jillian didn't know what to make of the comments. The picture of the crime scene the blogger posted to the site and the theme of the writing both suggested the writer was a student. Albano? Barrera? She didn't believe it was Pasquale. But Pasquale was smart and manipulative enough to fake the posting, and he could have gotten the photo from Albano or Barrera—or perhaps another Internet site.

Jillian showered and dressed in jeans and a light shirt, grabbed a jacket to combat the air-conditioning, and headed to the hospital. All else aside, she wanted to check on Eleanor, then planned to find out what Albano was up to. But where to begin?

***

The midday Sunday traffic along Oakland Park Boulevard jerked from one traffic signal to the next. Still, Jillian's drive to the hospital was a quick one, lasting no more than ten minutes. Visitors' cars filled the front lot, so she hung her employee permit from the rearview mirror, pulled into a spot near the front of the restricted lot, and entered the hospital through the Authorized Personnel Only entrance. She took a moment to wipe the perspiration from her forehead. Though the day was a scorcher, she soon shivered from the air conditioning.

Jillian found Dewey and Barrera in the waiting room outside the ICU.

Barrera glared at her, then looked away, scowling.

Jillian touched Dewey's shoulder. "What's going on with Eleanor?"

"Better today. She's been off the ventilator since six this morning. The nurse asked us to leave so she could change a dressing. We'll go back when he's done."

"Mind if I slip in for a minute first?"

"Go right ahead. She's been asking for you all morning. Um . . . Vincent heard you were in jail, and we didn't want to tell her."

"My lawyer and I convinced Zale and Brewer—well, Brewer at least—they were tugging on the wrong rope. They let me go. Told me to stay in town." Jillian forced half a tight-lipped smile and sat down next to Barrera.

Barrera met her gaze.

"What's happening with Shanna?"

"Don't know. Don't care. She's off the friggin' wall."

"Do you know where she is?"

"Not for sure." He paused a moment, looking thoughtful. "She sometimes works on Sunday. May be there. I don't know where she stayed last night. I found her at the apartment. She grabbed her stuff, told me to piss off, and left. I didn't try to stop her."

"I'm surprised. I thought you two were tight as oysters."

Jillian paused, considering what to say next. "I'm aware of Shanna's army record and your criminal record."

"How'd you get that stuff?"

"It wasn't hard. I gave copies to the police last night when they took me downtown—in handcuffs, I might add."

"Do they think I killed Bethany? I didn't, you know. I was at work."

"I believe you, but your friend Shanna wasn't. She went back onto the campus right before Bethany was killed."

Barrera crossed his legs and fiddled with his pants as if trying to make a crease down the front.

"What's the real story, Vincent? Bethany was blackmailing my ex. You all pretended to be his friend. I'm thinking you and Shanna put Bethany up to the blackmail, and when she didn't share the proceeds, you decided to kill her."

"That's not how it was at all. Shanna found the money trail on the computer at her office. One night while she waited for me to get finished at the bar, she told Bethany. Pascasio had been coming around pretty regular, hitting on Bethany. The two girls decided there would be some money in it, but Shanna couldn't come on to the guy because he knew she lived with me, and he knew her from the office. So Shanna put Bethany up to it."

"You didn't try to do anything to stop them?"

"No. I should have, I guess. Am I going to be arrested?"

"I can't say that I care."

Barrera admired his shoes. "There's something else."

"And that is?"

"One of the cops, Brewer, is connected with Shanna's boss, the Watson guy. Shanna told me how Brewer acted as if they were strangers when he and the other cop went into the office to talk to Watson. Said he even acted surprised to see her, but he's in there about every week, flirts with her."

"What's he doing, day trading?"

Barrera shook his head. "I don't think so. Shanna said Watson has another little business on the side. Brewer has a piece of it."

"What little business? I'm tired of riddles."

"He's loan sharking, covering gambling debts for people."

The smelly inconsistencies added up to a stinking pile of garbage for Jillian. She still didn't have an explanation for why Zale was intent on framing her. Maybe her father was right about someone feeding Zale false information, but she didn't believe it. Brewer had been respectful and almost supportive. She pondered how someone like Brewer could have mired himself in filth. Maybe Zale really was convinced she killed Bethany.

While mulling over the new information, she visited Eleanor and was pleased to find her alert, oriented, and breathing easily. Jillian expected doctors to discharge her in a couple of days.

"I need to tell you something," Eleanor said under her breath. "Lean close."

Jillian complied. "What is it?"

"Yesterday afternoon when the kids were here, they thought I was asleep or knocked out cold. I wasn't. Vincent and the little trollop were arguing."

"What about?"

"I'm not sure, but I think Shanna does more than push computer keys for Watson."

"Sex, you mean?"

"No, not that. It sounded to me like she collects money for Watson." Eleanor took a few moments to breathe. "I think she beats people up for him. She was going to take care of Pasquale today, no matter what."

Jillian tried to assimilate the image of a nursing student beating people. Maybe Eleanor dreamed the conversation.

Jillian spent a few more minutes at her bedside before leaving, scooting past the waiting room and waving to Barrera and Dewey.

After calling Shanna's work, then disconnecting when she answered, Jillian hurried through traffic. On Federal Highway, she rented a dark compact with tinted windows from the first leasing agency she saw. Perfect for surveillance, she thought, smiling at her own audacity. She called Warren and made arrangements to meet him. "Bring your gun, please."

"What exactly do you have in mind?"

She updated him, then said, "I want to follow Albano. See what she's doing."

"I can go with that. I'll be outside my building in ten minutes."

"So will I, probably in five." She glanced to the right, then drove over the causeway. Maybe this would be the day life returned to normal.

A few minutes later, with Warren sitting behind the wheel, they headed west toward Carnegie and Watson Investments. He stopped and parked a few doors away, settling in several car lengths behind Albano's black Toyota. "Now we wait. When does she get off?"

"Barrera said around three." Jillian checked the clock on the dashboard. "Soon, I hope."

The door to the office opened and Albano stepped out.

She looked both ways, turned around and said something, then redirected her attention to the street.

"Odd behavior," Warren said. "Maybe Barrera had second thoughts and tipped her."

"It could be guilt." Jillian studied Albano's appearance.

"Her blouse bunches on the left," Warren said. "She's carrying and is up to something. That's for sure."

"I see what you mean. I wouldn't have noticed." Jillian watched as Albano pulled into the street.

"We'll give her time to get into traffic and wait for a couple of cars." Warren let three cars go by, then followed.

"Hope we don't lose her."

Despite her earlier caution, Albano didn't seem aware anyone tailed her. She signaled turns and stopped for traffic lights, driving in the direction of the New River.

"She has to be going to Pasquale's. The only buildings on this street are residential."

Warren grimaced. "Can't be a good thing. She's armed. She's stressed. We saw the behavior at the bookstore. From what Barrera told you, she might be one chip short of a motherboard."

"That's putting it mildly." Jillian smiled. "He told me she's a whole lot stronger than she looks and has some awesome martial arts skills. Stuff she learned in the service. Eleanor could be right in saying she's muscle for Watson's side operation."

"Computers and martial arts. What next? She should have stayed straight. Could have had an interesting career with the FBI."

"Like someone I know."

"No special martial arts talents to speak of. Guns. They fascinated me long before I joined the bureau."

Albano parked two blocks from Pascasio's building on a one-way street heading away from the condo and stayed in her car.

Warren selected a space across the street and a block south. He kept the windows up and the air-conditioning running. The little car's cooling unit struggled to keep up with the brutal afternoon heat. "She's on her cell. I wonder who she is calling," Warren said. "The woman's behavior gets stranger and stranger. I say we call the police and have them meet us here."

"If there is nothing going on, it'll be embarrassing. It won't endear me to them."

"Call. This is about saving Pasquale from a beating and maybe his life."

"Brewer?" Jillian looked at Warren. "He seemed the most reasonable when it comes to me."

"I don't see we have a choice at this point."

Albano exited her car and stood on the sidewalk. Every few seconds she glanced up and down the street. Then she looked at her watch and walked toward the river and Pascasio's building. She stopped at the corner and swiveled both ways before returning to her car to set her purse in the trunk. She took some time putting things in her pockets before closing the trunk.

"Strange behavior," Jillian said. "On the path to no good."

Warren nodded.

Jillian extracted Brewer's card from her wallet and placed the call.

The woman answering said, "The detective isn't available. I'll be happy to take a message."

Damn, Jillian thought. But having no choice, she

continued. "Please tell him to go to Pasquale Pascasio's apartment. I think he's in bad trouble. Someone with a gun is entering his building." It took Jillian a minute or two to explain being there and watching. After disconnecting, she turned to Warren. "The operator took a message. I can't believe it."

"At least there's a record of the call. Nothing we can do about it."

Albano tapped on her cell phone, put it to her ear, said a few words, dropped it into her shirt pocket, and took off down the street at a brisk pace. This time, she crossed the street without a glance in either direction. A turning car missed her by inches.

Jillian and Warren waited until Albano was a block away before exiting the car. They followed from the other side of the street, holding hands, pretending to converse. Jillian stayed as close to the buildings as possible, hoping to be lost in the shadows should Albano happen to glance at them.

Albano entered Pascasio's condominium.

"I think we should wait for help before going upstairs," Warren said, holding Jillian's hand tighter to restrain her from following.

"I don't think so. She's armed, and she's moving with purpose."

Warren pointed at a white Taurus that screeched to a halt under the building's canopy. "Look. There's Brewer."

Brewer ran into the building.

Jillian said, "That was quick. He must have gotten the message."

"Much too quick, if you ask me. I think he was already on his way."

Jillian and Warren hurried down the street, peeking

around the corner and into the lobby as Brewer badged the guard. The guard pointed in the direction of the elevator and said a few words, but didn't make a telephone call.

When the elevator door closed behind Brewer, Jillian and Warren crossed the lobby.

"Excuse me," the young guard said in a thick Haitian accent. "Where are you going?"

"Pascasio's. I'm his ex-wife," Jillian said.

"Need to call first. Can I see some identification?"

Jillian showed her driver's license while the guard placed the call.

"He says you can come up."

As they walked across the lobby, Warren said, "I'm surprised Pasquale didn't tell us to leave. Why would he let us upstairs if Albano is there, maybe holding a gun on him? And, if Brewer is there, he has to be involved."

"Maybe they aren't in his apartment yet."

Warren raised a brow.

She squinted at the ceiling lights. "If that's true, when they knock on the door, Pasquale will open it without looking, thinking it's me."

As they stepped out of the elevator, Pasquale's apartment door clicked closed.

"I didn't hear him set the lock," Warren said.

"What do we do now? Zale might get the message and come."

"Pasquale might be dead before anyone gets here," Warren said. He removed a small handgun from an ankle holster.

Jillian gulped. "Maybe they're just talking."

"Right." He turned the pistol over in his hand. "I wish I could say I'm more than a computer jockey, but I'm not. I've practiced with targets."

"My dad says most cops only shoot targets."

Warren grimaced. "I think we should go in. Move away from the door."

Warren stood off to the side, gun in hand, then pushed the door open.

"What the shit's going on?" Brewer said, his voice tense.

"That's what I was going to ask." Warren took several steps into the apartment with Jillian following close behind. "Where's Shanna Albano?"

"Here I am." Albano struck Warren on the side of the head, knocking him to the floor. "I wondered how long it would take you two to have the nerve to open the door." She turned her gun on Jillian. "Sit next to your ex-hubby, bitch." Albano bolted the door.

Jillian lowered herself onto the sofa next to Pasquale. She noticed his hands were behind him.

Brewer pulled a pair of plastic ties from his suit coat pocket and tightened one bracelet on Jillian's left wrist. He jerked her forward, causing her to cry out in pain. He secured her hands. "You have a way of getting in the way." He turned and waved at Warren's unmoving figure. "Shanna, take his gun and cuff him." He tossed another set of ties to Albano.

Brewer dragged a chair over and positioned it facing Pasquale and Jillian. He hauled Pasquale off the sofa and dropped him onto the chair. Leaning close, Brewer said, "Okay, my friend, tell me where you put our money."

Pasquale glared at Brewer.

The bastard lied to me, Jillian thought.

Warren groaned and moved.

Brewer said, "You might as well tell me. If you refuse,

I'll have Shanna break your neck. But first, she'll do other damage—very painful damage I might add."

"I don't know what money you're talking about."

"The million dollars you ripped off from Watson and me. It was in your account and now it's gone."

"It was a brokerage error. I showed it to Watson. It has nothing to do with you."

"You lying son of a bitch. Where's our fucking money?"

Pasquale lowered his gaze.

Brewer slugged him in the jaw, slamming Pasquale's head back. Brewer grimaced and massaged his hand.

Blood trickled from the corner of Pasquale's mouth. His eyes rolled. He shook his head, squinted, and said, "Go to hell."

Brewer coiled to strike again, then relaxed. "Shanna, duty calls."

Having finished with Warren, Albano strolled to Brewer 's side.

He nodded.

She slapped Pasquale across the face, then delivered a vicious knife-hand blow to his left shoulder, creating a loud snap as his collarbone fractured.

Pasquale cried out.

Brewer said, "Feel like talking?"

Pasquale nodded. A steady flow of blood dripped from his split lip onto his white linen shirt. "When I was in the office, I saw Shanna put in the password for Watson's accounts. I used it to enter the system and discovered a lot of cash moving around. Small amounts, under ten grand. So I helped myself, a little at a time. I invested it, sold the investment, then altered my original records to make it look like a brokerage error. I went to Watson to discuss the windfall, hoping to cover my tracks."

"Watson's not stupid. Where's our money now?"

"I tucked it away. If you touch me or Jillian—or her friend over there—you'll never see it."

Albano delivered a solid punch to Pasquale's jaw, hitting the bruise from Brewer's earlier blow.

Jillian heard a crack and knew the jaw broke.

Pasquale screamed. Blood poured from his nose and mouth. His head lolled as he lost consciousness.

"You need to help him. He'll choke and die on all the blood," Jillian said.

"Lady, he's dying today anyway," Brewer said. "You and your boyfriend, too, for that matter."

Pasquale came to.

"Where's the money?"

"Fuck you." The words sounded garbled.

Albano slugged Pasquale again, this time in the gut, causing him vomit all over Brewer's shoes.

Jillian thought there was some justice in the world. She glanced at Warren. He was awake. She regretted pulling Warren into her mess. "Warren, I'm sorry."

Tears flowed. She pictured her daughter, granddaughter, and parents. She would suffer the consequences of Pasquale's misguided behavior one final time.

Brewer went into Pasquale's office.

Jillian heard doors opening and closing, papers shuffling, and then computer keys clicking.

Brewer returned. "Got it. Kill them."

Albano put one hand on Pasquale's broken jaw the other on his forehead.

As Jillian watched, she envisioned Newland in the same circumstance, and Jillian knew Albano had executed

Newland. She'd break Pasquale's neck as well. Jillian pinched her eyes closed, not wanting to watch.

The door opened with a crash. Zale's lean body filled the opening. He pointed his gun at Brewer.

"Kill Pascasio, Shanna. Do it now," Brewer screamed.

As Albano's hands moved, Zale fired. Albano staggered backwards, crumpling to the floor.

Zale moved to the side, allowing another officer to enter with him. "Take your gun out of your pocket, Sy. Two fingers. Toss it away." He collected the gun and cuffed Brewer.

Two uniformed officers stepped forward and escorted Brewer out of the apartment.

**

After paramedics loaded Pasquale and Albano on stretchers and hauled them away, Zale interviewed Jillian and Warren in Pasquale's ransacked office.

"Explain what happened," Jillian said.

Zale hiked one hip onto the desk and settled his weight. "We arrived at the same conclusion you did. Shanna Albano was dangerous and was going after Pascasio. But you had one piece of information we didn't. Your friend told you they were moving today. Good thing you called when you did. Internal Affairs intercepted your call to Brewer and passed it on to me. I've been working with them, trying to get the evidence on Brewer. We knew he was dirty, but we needed to get the proof. He was cheating on his wife, not a crime in itself, but he had too much money. Usually means a cop on the take."

"What I don't understand," Jillian said, "is how Bethany

got involved."

"Watson discovered his cash was short. When Pascasio discussed the fake brokerage error, Watson did the math. Albano overheard the discussion and put Newland up to the blackmail.

"Albano told Brewer she and Newland were blackmailing Pascasio. Then Newland realized the plan was unraveling and threatened to go to the authorities unless she got a bigger share. Brewer and Albano killed her to keep her quiet." He touched Jillian's hand. "He fabricated the witness who claimed to see you hauling something heavy across the parking lot. The science student who saw you near the trees actually saw Albano in a short auburn wig." Zale pointed to Jillian's hair. "Like yours. Brewer pushed for your arrest, even going so far as to ask for a warrant himself, but the judge refused. I'm sorry for what I put you through."

"But how did you know Brewer was involved?"

"Brewer and Albano were having an affair for some time. His wife questioned him, he made up the story about the rich aunt, then got her a big ring to pacify her, but it didn't work. I figure it forced him to grab Pascasio's loot for himself and take off.

"Then Vice hauled Watson in on a loan-sharking rap. Watson folded and made a deal, giving up Brewer and Albano. By then I knew you weren't involved, but I pretended to go along with Brewer until we could bust him. The information you brought in last night rocked him. He knew you wouldn't be taking the fall. He needed to cut his losses. We found Newland's school backpack in his locker and packed bags and airline tickets in his car. He was set to run, and he was taking Albano with him."

CHAPTER 34

Warren waited as Jillian dropped the keys to the rental car into the return slot. "How about a walk on the beach, dinner, a glass of wine?"

"Sounds wonderful."

Warren glanced at his watch. "I'll pick you up at six. Pack a bag."

Jillian raised a questioning eyebrow.

"The beach I have in mind is in Tahiti."

The End

ABOUT THE AUTHOR

Gregg E. Brickman was born in North Dakota. She migrated to Florida and completed her education, embarking on a varied career in clinical, administrative, and academic nursing.

Gregg started writing as a teenager, turning out pages of sappy poetry. In the mid-nineties, she bought a how-to book about writing a novel and committed the story burning in her head to paper. She recognized that first novel as a learner's effort—unfit to be published, joined Mystery Writers of America, and actively pursued the craft.

Credits include *the lord*, *Imperfect Daddy*, *Imperfect Contract*, *Illegally Dead*, Chapter 14 of *Naked Came the Flamingo*, a Murder on the Beach progressive novella edited by Barbara Parker and Joan Mickelson, and *On the Edge*, a short story [MiamiARTzine.com]. The Writers' Network of South Florida recognized *On the Edge* among the finalists in their Seventh Annual Short Story Contest.